MW00794969

PRAISE FOR RIOT

Four words: Don't forget to breathe! Seriously, only start reading if you don't need to stop to eat, sleep, work or do anything else. You won't be able to put it down.

LYNETTE EASON- AWARD-WINNING
AUTHOR OF THE LAKE CITY HEROES
SERIES.

With compelling characters like a Navy SEAL named Danger and a gutsy trafficking survivor who counsels others, *Riot* is unputdownable! Living up to its name, *Riot* has all the thrills, romance and danger readers want. Kendig and Myles hold nothing back when they send Danger and Paisley deep into the jungle to face evil head on. I loved it!

ELIZABETH GODDARD, CHRISTY AWARD
WINNING AUTHOR OF *COLD LIGHT*
OF DAY

Wow, this book was an adrenaline rush from start to finish. I could NOT put it down! From page ONE I was riveted - thrown into Ronie and JJ's ·world of heart-stopping suspense, thrilling action, and nail-biting rescue. But this world was also overflowing with mutual healing, breakthrough, and great love.

SARA A., GOODREADS

Wowzers!! Be prepared to be swept away on an overloaded suspense-filled adventure in the jungle! Danger and Paisley are in the fight for their lives! Luckily, they have Riot to show them the way. But through the suspense and the drama and the nail-biting, you're blessed with these awesome faith-nuggets! Do not start this before bedtime. You will not be able to put it down!

CARLIEN P., GOODREADS

I just love this series and the characters and especially the dogs! Love how they keep their purpose to work alive. Great story lines. Good clean suspenseful books. Highly recommend!

BRENDA, GOODREADS

This is an quick moving story with well drawn characters and lots of action. I truly enjoyed the ride and look forward to the next installment in the series.

LISA P., GOODREADS

Riot is another action-packed suspense story that features a military working dog as a focal character. Ultimately, Riot is a story about forgiveness and redemption. If you like military operation storylines, you'll enjoy this book.

LISA, GOODREADS

RIOT

A BREED APART: LEGACY | BOOK 3

RONIE KENDIG

JJ SAMIE MYLES

sunrise
PUBLISHING

Riot
A Breed Apart: Legacy, Book 3
Copyright © 2024 Sunrise Media Group LLC
Print ISBN: 978-1-953783-84-4
Hardback ISBN: 978-1-953783-85-1
Ebook ISBN: 978-1-953783-86-8

For more information about Ronie Kendig please access the author's website at roniekendig.com.

Published in the United States of America.
Cover Design: Kirk DouPonce

To my Savior, Rock and Commander—Jesus Christ.
May this work glorify You.

. . . The Lord is with you, mighty warrior.
Judges 6:12

PROLOGUE

CARACAS, VENEZUELA - 0134 HOURS

YOU CAN RUN, BUT YOU CAN'T HIDE.

Flanked by two of his teammates, his M4A1 Carbine at the ready, Petty Officer First Class Beau "Danger" Maddox pushed through the murky warehouse, scanning every pallet and beyond for movement and potential threats.

An animalistic scream ripped the chemical-laden air, bouncing back from tin walls and the grimy floor. Although Danger had no visual on their target, he could practically smell the panic roiling off him—A typical response when eighty pounds of muscle charged you and dug its choppers into flesh and tendons, all the way to the bone.

Shouldn't have run.

Danger, Bacon, and Cardenas advanced down the hall toward where screams were mingling with aggressive growls.

The comms crackled in Danger's ear.

"Base, this is Charlie One," Master Chief Tyron Moore—also Danger's brother-in-law—comm'd from one of the darkened offices. "We've secured the package. Moving to exfil."

"Good copy, Charlie One. Bird's five mikes out."

The "package" was politician William Nelson Sr. The guy'd had the stellar idea to travel to Venezuela and meet some big cheese to talk politics. Problem was, Venezuela was run by the Guerrero Cartel, who waited to demonstrate their power through people like Nelson Sr., seemingly begging to be abducted. And exactly that had happened—straight from his hotel suite in Caracas. And now Charlie Team risked their hides to save this poor excuse of a man from the grave he'd dug.

Not that Danger was complaining. He'd signed up for this, and so far everything was going according to plan. Wheeled in, breached the warehouse, neutralized about a dozen tangos, secured the package, and now moved to exfil.

The only hiccup had been a squirter, who was dragged into view by Special Operations Forces dog Cutter T041. The highly trained Belgian Malinois had his backside in the air and chest close to the floor, teeth chomped into the arm of the shouting hulk of a man.

The Guerrero struggled hard, swatting at Cutter with a beefy hand. His attempts to free his bloodied limb only deepened the military working dog's resolve. The Mal thrashed his neck back and forth with a demonic snarl as he hauled the insurgent backward with short, intense bursts toward Charlie Team.

If Danger didn't stop him, Cutter would drag the guy all the way to China. It seemed the older the Mal got, the stronger his prey drive. He'd never been that intense before.

After Cutter's last screening, Danger had been warned the Mal's retirement was near—he'd racked up some years and seen a lot of combat. And his joints were showing it. But Danger wanted to keep him in the game as long as possible. Their bond was unlike anything he'd ever shared with another dog or his two-legged teammates. Still, had to keep eyes out for signs hinting at Cutter's expiry date.

Eye on his four-legged partner and M4 tucked into his shoulder, Danger advanced toward the wrestling pack in quick strides. Hulk had surrendered to his fate and gone limp, Cutter dragging him like a ragdoll—

With a feral cry, the Guerrero yanked his free hand up. Something glinted in the dim light. Flew at Cutter.

Danger squeezed off two rounds.

The assailant snapped back and his body went limp. This time for good.

Sweat trickled down Danger's forehead into his eyes. Stung. While Bacon moved in and booted the knife away, Danger caught Cutter's harness. "Out."

The Mal continued jerking at the now-dead Guerrero's arm with guttural growls.

"Cutter, out!" Danger slid his fingers under his collar. Pulled it up—a safe and effective move to force him to unlock his jaws due to reduced airflow.

Huffing his discontent, Cutter backed off.

Until Bacon verified all threats were neutralized, Danger kept Cutter close and ready and double-checked he was unharmed by smoothing a hand over his body. Cardenas kept eyes on the back exit.

"Unfriendly down," Bacon finally said, still breathing hard. He keyed his mic. "One, this is Four. North end is clear."

"Copy that, Four. Let's move to exfil."

Danger roughed Cutter's neck. "Good boy." He patted the dog's thick chest, then clipped him back to the lead attached to his belt.

The rest of Charlie Team came up behind them with Nelson Sr. Though the politician had a busted lip and his clothes looked like they'd been through the wringer, he seemed in decent shape—physically. Not so much mentally—especially with the way his bulging eyes gaped at the dead Guerrero at their boots. Yeah, someone was about to wet his pants. Maybe already had.

Next time, think twice before strolling into a country like this, pal.

Tyron assessed the mess on the floor, then glanced to the back of the warehouse. "Alright, let's move it."

"Charlie One." Base again. "Be advised you've got a dozen hostiles approaching from the southeast, about two klicks out."

"I don't think they're coming to have a tea party," Cardenas muttered.

Danger's thoughts exactly, but a meet and greet was inevitable if they didn't get out of here ASAP.

Tyron keyed his mic. "Copy that, Base." He lifted his gaze to the team. "Cardenas, Crazy Rudy—buy us time. Mr. Nelson, stick with Miller if you want to stay alive. Clear?"

The politician nodded vigorously, his greasy hair flapping.

Tyron turned to Danger. "You good?"

Danger gave him a sharp nod, confirming he knew what his and Cutter's job was. They'd take the lead. This wasn't Afghanistan or Iraq, but the Guerreros liked IEDs just as much, and the field with the tall grass they were about to cross was perfect for hiding a small surprise gift.

With stealth and proficiency, Charlie Team slipped into the night. The moonless sky concealed their movement, and when Danger lowered his night-vision goggles, a green hue bathed the area. He followed Cutter through the dark, trusting that highly trained snout to guide them. The *whop-whop* of a helo grew louder as it zoomed over the tin shacks lining the airstrip of the small airport. Crouched at the edge of the field, Charlie Team watched the Black Hawk descend. As it neared the strip, they pushed into motion.

Cutter had his snout down, sniffing, running in a serpentine line.

Maintaining awareness of his furry partner, Danger scanned their surroundings. The bird waited two hundred yards out, a green field between the team and the line of tin shacks.

Pop-pop-crack.

In the chaos, Danger went to a knee as shots erupted.

"Move, move, move!" Tyron barked at his six.

The battle raging behind them, Danger shoved up, grip firm

on Cutter's lead. No more than a hundred yards left to the bird. *C'mon, boy.*

Cutter stopped short, and Danger shoved aside to avoid crashing into him. "What—"

Head up, Cutter opened his snout and sniffed. He angled his snout upward and took in draughts.

"C'mon," Danger said even as he spotted a dog spiriting across the field toward them. He snapped up his M4 and trained it on the dog. What was the mutt doing?

Cutter barked and strained at the lead.

No good. Shouldn't get distracted by a mutt.

Danger slowed him, grabbed the harness, and shouted, "Leave it!"

But the Mal strained violently. Took Danger everything to hold him back from breaking out. Had the mixture of penetrating odors in the warehouse messed with him? Or was it a female in heat? Wouldn't be the first time Cutter'd lost his manners at a time like that.

"Leave it," Danger repeated even as another option entered his head—what if Cutter had caught the scent of explosives? Was it the smell of the helo? That would be a break in behavior since they'd jumped together. But explosives . . . He leveled his M4 at the approaching dog again. In the darkness, he scanned the mutt's body for unusual bulges. Couldn't see much except the head because of the tall grass.

"What's the holdup?" Tyron's shout made Danger realize the team had closed the distance to the helo, but his buddy had doubled back.

"He really wants a piece of that dog." He lined his reticle on the mutt, but no way would he kill it. Especially not without proof of trouble. "Probably in heat—"

"Then move!" Tyron pivoted and sprinted toward the Black Hawk.

Danger tugged Cutter—but then his boot dropped into a hole, twisting his leg. He stumbled. Lost the lead. His balance.

Crashed down. He bit out a curse, only then seeing the Mal lunge toward the mutt. But the lead tethered him. Again, yanked Danger to the ground.

Barking like a psycho, Cutter bounced on his forepaws, straining after the mutt who raced straight toward the bird.

Even with the fingerless gloves, he felt the lead burning his hands, digging into his palms. Danger knew if he let him go, things would get ugly. Ankle screaming, he snapped up his M4. Again trained it on the mutt, who darted under the chopper. Right below the fuel tanks.

Oh cr—

BOOM!

Blinding light detonated. The world went upside down. Air punched Danger backward. Slammed him hard into the ground. A bolt of electricity zapped his lower spine, and he heard the lavalike spray of burning jet fuel raining down. Writhing, he tried to get air into his lungs only to inhale chemicals and smoke. Coughing exacerbated the pain.

Cutter. Where was he?

"Cut—" Another coughing fit. His ears rang, his head throbbed. *Always improve your fighting position.* He pulled himself up—pain wracked his body. Forced him back down. His hand hit something cold and hard right beneath him, digging into his lumbar. A rock. That explained the fire licking his back. He groaned, fighting the agony as he shifted his M4 on its sling. No question now—that dog had been rigged. Had to have been.

Where was Cutter? "Cutter, heel, boy."

Get up . . . get up . . . alert Base. He touched his mic—except it wasn't there. Neither was his helmet and NODs. What . . .?

His gaze hit the Black Hawk. Fuel spewed from it like lava—over the area . . . and team. Panic jammed his throat. Where were the guys?

He had to move. Help his brothers. His partn— "Cutter! Where are you, boy?" Danger rolled and fought to get on his knees. Another surge of electricity ripping up his spine buckled

6

him. Not able to make it into any kind of upright position, he low-crawled. "Cutter. Heel, boy."

What he saw froze him. That split-second moment seared into his mind so deep and hot that he knew he'd relive it for the rest of his life. With the helo's burning hulk as a macabre backdrop, bodies—seared, impaled with shrapnel . . . consumed by burning fuel—lay unmoving. He pitched to the side and retched at the acrid, horrific smell of burning flesh.

No . . . no no no.

A groan to his three yanked his attention. "Tyron!" He scrabbled over there, realizing his own hands were burning and aching. An invisible iron grip seized Danger's throat at the condition of his friend. Eyes burning from the smoke and chemicals, he scanned Tyron. The scalded flesh, material burned off. A large chunk of metal stuck out of his side, blood spilling out.

"Dange . . ." Tyron rasped out.

"Here. I'm here." He shifted to the side, snatching his CAT from his tac vest. "Let me get the tourniquet on—"

"No!" Tyron growled, hand flopping to Danger's vest. Caught hold. "Listen."

"Shut up so I can save you." Danger's gaze bounced from the CAT as he slipped it around, scanning the field. "Cutter! Cutter, heel!" Mind spinning a dozen directions, he refocused on his buddy bleeding out. But why wasn't Cutter responding?

"Too . . . late . . ." A wheeze riffled through Tyron's lungs. "Swear you'll watch . . . Lyr—" He slumped, hand falling away.

"Hey!" Danger threaded the band and secured it. Used the valve to twist. "Hey, Tyron! Don't do this to me. You know Rach will kill me if anything happens to you." One hand he twisted to cut off the blood flow while the other patted Tyron's chest. "C'mon, man." No response. "Tyron! Don't! Don't do this!" He slumped.

But he knew. Tyron might've survived the scalding burns over eighty percent of his body if the bird hadn't been hit and

the exfil could've happened right away, but with the wound . . .
Dead. They were all dead.

Panting and whimpering nearby snapped his attention to his four-legged partner. "Cutter!"

The Mal let out an almost inaudible whimper as his warm breath dusted Danger's face.

"Hey, boy." Danger hooked an arm over Cutter's shoulders. Fingers hit something sticky. *Blood. You're hurt!*

Hackles raised, the Malinois let out a low snarl, then frenetic barking. Ready to engage.

A shout—Spanish. Footfalls approached. Fast.

Danger slung his M4 to the front and pivoted around, kneeling in the grass, his ankle and back throbbing. Sighted a boatload of unfriendlies converging from all sides, muzzles trained on them.

Danger eased back the trigger. Dropped one. Two. Three—

A shadow flew at his head.

Thwack.

Pain exploded in his temple. Another blow, and he spiraled into gaping nothingness.

1

SIX MONTHS LATER

HARMONIA, TEXAS

EIGHTEEN YEARS AGO, DANGER HAD SWORN TO NEVER RETURN. YET here he was, caged in his stepfather's mansion crawling with Texas's high snobciety. The only reason he'd agreed to attend his mother's sixtieth birthday party was because his kid sister Rachel had insisted. He'd do anything for her and his six-year-old niece Lyric, especially since Tyron's blood caked his hands.

The memory of Tyron's last seconds on earth made Danger reconsider tonight's mission—steering clear of all booze. He eyeballed the marble-and-mirror bar that made his favorite watering hole in town look like a lemonade stand. Hank had massively expanded his liquor stash since Danger's teen years.

No. If he wanted his old life as an operator back, wanted to avenge his brothers and settle accounts with Osorio, he had to get a grip. Maybe the Navy had issued him a medical "separation," but A Breed Apart wanted to put him back in action. That was, if he didn't lapse. No way he'd waste that opportunity.

Or backstab Ghost, who'd hired him—past and all—as a dog handler.

"Danger, is that you?"

Of all people . . .

He tore his gaze from the liquor. "Mirabelle Berry." Even as he turned to every man's nightmare on two legs, old habit had him quickly scanning the glitterati conversing in the big hall—their greedy hands, posh suits or dresses, and Botox-distorted faces—then verifying the exits were still clear.

Gasping at his face—his opaque cornea—Berry covered her mouth. "Oh my!"

What would she say if she saw the rest of his scars? Probably would pass out. That'd be fun to watch.

Berry blinked. "Oh, *Danger*. I am *so* sorry!" She drew out the nickname he'd scored in high school—that'd haunted him straight into the Teams, where it became his callsign—and dug her manicured fingernails into his bicep.

He stared at her claws before meeting her eyes.

Her pity was as fake as everything else about her. Looked like someone hadn't made it far. Still happy to leave a trail of bodies to get all the juicy details of other people's lives.

As if there was anything left to say about his. The media had let the entire world know about the train wreck that was Operation White Scorpion. God only knew how they'd gotten their accursed hands on a mission with above-TS1 clearance. But hey, at least this way no rumors made their rounds about why he now resembled Blofeld in *Spectre*.

"It's good to have you back," Berry continued in a tone promising diabetes from just listening to it. Still clinging to his upper arm, she inched closer. "You are a true hero, you know."

Getting a drink suddenly didn't seem like such a stupid idea.

Sure have hit rock bottom, Danger. Needed a quick exfil before he caved . . . again.

He freed himself from Berry's death grip. "Gotta find the birthday queen." Not that he was eager to face his mother, but it'd be better than having Barbie stuck to him like old gum on the bottom of his boot. Even if she were sincere or his type—as long as he was wrestling his demons, he wouldn't let a woman into his life.

Ignoring the shocked glances when they noticed his scars, Danger navigated the crowd to where he'd last seen his mother. The cacophony of the live big band grated on his nerves as much as the fact that a single bottle of the champagne the waiters in penguin suits ran around with cost more than he got in a paycheck. Meanwhile, people were starving on the other side of town. Hank was one stingy son of a gun, but when it benefited his image, he threw money around like confetti.

The tension in Danger's shoulders ratcheted with every step he took deeper into this snake pit. Nevertheless, he kept moving, eyes now on his mother, Jill Westmoreland, who was engrossed in conversation with Mayor Lee. His mother's cream suit and heels matched her short, voluminous hair—none of which could hide the sadness that lingered in her eyes.

For a split second, Danger hesitated.

"Don't you see what you're doing to your mother? You're going to be the death of her."

The haunting voice made his insides churn. After all these years, Hank's words still had a death grip on him. What gutted him more, though, was that Hank had been right—his mother would've been saved a lot of grief without him.

Danger clenched his jaw. Definitely a stupid idea to come. Should've sent her flowers and her favorite wine instead. He pivoted to head back out when Mom's gaze locked on him and lit up.

"Beau!"

Great. Point of no return. Resisting the urge to keep his elbows out and plow people from his path, he closed the gap of polished marble between them.

"Beau, you came!" Mom wrapped her arms around his torso.

"Happy sixtieth, Mom." Her perfume ignited childhood memories as he bent to hug her bony frame. Yup, definitely lost weight. "You look stunning."

She held on longer than necessary. "I'm so glad you're here," she whispered, her voice thick with emotion. Finally letting go, she dabbed a tear from the corner of her eye before facing Mayor Lee. "This is Beau, the younger of my two sons, who moved back a month ago. Maybe you remember him. While Collin followed in Hank's footsteps, Beau became a warrior, like Scott."

Every cell in Danger's body went rigid at her pride in him— and the mention of his dad. There was nothing to be proud of. He'd failed his team, his country—heck, what he stood for with every fiber of his being. So no, he was no hero.

Mayor Lee, a lanky man in a tailored suit, extended his hand. "Thank you for your service, son." As an old friend of Danger's father, he was probably one of the few who were here for Mom and not to blow smoke up Hank's skirt.

Danger met the firm grip with his own. "Thank you, sir, but I'm just a dog handler."

"Serving our country for sixteen years deserves a thank-you." Lee's mouth quirked up before his expression turned stern again. "I heard about your last mission—my condolences. But welcome home."

And there it was—strangers knowing everything about him thanks to the press. Danger gave him a curt nod.

"You're not working at A Breed Apart ranch by any chance?"

"That's the one."

Lee heaved a sigh. "Then you knew Jordi Reyna."

"We were neighbors. Since Jordi's death, I've been in charge of his dog, Riot."

Or had been. Danger checked his timepiece. The new owner had to be picking up the Dutch shepherd from the ABA ranch just about now. He'd meant to be there for it, but Mom's party had priority. Hopefully whoever had adopted him understood that the former SDD with a specialty in narcotics detection wasn't a pet.

"We are still shocked by Jordi's suicide," Lee said. "He was such an astute young man."

"He was." Yet another veteran suicide. Too many of his friends had fallen prey to the dark, haunting thoughts consuming their lives.

Silence fell between them, leaving too much room for memories Danger didn't want to dwell on. He cleared his throat. "I'll leave you guys to it."

Lee nodded. "It was good talking to you, Beau."

"You too, sir." Danger turned to his smiling mother and kissed her cheek. "Enjoy the rest of your party, Mom."

Her hand on his arm stopped him. "Have you talked to Hank yet?"

The question raised the little hairs at the back of Danger's neck. "Haven't seen him." Technically true, but a skill he'd acquired as a kid—pure self-preservation—was to always know where his stepfather was, even if not in view.

Mom's smile dimmed. "You two should really sort out whatever is going on between y'all."

Not sure how to answer, Danger squeezed her arm. "Catch you later, Mom."

The pain flashing through her eyes haunted him as he snaked through the crowd. He'd never told her what'd happened when she wasn't around. She was clueless about her second husband's dark side. No surprise there. Hank was a master at camouflaging his true persona.

"Watch out, caveman!" a guy snapped.

The exclamation hit Danger at the same time cold liquid splashed his button-down, yanking him out of his thoughts. He shifted to the guy he'd T-boned, a slick dude in his mid-thirties like himself. "Sorry, man. Didn't see you."

The damage to his right eye during captivity left him lacking a good forty degrees of vision. He compensated by constantly scanning his surroundings and relying on that split-second recon. It worked until people, assuming he saw them, made sudden moves. Too acquainted with liquor, he guessed Slick had dumped whisky on him. He swallowed the mounting irritation.

"I'm happy to pay for glasses," the guy groused, looking down at his no-longer-white Oxford while holding out his tumbler.

Danger sniffed. "Glasses that restore eyesight? Guess I holed up too long in my cave."

Slick lifted his chin. "Don't be a smart—" His complacent glare morphed into shock when it locked on Danger's white cornea. "M-my apologies. I didn't . . . I . . ."

"No harm, no foul." Danger stalked past him toward the back doors leading to the porch. The humid evening breeze greeted him as he stepped outside. He took in a lungful, feeling the tension in his shoulders ease. Much better out here without these bloodsuckers making him want to hurl into one of the exotic plants.

Shaking out his arm, wishing he'd thought to grab a towel, he realized he probably smelled like a distillery now. Maybe the warm wind would dry his sleeve. He scanned the colossal yard with its neatly clipped lawn, planted palm trees, and the illuminated Olympic-sized pool. Memories of when he'd sunk Hank's golf cart made him smirk. That stunt would've landed him in juvie if it hadn't been for his mother's appeasement skills.

"Uncle D!"

At the squeaky voice, Danger turned and caught his six-year-old niece in his arms. "Whoa! Hey there, princess." He hauled Lyric into the air with an exaggerated groan, then poked her belly. "How much dessert did you eat? You're definitely heavier than this morning."

She giggled and tried to wriggle free. And just like that, his irritation over the evening evaporated, and the tickling morphed into a near-strangling hug by the little whippersnapper. "I missed you," she whispered.

It wasn't her arms around his throat that choked him. "Not as much as I missed you."

One day, would she blame him for having to grow up without her dad? For having Tyron's blood on his hands?

Lyric shoved away. "You stink!"

Right, the booze. He let her down.

"Here you are." Rachel stepped outside, her gaze raking over Danger. "No time to get changed?"

He reached out and pulled her into a side-hug—with the dry, non-booze-drenched arm. "Couldn't find my favorite dress."

Laughing, his sister hugged him back. "I'd love to see that." Before Danger could answer, she recoiled. "Are you *drinking*?" She mouthed the last word, probably for Lyric's sake.

Danger scrubbed a hand over his chin. "A guy dumped his drink on me."

When Rachel's eyes—no more than slits—swept over him like a vulnerability scanner, he held his sleeve to her face.

She yanked back, her nose scrunched. "Okay, okay. I believe you."

Good, because the last thing he wanted was for her to think he'd fallen off the wagon again. By getting her husband killed, he'd already caused her enough pain.

"Can we play soccer, Uncle Danger?" Lyric pulled his hand so hard he could swear it was about to rip off.

"No, honey," Rachel said. "We're going home. It's late."

"But I want to be with Uncle Danger!"

"I'll give you a lift." Anything to get out of this place. Needed to work the punching bag in his garage before he succumbed to old habits.

"Son."

Danger stilled. They hadn't seen each other in eighteen years—not in person, anyway—and this was the one word Hank used? Swallowing the spiking fury, he dug out the keys to his Tacoma and passed them to Rachel. "I'll be right there."

"Be nice to Dad."

Danger held on to the keys. "He's not my dad—or yours." Or Collin's.

"He's the only dad I know."

That was on Danger. She'd been three when he'd gotten their biological father killed.

Rachel sighed. "Look, just because you don't get along with Hank doesn't mean he's a bad father."

Easy to say with the treatment she and Collin had gotten. But Danger let it go. The keys too. Wouldn't allow Hank to get between them one more time.

He watched Rachel kiss Hank on the cheek and disappear with Lyric into the mansion, then locked eyes with his stepfather. "Hank."

The guy hadn't changed. Still reeked of power and money. The navy three-piece suit molded to his built physique like a second skin. Thick gray hair shadowed a deep crease in his forehead. "Son, you lost weight."

The comment aggravated Danger almost as much as the *son*. "Like you'd know."

Hank's cheek twitched. "Your mother showed me some pictures . . ."

Danger grunted, moving on. "Didn't like the food the captors served," he said, shoving down the rising memories of Cutter refusing the rice he'd tried to feed him. The Guerreros had nearly starved Danger to death, and being trapped in the hospital had slowed the rebuilding of his muscle mass. While he'd made some decent progress over the past three months, he was far from where he'd once been.

Hank shook his head. "You sorry lot got a respected politician killed."

Danger grabbed him by his lapels, thrust him against the

wall, and crushed his forearm into his windpipe. "Say that again."

His stepfather stared at him with bulging eyes, seeming to grope for what was happening.

"Beau!" Mom's cry dug into Danger's rage.

Realizing he was about to put his stepfather on a liquid diet, he backed off. Trembling from the rage, he let out a ragged breath. Felt the tattered control returning . . .

Mom rushed to Hank, who was hunched over, gripping his throat. "Darling, are you all right?" The horror in her voice matched her expression.

"Keep his body upright and he'll be fine." Danger's words emerged hoarse as he backed away. One last glance at Mom, then he turned and beat a retreat.

THE ABILITY TO CONTROL MY EMOTIONS AND MY ACTIONS, REGARDLESS OF CIRCUMSTANCE, SETS ME APART FROM OTHERS.

The SEAL Creed seared a hole into his conscience as he hoofed it to his truck and climbed in.

"Everything okay?" Rachel asked.

"Fine."

Except that on the way home, the creed kept assaulting him. He'd always done everything to not only keep it but excel in it. What he'd just done proved how far away he was from being an operator again.

As a trauma counselor, Paisley Reyna could never predict the level of urgency for the incoming calls, but something told her this one was serious. She released a hand from the steering wheel and swiped her phone attached to a car holder. "Tara?"

The headlights of her 1988 Ford Bronco II lit the dimly illuminated street of her new neighborhood with the generously spaced, beautiful homes. Almost there.

"Miss Paisley?" Her client's—*former* client as of two days ago—words oozed panic.

"Yes, it's me, honey. What's wrong?"

"I-I can't . . . I just . . ."

"Your destination is on the right," her GPS announced.

"Tara, take a deep breath." Paisley pulled to the curb of her cousin's home—a onetime large work garage that had been converted to a one-bedroom cottage—and parked. "Let's do it together. Four seconds in"—she counted silently—"and seven out."

Deafening barking from the back of her vehicle made her jump. She whipped around. "Shh, Riot. Quiet!" She'd totally forgotten she'd put Jordi's dog back there in a crate.

Riot barked louder, incessantly.

Oh, for Pete's sake. She couldn't hear—she had to get inside the cottage. "I'm so sorry, Tara. I'm right with you." Paisley cracked the window on her side, slipped into the humid night, then grabbed her bag from the passenger seat and locked the car. "Okay, let's take another deep breath."

As they repeated the exercise, Paisley shot off a text to Amara—a counselor friend living near Tara—and fled through the yard to Jordi's home, Riot's barking chasing her. He could wait ten minutes; Tara needed her full attention. She unlocked the door to the cottage, slipped into the rustic, sort of farmhouse-style space, and flicked on the light. "Now, tell me what's wrong." She navigated around the moving boxes she'd unloaded before picking Riot up from the A Breed Apart ranch and sank into the two-cushion couch in the small living area.

As Tara brought forth her doubts and fears, Paisley listened attentively. Although two days ago she had quit her job at Serenity Chicago, an organization serving trafficking survivors, to move to Texas, she'd told her clients they could reach out anytime.

"Remember what we talked about last week?" she asked once Tara was done.

"I . . . no." Thank God the girl had calmed down.

"That it's normal to feel lost, even to want your old life back. But that's only because the familiar is sometimes hard to let go of."

"But I don't understand why I want to go back to him. Something is wrong with me!"

The desperation tugged at Paisley. If only she could be there with her. Instead, she was over a thousand miles away. "At first, I wanted to go back too."

"Really?"

"Uh-huh." As she told Tara about her struggle to start a new life, Paisley continuously ran her fingers over a moving box. She'd unpack tomorrow. Driving down here from Chicago had taken two days and completely worn her out. All she wanted tonight was sleep. "You have a new life ahead of you, Tara. Get excited about it! Discover what the Lord has in store for you."

Huh, a great reminder for herself. While no doubt God wanted her here in Texas, she was still trying to figure out what exactly His plan entailed. Not knowing frightened her.

All because of Jordi bequeathing his possessions to her.

"I'm feeling much better," Tara said. "Oh, Amara is here."

The knot in Paisley's gut loosened. *Thank You, Jesus.* These girls had been so much more than clients.

After ending the call with a prayer, Paisley slumped into the cushions. She let her gaze sweep over space she would now call home. Life in Chicago had been okay, but working for a charity had meant funds were thin. So this unexpected blessing from her cousin felt like a kiss from God.

Though small, it perfectly met her needs. The kitchen and island were set right by the front farmhouse door with high windows, a small dinette tucked on the other side. Opposite the living room was a wall that gave a semblance of privacy for the bedroom, enhanced by a sliding barn door. The stained concrete was low-maintenance, but the short-pile rugs redeemed the coziness.

Even in his death, Jordi had been looking out for her. He'd been closer than a sibling to her—her best friend.

And she hadn't seen his suicide coming.

Oh, Jordi. The deep ache Paisley had been wrestling since his death welled up. Two weeks had passed, but the days weren't getting any easier. She felt so . . . lost.

Outside, a car pulled up. Probably the neighbor's son checking in on his mother. Paisley had met the sweet elderly lady three months ago while visiting Jordi. She was also the one who'd converted this place and, once her grandson who'd lived in it off and married, let Jordi buy it.

Paisley glanced at the urn with his ashes sitting on a rack above Riot's wire crate. Once again felt the guilt of not yet having spread them.

She hauled in a gasp. "Riot!" Scrambling to find her car keys she'd tossed somewhere, she growled. Found them on the kitchen island, jerked open the door, and charged into the night.

Barking erupted as her foot hit the lawn. Why on earth had Jordi left his working dog to her? Worst decision ever!

Remembering the way the A Breed Apart owner had had to help her get Riot into the crate at the back of the Bronco, she cringed. "Whatever your reason, cuz, I'll do my best to take good care of him. Promise."

The moon and the streetlamp hovering over her SUV offered little light, but it was enough to make out a man at the rear hatch, ogling inside.

Sweet mercy! He'd get his face bitten off if Riot got loose. She hurried down the shared driveway toward the street. "You need something?" When he didn't respond, she realized Riot's barking was eating her words.

He stalked to the passenger door, slipped off his dress shirt—revealing a T-shirt beneath—and wrapped it around his right hand. His moves were confident, like he was on a mission.

She wasn't one to confront powerfully built strangers—he wasn't a tank like Crew Gatlin from the ranch, but still strong enough to harm her—but she also wasn't willing to have a lawsuit or a dead body on her hands. "Sir. Excuse me."

Either he couldn't hear or didn't care. He drew his padded fist back and—

Paisley gasped when he punched the passenger window, shattering it to tiny pieces.

The heat spiraling from the pit of her stomach propelled her forward. "Are you out of your mind?"

The stranger whipped around.

Paisley came to an abrupt halt a good nine feet away, heart in her throat. His right cornea was white, a long scar running from his forehead across the eye and down his cheek.

Suppressing a shudder, she lifted her chin. "What're you doing?"

"That your dog?" His good eye drilled into her as he stomped closer till his six-foot-plus frame towered over her five-three.

Jutting her chin, she glared up at him. If he thought this would scare her, he was wrong. "Is that a problem?"

"The only problem here is you. What person with more than three brain cells would leave a dog in a car in this heat?"

"Heat? It's night! And I cracked two windows. Besides, he was only in there for ten minutes."

Without taking his eyes off her, Macho Man backtracked, reached through the broken window, and pulled the lock knob up. Then he opened the front and back doors. "This is Texas, *darlin'*, not Illinois. Let me stick you in there for five minutes and see how long it takes you to cook." He cocked his head at her. "I'll even crack a window for you."

Darlin'. The word slithered through Paisley. No one got to call her that, and the way he'd said it with an extra thick Southern drawl . . . *ugh.* Who did he think he was? And how did he know she was from—

Oh, the license plate. Maybe he acted like an idiot, but he sure wasn't one.

Sweat dribbled down her spine, and she realized he was probably right about the heat. Oh no, had she really put Riot in danger right after promising Jordi she'd take good care of him?

The guy squared his shoulders. The way he held himself screamed military. "Someone who doesn't know how to handle an MWD shouldn't have one."

"Excuse me?" Paisley's voice pitched. Just because she'd made one mistake didn't mean she had it all wrong.

"Did I stutter?"

She was pretty sure her jaw just dropped to her chest. How *dare* he? Riot was *her* dog now—thanks to Jordi—and this man had absolutely no business telling her how to handle him.

She stomped up to him. "Listen, pal. Riot—"

The ripping of fabric drew her attention to the Bronco.

Riot sank his teeth into a long swath of the rear seat and played tug-of-war with it. The rest of her back seat looked like it hung in shreds . . . No, this couldn't be happening. How did he get out of the crate?

"No!" She pushed past Macho Man to intervene. "Please, no! Riot, stop. Please!"

He'd shredded not just one seat. All—save one—were destroyed. Foam material littered the floor.

Riot looked at her, then at the seat. Back at her. Like a dare.

"Don't!" Paisley leaned into the vehicle to grab his collar.

"I wouldn't do that."

Riot barked, startling the tar out of her. She yanked back her hand. With a huff, the Dutch shepherd resumed his attack and tore out another chunk.

The command. Crew had told her what to say. What was it? "Riot—uh—out!"

More foam tumbled to the floor.

"Stop it!" Paisley whimpered, hating to see her beloved Bronco destroyed. Feeling powerless to stop this military working dog. "Pleeeease."

"We gotta lie in the bed we make," the guy's voice rumbled behind her. "Serves you right for locking him in."

The smug tone made her whirl around. "This wasn't my choice, okay? I wasn't even asked if I wanted him. Yet here I am, all of a sudden responsible for a crazy"—she clenched her fingers—"retired military working dog. He doesn't listen. Doesn't do anything I ask—"

Macho Man emitted a whistle. "Riot, out."

Those two words thudded into Paisley's chest. She watched in disbelief as her dog immediately stopped wrecking her SUV, angled his head to the guy, and sat, tongue dangling in obvious pleasure at his kill.

Giving his leg a double pat, the guy said, "Heel."

With a lethal grace, Riot leapt out of the Bronco and landed in the grass. Then, dragging the leash behind, shot to Macho Man's left side. Panting, he watched the man's every move.

"How . . ."

"Of course it's the dog's fault." Macho Man plucked the leash from the lawn and attached it to Riot's collar. "Why blame yourself when you've got the perfect scapegoat."

"That's not—" Paisley pressed her lips together. Nope, not worth the little energy she had left. "You know what? I don't even know why I'm talking to you. My dog is none of your business."

Hard eyes bored into hers. "If he's locked in a car in this heat, he sure is."

Paisley shot him a one-more-word-and-I'll-scratch-out-your-good-eye glare. Oh yes, she absolutely meant it. But first she had to get Riot back.

She focused on him. "Riot, heel!"

The dog's attention remained on Macho Man as if he hadn't just been given a command. Was he for real?

"Riot, heel!" Paisley repeated, trying to keep the desperation from bleeding into her words. This was the exact command Macho Man had used. Why wasn't it working? She was about to demand the leash when Riot's focus shifted to something behind him, his tail wagging slowly.

Macho Man had his gaze cast down and to the side as if listening to something.

Paisley stared into the dark. What had they heard?

"What's going on here?" a woman's voice intruded into the standoff. "You're yelling down the entire neighborhood."

It sounded so much like . . . "Rachel!" Paisley stumbled to her friend and into open arms. The familiar smell of honeysuckle enveloped her like a warm blanket, letting the tension flake away. "I thought you were out of town."

"Change of plans." After another squeeze, Rachel let go. "I'm glad you got here safe, Pais. I wanted to reach out, but I had so much organizing to do."

"Don't worry about it." Paisley grinned. "This is the best surprise."

"True." Rachel's gaze landed on Macho Man, still hovering nearby. "Now, what's going on?"

"Macho Man here"—Paisley jutted her chin at him— "decided to break into my car while I was in my home, taking a call."

He scoffed. "You forgot the part where you almost killed your dog with heat exhaustion."

"I did not—that—" She huffed, forcing her attention back to her onetime college roomie. "The call was important, and when I couldn't hear anything because Riot was barking nonstop, I went inside."

"Must've been very important for you to sacrifice him," Macho Man said.

"It was a suicide call!"

"Sure."

Rachel raised a hand. "Guys, please." Her gaze bounced between them, then she pursed her lips as she focused on Paisley. "Danger is a dog handler at ABA, and he's right about

RIOT

the heat. Even at night and with cracked windows, vehicles become ovens, and with that, death traps."

Wait. Macho Man was Rachel's brother Beau, aka Danger?

Paisley slipped another glance his way. How had she not recognized him? She'd seen pictures, even met him at Rachel's and Tyron's wedding seven years ago. Those intense blue eyes had rested on her almost the entire night.

His hair was shorter now, his beard shaved to a five-o'clock shadow. Also, hadn't he been more . . . built? And the scars . . .

"We finally found him, Pais. He's in bad shape, but he'll pull through. He's a warrior." The memory of Rachel's hopeful words four months ago sucked every bit of anger out of Paisley. This man had been through the unthinkable. Not that she knew details. Rachel had only mentioned that he'd been the sole survivor of an ambush and forty-nine days of captivity in Venezuela. That he'd escaped, hiked thirty miles through the jungle, and swum another ten to Trinidad and Tobago.

But the scars told a story of gruesome pain.

Now it also made sense why he knew Riot—they were both connected to the ABA ranch.

"Still," Rachel continued, raising both eyebrows at her brother, "you can communicate in a civilized manner. Paisley is a trauma counselor, so if she says it was a suicide call, it was a suicide call."

Paisley waited for another retort, but Beau seemed too busy working his jaw.

With two quick strides, he cut the distance between them. "Take better care of this combat hero, or I'll make sure you don't have to worry about him anymore." He shoved Riot's leash into her hand, then made some kind of gesture that had him sit by her side.

The fear his words spiked silenced her. She wouldn't put it past him to follow through if he caught her making another mistake. But good luck trying to take Riot from her.

She narrowed her eyes at him. "I don't like being threatened.

But don't worry—we'll stay out of your hair." By never again crossing paths with him.

His shredded eyebrow drew up ever so slightly. Then he grunted, turned, and stalked off.

Right to the house next to Jordi's.

Paisley's jaw slackened. Neighbors? They were *neighbors*?

2

HARMONIA, TEXAS

"He doesn't take risks when it comes to dogs," Rachel said, her gaze—not unlike Paisley's—glued to Beau's single-family home. "Never did, but even less since he lost Cutter."

The words fueled Paisley's guilt. As a counselor and a Christian, she was supposed to build people up, not tear them down. The way someone treated her shouldn't affect how she treated them. Exhaustion and grief were no excuse.

She wrenched her gaze from the closed door and looked at her friend. "Was Cutter the dog he lost in the ambush?"

"Yeah, he died during captivity." Rachel sighed. "The two shared a powerful bond."

Like Riot and Jordi. Her cousin had once explained how their connection went beyond anything he'd ever shared with a human being. Maybe it had been the same with Beau and his dog.

Glancing down at Riot, Paisley found his gaze fixated on Beau's house as if expecting him to come back any minute. *Please don't.* Despite all the sympathy she felt toward Beau, she wanted no business with him. Impossible, considering their homes sat on the same property with only fifty feet of grass separating his drive from her house.

Very funny, God.

"When did he move in?" she asked Rachel. "When I visited Jordi three months ago, an elderly lady lived here."

Her friend smiled. "Ah, Mrs. Timmons. She moved to an old folks' home about a month ago."

Yes, sweet old Mrs. Timmons. Paisley wanted her back, please.

"All the houses on this street belong to Dad, so when it came available, Danger asked for it."

Light penetrated the two small windows of Beau's garage, and subdued hard rock started booming.

"He's probably blowing off steam in there." Rachel pulled out her phone, the light illuminating her delicate features. "He's been working out like a maniac. His way to deal with stress." Her eyes widened at the screen.

"Everything okay?" Paisley asked softly.

Rachel looked up. "Mom just texted that Danger and Dad got into a scuffle at the party." Exhaling, she dropped her hand. "What did you do now, dear brother?"

"Are they still not getting along?"

She shook her head. "I'd hoped after not seeing each other in eighteen years and Danger's near-death experience that things would change. But nope."

Paisley drew up her brows. "They haven't talked in eighteen years?"

"Danger never came back after he signed up. He'd meet Mom anywhere but here when he was stateside." Rachel lifted a shoulder.

Riot pulled at the leash, staring into the dark, a low rumble coming from his chest.

"Do you mind if we continue our conversation inside?" Paisley asked, clutching the leash with both hands. "I'm scared he might run off."

"Actually, you look exhausted. How about Lyric and I come by tomorrow and help you unpack?"

The thought of having them help her warmed Paisley's chest. "That'd be amazing." She pulled her friend into a hug. "I can't believe we're living on the same street. All I have to do is walk up the street and you're there. Remember how in college we joked about moving in together with both of our families?" Only she didn't have a family. With Jordi gone she had no one at all.

As always, she ignored the sting the thought caused.

"I remember." Rachel's voice sounded muffled. Nevertheless, a smile was audible. "God has His ways, although they usually look different from our expectations." Maybe she was thinking about being a widow now. "I think maybe God timed this—for us to be here together, to grieve our losses and support each other." She gave a wavering smile. "We'll get through this, Pais. Together. Promise."

Paisley nodded. "By God's grace."

After bidding goodnight, Paisley escorted Riot inside. Or tried, because he kept pulling toward Beau's home, whining without pause. Finally in the cottage, he trotted to Jordi's boots and curled up on them, his muzzle resting on his paws. For some reason, he was obsessed with them.

Paisley slumped down before him and smoothed a hand over his brindle coat. "I'm sorry for locking you in there. I guess I deserve the shredded seats." How on earth would she afford to repair that?

Riot's chocolate eyes met hers, and her breath caught at the sadness in them. He looked like a big, sad teddy bear.

"You really miss him, don't you?" she whispered. "Me too. Everything here reminds me of him." She wiped away a tear with the back of her hand. "Remember my last visit, when I tried to make *catalinas*?" The Venezuelan soft cookies had been Jordi's favorite, and she'd wanted to make them like their grandma used to. "Although I meticulously followed Abuela's recipe, I managed to burn them to a crisp. Jordi laughed so hard that coffee came out his nose."

The memory elicited a chuckle, which quickly turned into choked sobbing. What was she going to do without her best friend? She rose and, clutching her fists, turned to the urn. "Why didn't you tell me that you were struggling? I could have helped!"

Instead, he'd gone without a word. Not even a note. Only that stupid will, stating she inherited everything.

Paisley buried her face in her hands. Okay, she was losing her marbles. Sleep. She needed to get some sleep. Tomorrow the world would hopefully look a little brighter. Rachel and Lyric would come over, and she had to conduct lots of research on how to train Riot.

She moved to the Dutch shepherd's crate and pointed at it. "Riot, inside."

He didn't respond, not even cracking an eye open.

"Riot, inside!"

No reaction.

"Oh, come on. I need to sleep." Paisley stomped over to him. "Fine. If you're not willing to cooperate, I'll help you." By putting Jordi's boots in the crate.

She reached for them.

Riot jerked his head up with a snarl, making her yank her hand back.

The force of her own movement knocked her to her backside. Breathing hard, she stared at the sharp, glistening teeth Riot bared. "Okay, how about you're not sleeping in the crate tonight?" She slowly scooched away. "You sleep on the boots, and tomorrow we'll figure things out. Sound good?"

Riot lowered his head back to his paws. Looked like they had a deal.

Sleep came fast and hard. When Paisley awoke, she found herself in complete darkness. Lying still, she strained to hear what had roused her.

There. It sounded like . . . someone was in the kitchen. Pushing dishes around on the counter? Something shattered, making her jump. Her heart galloped as she scrambled out of bed and pulled open the sliding barn door. She reached for the light switch on the wall. The brilliant glow assaulted her eyes and it took a moment until they adjusted—

She gasped at the sight. Cardboard from the moving boxes was strewn all over the cottage, along with shreds of clothing—hers!—and psychology books. "No no no no . . ." A stool from the island lay on its side, and fractures of ceramic scattered the kitchen area.

Riot was crammed onto one of the counters, his nose in the cabinet above him. He sniffed Jordi's favorite cup, emitting loud huffs in the process.

"What did you do?" Paisley cried.

His head swiveled in her direction, then he turned and nudged the cup. It slid to the edge.

Paisley scrambled into the living area. Tripped over something and tumbled in a pile of clothes. Lying there, she was forced to witness Riot give the cup another nudge. It went over the edge and shattered on the concrete floor.

Paisley buried her face in the clothes. *Help me, Lord. I can't do this.* The grief, the move, the unknown future . . . She didn't have the energy to deal with a crazy dog. Heath Daniels, the co-owner of A Breed Apart, had offered a staggering sum for him. Accepting it could solve a lot of problems.

"My goodness, why am I even thinking about this?" Jordi wanted *her* to have Riot, and even if it weren't for his maddening will—the dog was the only thing left of her cousin.

Air tickled her arm, then something wet nudged her cheek. She opened her eyes and found Riot standing over her. "You're a varmint, you know that?"

He continued huffing into her face, causing her to laugh. Then he turned and found something to chew on.

Paisley jolted upright. "No, no, no. Not Kala! Riot, out!"

31

RONIE KENDIG & JJ SAMIE MYLES

Of course he didn't listen. He chewed away at her hand-sized crocheted monkey like it was his KONG.

The *KONG!*

Paisley rolled to her knees and frantically rifled through the mess. Where had she put his stuff? The car. After last night's ruckus she'd forgotten to bring it inside. She slumped back down. Was there anything she did right?

Riot dropped Kala and gagged, then pawed at his mouth. He'd probably gotten a taste of the vanilla oil she'd dribbled over her.

Taking in a steadying breath, Paisley picked up Kala's slobber-drenched body and severed head. Enough! "We're going back to the ranch for help."

Huffing a breath, she opened the bag of dog food but realized she had to hunt down the bowl. She pivoted and found it tucked in the corner between the living room and island. Bowl retrieved, she turned. And sucked in a breath.

Riot was on the counter, head thrust neck-deep in the food bag.

"No, no! Down—" Wait. No, that meant to lie down. What was . . . "Off! Off off off!" When he didn't comply—*no surprise*—she snatched away the bag. Inexplicably, kibble splattered across the counter and onto the floor. "No!"

And finally, Riot complied, hopping down, but only to devour what had been spilled.

Deflated, she eyed him inhaling the food like a vacuum. *I'm never going to survive this dog.* Definitely needed to go back to the ranch. No point in trying to clean that up. Taking advantage of his distraction with chasing the kibble that had slid under the table, she clipped on his lead. Purse on her shoulder and keys in her pocket, she wrestled Riot outside and back into her Bronco. While duct-taping the broken door of his crate, she eyed Beau's house, sitting quiet in the dawning day. His pickup was either in the garage or gone. Running into him would be the crowning glory of her wretched morning.

The sun crept past the horizon as she pulled up to the ABA ranch. She depressed the button at the gate. Rather than hearing someone answer, the gate clicked and rolled open in response. Guess someone else was up at this ungodly hour. When she parked at the main building, she found Heath Daniels awaiting them in cargos, a patriotic T-shirt, and a tan baseball cap with the A Breed Apart logo.

"You're back," he greeted her. "Glad you reconsidered. Smart move."

Paisley froze, mid picking up seat stuffing that had fallen out. "What? No! I-I . . ." Had Beau said something? Were they going to take Riot away from her now?

Clutching the foam, she straightened slowly. What was wrong with her? Heath had just asked if she'd reconsidered the offer. He wasn't taking Riot away. She willed her heart to slow. "Actually, I came because I'm hoping to get help with him."

Eyebrows drawn together, Heath eyed the rear of her Bronco, where Riot was barking. "He alright?"

"No. I mean, yes." Paisley briefly closed her eyes. "I think he's going crazy. He tore apart Jordi's entire place and shredded my Bronco seats." She displayed the foam, then tossed it into the vehicle and shut the door. "Fine, I deserved that one. But no matter what I say or do, he doesn't listen." Oh, she sounded desperate. Maybe because she was.

"Let's bring him out."

"Okay." Paisley walked around the vehicle and unlocked the tailgate, then opened it.

Riot's barking turned into whining, his tail wagging slightly. Oh, look who was back to being a sweet angel.

"Hey, boy." Heath snapped the duct tape like it was paper and made a fist.

Riot lowered into a sit, and Heath clipped on the leash that'd been sitting beside the crate. "Let's go." Riot leapt out of the Bronco and started inspecting the ground eagerly.

Heath walked him up the green and back, gave him a few commands, which the traitorous dog did with vigor. "Seems fine to me," Heath said as he smoothed a hand over Riot's spine. "What's going on that you need help?"

"He obeys everyone but me." Paisley let out a huff. "I don't know what I'm doing wrong."

Rubbing Riot's ears, Heath considered her. "Working dogs are either alphas or need to be alpha'd. You can't half-cock anything, or they'll steal control out from under you." He squinted at her. "We can train you to handle him, but it's not easy and it demands consistency. I have plenty of handlers and trainers who'd be willing to step up so Riot can have a successful retirement."

Paisley chewed the inside of her cheek. This actually sounded like a good idea. If a professional taught her everything she needed to know, she could keep Riot. Sure, it was a lot of work, but she'd do anything to provide him the best life.

She nodded. "I'd love that, but I'm not sure I can afford it." With Serenity Chicago being a nonprofit, she hadn't been able to put much aside.

Heath produced a black KONG and pitched it down the green. A second later, he sent Riot after it. "I hear that." When Riot bolted back with the toy trapped in his teeth, Heath considered her for a second. "Okay, how about we train you, and in return you lend us your skills."

"Mine?" she balked.

"Yeah, you're a trauma counselor, right?" He nodded to the ranch. "Not uncommon for the dogs or the people to encounter trauma on missions." He gave her a look. "And if I'm honest, I'm also hoping to capitalize on your experience with the Guerrero Cartel."

Shock pushed her back a step, her heart thundering.

"Jordi told me you've been giving a hand to anyone going

against them." Heath readjusted his ball cap, oblivious to her visceral reaction. "They're getting a little too cozy on our soil. Sheriff's been talking about putting together a task force and using a dog or two from here to address that."

Briefly closing her eyes, Paisley willed away the all-too-familiar feeling the name Guerrero—or Lyonel—left in its wake every time it popped into her head. Not many people knew about her involvement with Venezuela's most lethal cartel. They were absolutely ruthless, trafficking anything traffickable: drugs, arms, organs, and the worst, humans.

Like her.

Now they were invading the US, her home.

She suppressed a shudder. *But the Lord is faithful, and He will strengthen you and protect you from the evil one.*

No matter how often she pondered this verse, the words found her head but not her heart. She wanted to believe it, that God protected her, but there was a nagging anxiety lodged deep within her. Yes, healing needed patience—as a trauma counselor she was more than aware of that. But the scars on her soul would never go away.

"Think about it," Heath said. "While you're doing that, we can get underway with training you to also ensure Riot doesn't regress. I can introduce you to the guy I have in mind. Speaking of—" He jutted his jaw toward a big vehicle rumbling up behind them. "This almost seems like providence."

Turning, she spotted a silver Toyota Tacoma. Her gut tightened. That looked a lot like Beau's truck. *Please, no, Lord.* See, that's why she didn't make any rash decisions.

The Tacoma stopped, and the guy stepped out of the truck. Riot tore across the grass toward him. Paisley watched in horror as he rammed straight into Beau—of course it was him—who deflected the incoming assault. Patted the Dutchie's sides. Then Riot rose up on his hind legs to his full size, planting his front paws on Rachel's brother's chest. His tail wagged as hard as if it were . . . Jordi.

Paisley groaned. Divinely ordained or not, she most certainly would *not* work with this guy.

Danger had come to the ranch early to discuss mission readiness with Ghost, not to deal with his new favorite neighbor. Yet they both lurked in the main parking lot, watching him like a dog tracking his KONG. At least having Reyna around meant Riot was here too. The Dutchie had his paws firmly planted on Danger's chest, his excitement digging into Danger's foul mood.

"Hey, bud. Glad she didn't kill you overnight." He smoothed both hands up and down the dog's sturdy ribcage.

Riot squinted, that long, pink tongue trying to find its way into Danger's face.

"Thanks, already had a shower." He gave him a thump on the side, then pointed to the ground. "Down."

Riot backed off and parked his rear at Danger's nine. Man, the more time he spent with him, the more he reminded him of Cutter. For whatever reason.

"Riot's growing fond of you," Ghost said with a jut of his jaw.

"It's mutual." Danger's gaze struck Reyna over his boss's shoulder. She had her hands buried in the back pockets of her faded jeans, long black waves cascading down her shoulders.

That hair was one of the things that had caught his eye seven years ago at Rachel's wedding. He'd been kicking it with Tyron's Team Six, which he later joined, when Reyna showed up in that flower dress hugging her lean, curvy body and highlighting her golden skin. He'd nearly ignored the fact that God had given him two left feet and asked her for a dance but then chickened out. Crazy Rudy had seized the opportunity instead.

Ghost stepped aside and nodded at her. "This is Paisley Reyna, Jordi's cousin. Paisley, Beau Maddox."

Danger planted his hands on his tac belt. "We've met."

Riot barked as if agreeing.

"I went to college with his sister," Paisley explained when Ghost drew up a brow. Her gaze landed back on Danger. "And now we're neighbors." She said it matter-of-factly, almost cheerily, but her hazel eyes flashed.

Ditto, woman.

"Right," Ghost muttered, then locked eyes with Danger. "A word."

When Danger took a step to follow his boss, Riot moved right with him, his shoulder pressing into his leg. Looking for his handler—which he hadn't found in Reyna. Made sense he came to Danger for structure. After all, he'd been working him daily, from sunup till sundown, for the past two weeks.

Still. He needed to know his place. Danger pointed at Reyna. "Guard."

The Dutchie trotted to her side and sat, his watchful eyes remaining on Danger.

"Rough night?" Ghost asked once they were out of earshot.

Danger sniffed. "No different from any other." Which meant working out till he was ready to hurl—the only way to subdue his demons and steer clear of booze.

Over on the green—an open, park-like area with a watering fountain—Reyna tried to make Riot heel. The Dutchie tilted his head, then rose and scampered away, ignoring her command to come back. When she chased after him, Danger hollered "sit," relieved when the dog complied without issue. Chasing an MWD like Riot, who had aggression training, was begging for trouble. And it was painful to watch her scampering around, putting herself in danger.

"You know we've always got your six," Ghost said, eying the woman and Riot, then him again.

Danger met his gaze. "Appreciate it." He did, but this was his battle alone. Enough people had already paid for his wrong calls. Wasn't gonna drag anyone else in.

"What's with the aggression toward Paisley?"

Danger gritted his teeth. "She locked him in her Bronco last night—in the heat. Had to break him out." Just thinking about it had him fuming again. He indicated to her on the green. "She doesn't know what she's doing. Sooner or later she'll get him killed. Why's she even have him?"

Ghost's frown deepened as his gaze scanned the pair. "Jordi's left Riot to her." He turned back to Danger. "Offered to buy Riot. She refused. Twice."

"Then why's she here?"

"She needs help. Riot tore her place apart."

Danger couldn't help the smirk. Served her right.

"Made a deal with her—in exchange for specific intel and experience she has, we'll train her to handle Riot."

"You want to put her in the field when she can't even function with him in a one-room garage?"

Ghost held his gaze without answer.

"And who's supposed to train her?" When his boss kept staring, Danger's amusement died. "C'mon, man—"

"You know Riot better than any of us."

"—if I wanted to work with people, I'd be a cashier at Target. I handle *dogs* for a reason."

Warning flashed in Ghost's expression. "You wanted to talk about mission readiness? Then let's talk. Going up against the Guerreros means we need a narcotics detection dog." He nodded. "Riot is the only NDD on property right now—that is, if Paisley cooperates. That means to go on the mission, you go with him. Them."

The last thing Danger wanted was to go against his boss—the man had done so much for him. Still. The *very* last thing he needed was a shrink up in his business. "You know I'll do anything you ask, but not with her."

"You think I'm asking?" He scowled. "Put your ego aside for a second and think about what taking down the Guerreros could mean, not to mention what it'd mean for Riot, since she won't relinquish him. That dog needs to work."

That one was so well aimed Danger felt it physically. Ghost was right. By training Reyna, he could ensure Riot had a good life. Even if it was with her.

Ghost slapped his back. "Think it over and get back to me."

Barking and a yell snapped Danger's attention to the green. Riot chased a rabbit across the lawn, right toward the road where Crew Gatlin was coming up in his Raptor—not fast, since all handlers knew dogs were here training, but still a danger if the dog proved unpredictable. Like Riot right now. Reyna yelled commands like a madwoman, her voice shrill. What the—

Danger emitted a whistle.

Riot banked the same time Crew hit the brakes only inches from him. Stance squared, he swiveled his ears in their direction but didn't return.

Muttering an oath, Danger jogged down the road. "Riot, heel." He patted his leg.

Riot met him halfway, panting up to him.

Holding his collar, Danger escorted him back to the lawn, the Dutchie giving a quick snarl before getting a grip. "Not a fan of her either, but you gotta listen to her, bud."

Gatlin rolled up to them, a log-like arm hanging out the open window. "Please tell me she accepted Ghost's offer."

"Negative." Danger sliced a glance Reyna's way. She'd frozen on the spot, mouth slightly agape. "His new offer is to teach her how to handle him."

Gatlin snickered. "Well, he did get your sorry carcass turned around."

"Unnecessary."

Laughing, Crew pulled in his arm and drove on, leaving Danger alone with Riot and Reyna.

"Thank you," she breathed when they stalked up to her. At least she had the decency to look contrite.

His temper flared anyway. "Yelling won't get his attention," Danger ground out.

Her brows rippled, then she jutted her chin. "Makes sense. It doesn't get mine either."

A string of curses shot through Danger's mind. See, this was exactly why he couldn't work with her. "You think this is a joke?"

"Of course I don't!" Her voice shook, but her hazel eyes remained on him. Steady. Sincere. "I know I made a mistake, but that doesn't mean you have to be a jerk about it. Or do you never make mistakes?"

Her words drew Danger back. If only she knew. She'd understand that the reason he'd yelled at her last night had been panic talking. Seeing Riot in a deadly situation had thrown him right back to Venezuela, where Cutter died because of his mistake.

Cutter. The way he'd looked at him, lying there, bone thin, those faithful eyes boring into his soul. *Why aren't you helping me, Dad?*

He'd wanted to, but . . . Turning away from Reyna, Danger roughed a hand over his mouth. Swallowed the acid pooling at the back of his throat and faced her again. "When you give a dog a command, the tone is more important than the words. Keep your voice firm and controlled. He feeds off emotions. If you're amped, he's amped." He focused on the Dutchie. "Riot, sit."

He sat.

"Down."

He lay flat on his belly.

"Up."

Back on his paws.

"See? No yelling necessary." His phone went off in his pocket. Probably Rachel wanting to talk about Hank. He let the call go to voicemail like all the others. There was nothing to talk about.

Reyna's gaze traveled from Riot, sniffing his pantleg, back up to him. Strangely, she wasn't the least bit irritated by his damaged eye. "I wasn't aware I was yelling." Her words sounded small. She sucked in her bottom lip, then her brows knotted. "What's in your pocket?"

"Oxy." He dug out the orange bottle with the oxycodone pills he needed since cracking his back on that rock in Venezuela. Usually left them in the car. "Riot's an NDD—narcotics detection dog. Trained to sniff out opioids."

The corners of Reyna's mouth dipped, her eyes hardening. "Pretty strong stuff."

"The only thing that works for my busted back."

"Mm-hmm. High risk for dependency and addiction." She muttered it just loud enough for him to hear. Sounded like she had experience—personal experience. Herself or someone she knew.

He nearly joked his only addiction was booze, but saying things like that got him into hot water. If she took his word for it and reported to Ghost, or even Rachel, he was a dead man.

No, he had the drinking under control.

For the most part.

"I only take them when I'm close to dying." No idea why he felt the urge to reassure her, but he did. He pocketed the bottle and redirected this convo. "The dog's sense of smell is far superior to ours. We've got about six million olfactory receptors in our nose, but dogs have up to three hundred million. That's why Riot can sniff out the oxy through the bottle. He'd find it buried six feet under."

"That's crazy." Reyna's face lit up as she studied the Dutchie. "Jordi always talked about how special he is."

Seizing the opportunity, Danger tucked his hands under his armpits. "He is. That's why he needs to have a responsible owner. And he wants—needs—to work. That's what he's born for."

Reyna eyed him, apparently already on to him. "I know, and I want only the best for him. But I can't give him away."

Obviously she *didn't* know, or she'd release him to ABA immediately. What made her hold on so hard?

Danger dipped his chin to look her square in the eye. "What's your plan?"

She blinked. "What do you mean?"

"You coming every day to train him? Is he spending the nights at the kennels or in your home? How will you keep his joint issues in check?" The reason he'd had to retire.

"I-I don't know." She glanced at the Dutchie. "That's why I'm here—to get help."

Heat swelled in Danger's gut. "So you expect us to fix him."

"N-no. I want to learn. Figure this out."

He grunted, not sure he believed her. Too many people screwed up their dogs because they had no idea what they were doing. And when the dog acted out or attacked somebody, they blamed someone else, like him.

Easy, man. At least she'd come for help. This way, he could keep an eye on Riot, even if he wouldn't be the one training Reyna. Whoever that poor punk was going to be—good luck.

3

HARMONIA, TEXAS

PAISLEY'S PLAN TO USE THE REST OF THE MORNING TO CLEAN UP Jordi's place while pondering Heath's proposal went to waste when Riot dove right back into destroyer mode. On the verge of a meltdown, she let him out the back, where he tirelessly ran circles in the small yard with its six-foot wooden fence.

Standing in the open door, she sewed Kala back together—never letting Riot out of sight—while begging God to send help. Help that didn't include her abrasive and crude neighbor.

The first part of Heath's deal, her supporting ABA in the fight against the Guerreros, was a no-brainer. She was ready to do anything to stop them before more people went through what she had at their hand.

But Beau teaching her to take care of Riot? Nope. No, thank you. She didn't need to be yelled at every time she made a mistake. Surely there had to be someone else who could train her. *Right, God?*

Riot started barking as he paced the length of the fence. Oh boy, what was it now? She couldn't see through it.

"Riot, quiet."

A knock sounded at the door. This had to be Rachel and Lyric, coming to help with unpacking.

"You be a good boy and stay here, okay?" Paisley slipped into the cottage and closed the door. She placed Kala on the kitchen counter, then climbed over the mess to invite her guests inside.

"Auntie Paisley!" Lyric wrapped her skinny arms around Paisley's waist and squeezed tight.

Warmth curled through Paisley as she bent to hug her back. The little one was a ray of sunshine. "Hello, sweetie. Thank you for coming and helping Riot and me unpack—"

A blur of brindle came up behind Rachel. Riot! How— He cleared the six-foot fence?

Her heart nearly stopped, imagining him targeting Lyric. "Riot, no!"

To her shock, he simply circled her, then Rachel, then pranced back to Lyric and licked her fingers.

Rachel's daughter giggled, her dark eyes shining. "That tickles."

"He's so sweet," Rachel cooed.

Paisley huffed. "Until he turns into a little demon." She caught Riot's collar, drew it straight up the way she'd seen Heath do in order to get Riot to stop thrashing against her restraint, and led him inside. "See for yourself."

Rachel gasped as she stared at the mayhem. "Was this him?"

"Yep."

"So he's still not obeying?"

"No, he does. Just not me." The memory of the beast darting in front of Crew's truck turned her stomach. Beau had saved him. Again.

"A monkey!" Lyric rushed to the kitchen island and picked up Kala.

"Careful, the needle is still in there," Paisley said, chiding herself for not having thought of the danger.

"Can I have it?" Lyric bounced up and down.

"No, honey," Rachel said, taking it from her. "This is Auntie Paisley's."

"How about this?" Paisley pointed at Kala. "I sew her back together, then she's yours."

Lyric clapped her hands. "Yes!" She marched to the sofa and dropped the pink backpack on it. "I brought books so I can read them to Riot. Come on, Riot."

The Dutch shepherd launched himself out of Paisley's grip and onto the cushions.

Paisley gaped. *Um, what?* He even obeyed a six-year-old but not her? Wow, she really was doing something wrong. She looked at Rachel, who was leaning against the island. "See? That's what I mean."

Her friend blew her blonde bangs out of her eyes, something she'd done even in college. "What're you going to do about it?"

And here they were, diving right into the topic she didn't want to discuss. Oh well, maybe Rachel would have some advice. "I went to ABA this morning to ask for help, and they're willing to train me."

"Oh, that's good." Rachel moved to one of the torn moving boxes and opened it. "Where do you want these?" Waving a psychology book in the air, she looked around the cottage. When Paisley didn't answer, she turned to her. "What's the matter?"

She sighed. "They want your brother to train me."

"That's great! He's really good at what he does."

"Did you forget about last night?" Paisley hissed, not wanting to alert Lyric and Riot. "He bit my head off for no—" She faltered. "Okay, *no reason* is not true, but still. I don't want to be yelled at every time I make a mistake." She shook her head. "I won't let another man trample me." She'd made this vow to herself years ago and would stick to it. Breaking rules got people hurt.

"Oh, Pais." Rachel dropped the book and stepped up to her. "Danger is nothing like Lyonel. He'd never hurt you." She caught Paisley's hands. "Last night . . . that wasn't like him at all."

"You literally call him *Danger*. Why, again? Oh, because in high school he ended the quarterback's promising career by breaking his arm in three places."

"That was different," Rachel argued. "That quarterback picked on Mick. Beau is only a danger to those who pose a threat to his loved ones."

Paisley looked at their interlocked hands. "I don't know, Rach. I'm not sure I'd feel safe around him."

The words had their impact—hurt splashing over Rachel's face. "Give him a chance, Pais." She smiled and picked up the book again. "Try a week, or even a day, and if you don't feel comfortable, I'm sure you could ask for someone else to help."

Hmm . . . not a bad idea, but also not convincing. "I'll pray about it." Or keep praying, because she already had.

"Good. Now tell me where to put the books."

"Right there." Paisley pointed at the rack over Riot's crate in the corner by the couch, stomach tightening at the urn there.

Rachel eyed her. "Jordi's . . .?"

Chest aching, Paisley nodded. "Uh . . . yeah. I still have to spread them." Paisley busied herself with the kitchen box and started putting her mugs away. The girls at Serenity Chicago had gifted her a new one for every birthday as a joke, all of them with Bible verses.

"Do you know where?" Rachel asked over her shoulder as she placed some books on the rack.

"He loved that waterfall near the ABA ranch."

"The Pedernales Falls? I'll come with you."

Sighing, Paisley closed the kitchen cabinet. "I'm not ready yet, Rach. I know it's time to let him go, but I . . . can't."

"Take all the time you need." Rachel's lips tugged into a small smile. "You told me yourself everyone grieves in their own way and at their own pace."

Paisley nodded, swallowing against the burn in her throat.

"Thank you—for being here, for caring. I wish I could've done the same for you after Tyron passed."

"What? You came all the way down to Virginia Beach to his funeral and stayed with us an entire week. That meant the world to me. And now I'm here for you. This is how God takes care of us."

"Carry each other's burdens, and in this way you will fulfill the law of Christ," Paisley recited Galatians 6:2. "I'm so grateful to God for our friendship."

"Me too." Rachel smiled, then indicated the sofa. "Look at them."

Lyric was reading *Frozen* to Riot, and the way his gaze followed her finger gliding over the pages made it look like he was actually reading with her.

Paisley laughed quietly to not disturb them, but suddenly, her heart felt heavy. *When do I get to have my own family, God? A husband, a daughter or a son . . . * Was she asking for too much?

While they kept unpacking, Paisley prayed over her problem with the Dutch shepherd. The more she talked to Jesus, the more she felt like He wanted her to give Beau a chance. Frankly, she had known it all along, but her stubborn heart had hoped she'd misheard Him. *Can You give me a clear sign, Lord?*

"I think Danger might have PTS."

Paisley picked up a pair of jeans and turned to Rachel. "What makes you think that?"

"He's always been tense, but ever since Venezuela . . ." Rachel's gaze flicked to Lyric, who'd fallen asleep, and she cut her voice low. "He's just . . . harsh. Almost always irritable. Snaps for no reason. And I think he's drinking again, though I know he's trying hard not to. He compensates by working out like a maniac."

And you tell me he's safe?

Classic signs of post-traumatic stress. Paisley immediately felt ashamed for thinking about herself instead of him. PTS wasn't surprising after all he'd been through. She needed to give the man a break.

"I don't think he's ever talked to anyone about what happened to him," Rachel went on. "Well, maybe when he had to give his report about the incident, but . . ." She fidgeted with her wedding band and wrinkled her nose at Paisley. "I—do you think maybe you could help him? Like that verse you mentioned."

"Carry each other's burdens, and in this way you will fulfill the law of Christ," Paisley repeated slowly. Wow, talk about conviction.

"Yes," Rachel said, as if she found hope for the first time too. "And I know Da—Beau can help you carry your burden with Riot."

Chewing her bottom lip, Paisley glanced at the dog. He had settled on Jordi's boots, his nose tucked under his tail. She wanted what was best for him, and Rachel was right—Beau was good at what he did. He'd proven it more than once.

And yes, she not only wanted to help Beau because of Rachel but because of him. Maybe it was the counselor in her, maybe something else, but she realized she wanted to help ease his pain. Do for him what she couldn't do for Jordi.

But what if he is like Lyonel, Lord? If he really suffered from PTS, that meant he was unpredictable.

A snarl snapped through the space as Riot whipped to all fours and leapt at the kitchen island.

Where Kala still lay.

"No!" Paisley dove forward, but the beast already held the crocheted monkey hostage. With a deep growl he thrashed his head back and forth.

The needle! What if he swallowed it?

"Out, Riot! I said out!" Paisley wanted to grasp Kala, but she didn't dare get anywhere near his razor-sharp teeth.

Jesus, please!

Riot paused, canines clamped on the monkey, then recoiled.

A sneeze shook his striped body, forcing him to release Kala. Paisley snatched her out of reach even as another sneeze hit Riot.

She spun to inspect the monkey—a pinch poked her finger. "Oh, thank God!" She extracted the needle and put it back in her kit, then put Kala atop the fridge. This place needed to be dog-proofed. She took Riot by the collar, narrowly avoiding a small snap, and led him to his crate. With a dissatisfied moan, he slumped down, turning his back on her.

"Yeah, I feel that too."

If this wasn't the sign from God she had asked for . . .

Paisley slumped into one of the chairs. "Fine, I'll do it. I'll accept your brother's help."

BLANCO COUNTY, TEXAS

"I heard you moved on from handling dogs to training people."

"You heard wrong." Danger sent his right followed by a quick hook at Mick Caffrey's head. His childhood friend blocked the attack with raised fists, then ducked out.

Since Danger had moved back to Harmonia a month ago, they'd spent their free evenings at Amadore's Fight Club, bashing each other's heads in. Owned by a former pro boxer going by that very name—who was also the grandfather of an ABA handler, Aspen Courtland—the club was located on the outskirts of Austin and a favorite with the ABA staff. Some of them were here tonight. Jibril Khouri was over at the free weights, and Ghost was working the speed bag.

Danger had to catch his boss before he left. They needed to talk. "Never agreed to train Reyna," Danger snarled around a breath as he backed away. Sweat ran from his forehead into his eye, stinging. His resolve hadn't wavered once since this morning, and it'd stay that way. Didn't have the nerve to teach someone so inept with dogs.

Mick shook his head. "How can you pass up an opportunity like this, man?"

Danger faked a high knee, then planted the foot back down, pivoted, and thrust his other foot into Mick's chest. A grunt washed out of the giant, but he barely moved an inch. Really? Fighting a brick wall was easier than this guy.

Backtracking, he gave Mick space. Or maybe saved his own hide. "She doesn't know a rat's—" He snapped up a block to Mick's kick, which hit his gloves and reverberated down his arms all the way into his lower back. He ignored the searing pain.

Mick flashed him a wicked grin, his red mouthguard making him look clownish. "C'mon, man," he said around the guard. "I was at Rachel's wedding when you couldn't take your eyes off Reyna all night."

"That was seven years ago," he growled.

"Exactly. Don't you see the second chance smacking you in the face?"

After a quick jab and cross, Danger angled away. "She doesn't want anything to do with me."

"That's true, but too bad." The intruding voice jerked Danger to the side where Ghost hooked his arms over the lower rope of the ring. "Just called—she's in."

"Seriously?" Focus fractured, Danger missed the incoming hook from the blind spot of his damaged eye. Mick's blow hurled him sideways and sent the world into a merry-go-round. He blinked violently to clear his vision, but it did nothing. He'd swear his brain just face-planted into his skull.

Where was Mick?

Thud.

A shoulder rammed into Danger's side, driving the air from his lungs and him to the mat, alongside his dignity. Mick had gone down too and was right behind him, trying to get on his back. Danger wrestled against his buddy's plan to go for a rear naked choke. If he failed, Mick's victory was sealed.

Why would Reyna agree to work with him? Didn't make any sense. He'd seen the aversion in her eyes, her posture. Something must've changed her mind since this morning.

Or someone.

Rachel. What had she said to her?

Legs snaked around Danger's waist, and he bit back an oath—Mick had managed to get into rear mount.

Get it together, man. His head was everywhere but in the fight. Since when did he get so easily distracted?

He drew up his shoulders and tucked his chin to protect his neck, but Mick grabbed his forehead and yanked it back, forcing Danger to give him access to his weak spot. Danger clamped his arm on Mick's left while gripping his buddy's right wrist with both hands, preventing him from linking them and getting him into the schemed choke hold. Sweat made it hard to keep a good grip, and Mick digging his heels into Danger's thighs wasn't exactly helping.

"Can I tell her you're in?" Ghost asked. Due to the elevation of the ring, he was nearly on eye level with Danger.

"No—"

Mick's hand slipped free. Snaked around Danger's throat. Cut off air supply. "C'mon, man," he grunted into Danger's ear. "Tap out." Thankfully, he wasn't yet applying full pressure.

"That all you got?" Danger growled while reaching back with both hands to find Mick's left wrist. If he caught it, he could break the grip and turn the tide in his favor.

If knocked down, I will get back up, every time.

Words he'd learned from his dad at six. It'd been their motto, and Danger had later discovered it was part of the SEAL Creed. Maybe he didn't wear the trident on his uniform anymore, but in his heart he did.

"He's a SEAL," Ghost growled. "He'll die before giving up."

And he'd also die before he worked with Reyna.

Mick flexed his bicep, turning Danger's words into a

strangled grunt. Instead of placing his hand on Danger's head, he had it on his own shoulder, making it impossible to reach.

"Don't kill him, Caffrey. He owes me an answer."

Danger could barely make out his boss's face through the blotches clouding his vision. His head was about to explode.

"His answer is yes," Mick half chuckled, half grunted. He sounded miles away. "He has the hots for her."

Danger writhed, fire licking his lower back. Darkness sucked him in.

His head was yanked back by the hair, a cloth placed over his face. "Let's see how long you last this time, Beau Maddox." The guy had a strong Spanish accent. Osorio.

Danger fought the hands pinning him to the metal table. Too strong.

Water seeped through the cloth into his mouth and nose and down his throat. Despite all the training, his body responded with a gag and a rush of panic. Drowning. He was drowning.

No, he wasn't. The Guerreros wouldn't let him die, just wanted him to believe it so he would talk. Not over his dead body. He would get out of here. Go home to Lyric and Rachel.

He lashed out. Punched, kicked. Neutralize the threat. *Punched again.*

A thick arm shot around his chest. "Maddox! Stand down." Ghost's voice was low in his ear.

The present rushed back. Danger found himself on all fours, one arm wrapped around Mick's neck. His buddy lay on his side, face purple from lack of oxygen.

Stunned to find himself strangling him, Danger recoiled. Shoved back. Again, the ropes of the ring thumping his shoulder blades. What the heck just happened? How'd he get from nearly tapping out to nearly killing Mick?

He stared at his trembling hands, then at his buddy. Mick was sprawled on his back, eyes closed and his chest heaving with every wheezing breath.

"Both of you breathe." Ghost was on a knee between them, his expression lethal.

Freaking flashbacks. Would they ever stop? The Guerreros were over four thousand klicks away, yet they still had a vise grip on his head. Inhabited him like a deadly virus, threatening everyone who got too close.

"Drink." Ghost passed him a water bottle.

Danger held up a hand, the drowning sensation too recent. "I'm good."

Face a normal color, Mick sat up. "You're not good, not in your head." His voice held no anger, not even accusation. More like concern.

"My head's fine." Danger punched to his feet and extended a hand to his buddy. "Sorry, man."

Accepting the olive branch, Mick let Danger haul him up. "Yeah, okay. But next time I tap out, let me go."

He'd tapped out? "Copy." He ducked through the ropes and hit the floor.

A grip caught his shoulder. He pivoted and found Ghost there, watching Mick lumber toward the men's locker room, rubbing his neck.

Ghost angled in. "Flashbacks?"

Danger clenched his teeth.

"Since when?" Ghost asked quietly. His brows were drawn low, mouth a thin line.

The club had cleared out, only Amadore himself left. The former pro boxer was working the speed bag in a blur, like machine gun bursts.

Kind of like Danger's pulse right now. He removed his gloves and mouth guard. "I'm fine." Hadn't told anybody about the flashbacks and wasn't starting now, especially not his boss. He'd never clear him for ops.

Ghost stared at him, his expression tight. "Talk to Reyna."

"Look, training her—"

"Not for training . . ."

53

Danger frowned. Then what— "Oh man. No. C'mon." He shook his head. "Let the shrink dig in my head? No way." With his demons, he was every counselor's dream. Or nightmare until he dumped his entire story on them.

"She has experience with the Guerrero Cartel."

Danger stilled. Hold on, what? *Her,* tangled up with Venezuela's—scratch that, South America's most lethal cartel? Fat chance.

"Not what you'd expect, right?" Ghost's mouth pulled into a grim smile. "She works closely with forces going against them. More than once provided Cord Taggart and his MiLE organization vital intel to free those caught in trafficking."

Okay, this intel ambushed him. Sure, Reyna had Venezuelan roots—at least, that's what Rachel had told him—but ties to the Guerrero Cartel was the last thing he'd expected. "How was she involved?"

"Ask her." A smug expression built on Ghost's face as he made for the lockers. "When you're out in the heat teaching her how to handle Riot."

Son of a . . . Snorting, Danger followed him. Smooth, had to hand it to the guy. "You seriously gonna make me work with her?"

Inside the locker room, which was really a converted broom closet, Ghost retrieved his bag and propped it on the bench. "Your call. But if she gets help elsewhere, Riot's gone. That"—he gave a cockeyed nod—"would tick me off."

No Riot, no missions. But that was the least of Danger's worries. If Reyna got the Dutchie into the wrong hands . . . Danger tossed his equipment into his bag and stripped out of his shirt. Stared at the scars covering his torso. No, this wasn't over. "Fine."

Ghost looked up from his bag, his gaze skimming the scars before meeting Danger's good eye. He gave a curt nod. "I'll read her in. You start tomorrow." He hesitated and eyed Danger again. "You seem reticent."

Danger looked down, thinking.

"Get your head on straight. We work dogs—you know that. Helping her is the right thing."

Digging his own grave didn't sound like doing the right thing, but for Riot, he'd even make his own coffin. Not to mention Reyna could have vital intel on Osorio. If she did, the Guerreros better be on their watch.

4

TEXAS HILL COUNTRY

PAISLEY'S STOMACH TIGHTENED AT THE SIGHT OF BEAU'S SILVER Tacoma rumbling up the road of the ABA ranch, heading past the training yards. Heath's call had taken her by complete surprise. *"You start training tomorrow. Eighteen hundred—uh, that's six. Sharp."*

Poof, just like that.

The sun was about to drop behind the hills the ranch was nestled into, casting its last rays of the day on the over-three-hundred-acre sprawl. Before Beau's arrival, a serenity had engulfed the facilities and natural pond, but now Riot was barking his lungs out, racing up and down the fence that separated this training yard from the parking lot across the green. No doubt he'd recognized Beau's pickup—Jordi had said dogs could distinguish different car engines and link them to people.

It stung that Riot got more excited over seeing a stranger than her.

Riot stopped, his snout stuffed into the fence, huffing, his gaze locked on the Tacoma, then started barking and patrolling the fence. She had deployed Beau's terse tips from yesterday morning and used a firm tone with the commands, but Riot only obeyed sporadically. Hopefully there was a better way to make a dog listen. Otherwise, she was officially incapable of handling Riot and . . .

Oh God, please don't let me lose him. I just . . . can't. Help me to become a good handler. The best.

And give me the patience to learn from Beau.

Said guy came stalking across the grassy area leading to the entrance. Like yesterday, he wore cargos, a tan T-shirt with the ABA logo on the back, a black ball cap, and his Oakleys. She remembered what lay beneath those shades . . . A white burn scar she'd missed two nights ago that circled his right eye, begging the question whether its opacity was from that or the long cut. His eyebrow was shredded too.

That handiwork had one signature—the Guerreros'. She'd seen many end up like that. And her stomach clenched, thinking about Beau held by those savages.

Riot lunged at the fence with exuberance, barking hard.

"Off." Beau opened the gate, and Riot jumped up at him.

Paisley winced. Why did he have to keep doing this? There were dozens of people on this ranch, but Riot only did this with the one guy who would chew her out for it.

"Sorry." It was lame but better than trying to call him back and getting ignored again. Shoving her hands into the back pockets of her jeans, she strolled over. "Hi."

Beau rubbed Riot's sides, eliciting a moan from the Dutch shepherd—um, traitor?—then cocked his head at her. The usual intensity rolled off the man. His stance was broad, like nothing in the world could shake him, his shoulders were drawn back, and his expression was stern.

"Thank you for doing this, Beau. Heath told me you're one of the best." Why was she rambling?

His mouth pulled into a hard line. "Danger."

"Pardon me?"

"No one calls me Beau."

Oh. "Right." She still didn't get why anyone would call him Danger. It sounded like a warning label.

He ordered Riot down, then fully stepped into the training yard and closed the gate. "Take your hands out of your pockets and pay attention. Riot's a working dog, not a pet."

Wow, he couldn't even go a minute without being rude. Maybe she should teach him how to communicate like a civilized person while he taught her how to handle Riot.

Chastised, she pulled her hands out of her pockets and, copying his posture, lowered them to her sides. For some reason he was good at triggering her long-buried defense mechanism. The one urging her to make clear she wasn't the kind of woman who let men push her around. But she was long past that.

"The way you convey yourself is crucial to your relationship with Riot," Beau went on, unaware of her inner debate, "and that relationship is key. It's all about trust and respect. Forging a bond." He jerked his chin at Riot, who came to his paws, looking up at him like a child admiring an adult. "He relies on nonverbal cues, which means you have to be aware of the head-to-toe signals you're sending. That's essential because most dogs look for a leader who exerts power and control over them, like their mother when they were puppies."

Oooh, now it made sense why Riot kept running to Beau. The guy was the embodiment of a leader. Meanwhile, she had no idea what she was doing. "Heath said something about alphaing the dog."

Beau nodded. "When we don't assume the alpha role, the dog will. And he'll do whatever he wants."

Paisley laughed. "And shred all of your possessions."

A muscle in Beau's jaw tightened. "Or attack someone, and then the dog—doing what he's been trained to do—is seized by animal control for being aggressive, and euthanized."

Paisley's heart dropped. "C-can they really do that? I mean, I've heard stories, but—"

"Can and will. Especially with a dog who has the training MWDs have."

Swallowing hard, she looked at Riot sitting at Beau's left, those keen brown eyes fixed on him. The responsibility of owning a retired military working dog all of a sudden weighed heavier on her than ever before. She'd never thought that *she* could get *him* killed.

"That's why our goal is to make you the alpha," Beau said as if reading her thoughts. "Tell me—do your clients open up when they don't trust you?"

She shook her head, feeling called out.

"Exactly. Same thing with Riot—earn his trust and respect and he'll cooperate."

"This makes so much sense," Paisley muttered more to herself than him. Especially the simile with the counselor-client relationship. Trust could be built over time; she'd experienced it with some very challenging clients. Knowing she could do the same with Riot loosened the knot in her gut tremendously. "So, I feign confidence until I actually feel it?"

"The dog will know. Faking it can have fear, and they'll rout that in a heartbeat. Learning, training, will give you the confidence you need." He nodded. "Now. Watch your posture and keep emotions out of the equation—they travel down lead, so Riot literally smells them."

Okay, she could do that. He was right—counseling wasn't much different in that regard.

Beau produced a ropeless KONG from his pocket, and Riot's eyes immediately locked on to it. His entire body shivered with anticipation, but he remained in his spot.

Beau handed her the black rubber toy. "Toss it."

She took it and flung it across the yard. Surprisingly, Riot didn't take off after it.

"Tell him to go get it."

Wetting her lips, Paisley looked at Riot, whose gaze was still trained on the spot where the KONG had landed. "Riot, go get it."

He took off. Grass and dirt flew as he chased down the yard. Once he'd reached the toy, he snatched it up, flattened to the ground, and started chomping on it while holding it between his paws.

Beau adjusted his ball cap, letting her glimpse his light brown hair. "Now tell him to heel."

Wrenching her gaze away, Paisley refocused on her dog. "Riot, heel!"

The Dutch shepherd looked at her, but didn't budge.

Oh no.

"Remember your posture and tone," Beau said. "Firm and controlled."

Paisley squared her shoulders. Widened her stance. *Firm and controlled* . . . "Riot, heel."

The KONG locked between his jaws, Riot shot to his paws and came darting back. He circled her and, halting at her left side, pressed his shoulder into her calf.

Her belly somersaulted. "I can't—did you see that?" she sputtered. "It—it worked! He totally listened!"

"Tell him to release it with 'out.'" Although Beau's expression remained unchanged, his countenance had softened.

Paisley gave the command, and Riot dropped the slobber-drenched KONG at her feet. He didn't back up but instead kept his snout an inch from the reward, anticipation rippling through his sleek body. More exhilaration swept through her. But doubt wiggled in—what if this was just a one-time fluke?

"Now tell him to stay, pick up the KONG, and repeat the process."

The "heel" command struck Paisley as the hardest, and when Riot obeyed immediately, darting back to her side, her chest was about to burst. If only Jordi could see them. She furtively eyed Beau, who scanned their surroundings. He stood there, legs planted, his T-shirt stretching over his solid chest.

She had to admit he was a great teacher. "This is amazing. Thank you," she said quickly when he turned back to her.

He ran a hand over his chin. "Once, twice is good. A hundred times is great. But a thousand is ingrained."

In other words, keep practicing. They continued, and with every success, Paisley felt more confident. At some point, Beau pulled a KONG with a rope from his cargo pocket. Riot snapped to Beau, eyes big, teeth chattering as the black toy dangled before him, all other interests abandoned. Even the top of his skull was bouncing.

"Is that normal?" Paisley asked, stifling a laugh. "I've never seen that before . . ."

"This right here's true love." The right corner of his mouth curved upward.

Now Paisley was the one about to start chattering over the tiniest of grins that came so unexpectedly. And oh, it looked good on him.

He gave some kind of hand signal she missed, and Riot lunged. Sharp teeth met the KONG with a hollow *thump*, sending the two in a tug-of-war.

"That all you got, hmm?" Beau slapped the Dutch shepherd's brindled side. "C'mon, boy. I know you can do better than that."

The gruff play seemed to amp Riot's resolve to gain the victory. His growl deepened, his head jerking from side to side. When Beau let go, Riot dashed off but kept looking back as if he were doing something forbidden.

Paisley laughed. "He's testing you."

"You have no idea." Beau commanded Riot back, and once he was in possession of the KONG, let it disappear in his cargos. "This time no words." He made a fist at his waist.

Riot shot to his side and heeled. When Beau took a few steps, Riot followed without missing a beat, never breaking eye contact. He was so eager to please, to do everything he was told. What a special dog. *Her* dog.

Beau cocked his head at her. "Your turn."

Paisley licked her lips. "So . . . I just have to make a fist at my hip?"

He nodded.

Okay, couldn't be that hard, could it? When Riot looked at her, she made a fist like instructed.

As if confused, the Dutch shepherd tilted his head.

Paisley dropped her hand. Fisted it again, but still nothing. "What am I doing wrong?"

Beau reached around her and placed his hand over hers.

Her breath hitched, skin tingling where he held her. *What's he doing?*

"Right"—he moved their hands in a circular motion, then touched them to her hip—"here. See?"

No, she didn't see anything. But she smelled his rugged scent and felt a whole lot. Beau's hand was warm, his grip steady and confident, and his arm across her back hot.

And it felt . . . good. Safe.

Wait, why *safe*?

"Try again," he said, clearly not affected the way she was. He'd let her go without her noticing.

She swallowed. *Just breathe.* She was fine. Everything was fine. Except for her quivering fist when she drew the circle and the warmth of his proximity lingering. Why did she want more of it?

A whistle behind them made her jump and whirl around.

Heath stalked toward them, urgency in his step. "Danger, Riot's been called up for a mission. Let's go. You too, Paisley."

Beau commanded Riot to his side, clipped on the lead he produced out of the blue, and made for the gate.

"Heath, wait." Paisley squeezed past Beau and Riot, hurrying out of the training yard. "What do you mean? What mission?"

"Local LEOs have intel that the Guerreros are in the area," he tossed over his shoulder as he continued toward the office.

Paisley froze, nearly causing Beau to run her over. "They're *here*?"

"It's too dangerous for her to come," Danger hissed to Ghost as they neared the main training building, which had been turned into a makeshift command center.

Twilight was falling on the ABA facilities, the air becoming more breathable. The number of vehicles—civilian and law enforcement—pulling into the main parking lot proved alarming. Handlers and officers wearing full tac stalked past them into the training building, all giving Ghost a nod of acknowledgement.

His boss hadn't disclosed more intel, but this looked like a joint operation. Strangest thing Danger had ever seen, and he'd seen a lot of strange things. But he was here for any opportunity to stick it to the Guerreros and at the same time cement his path back to his old life as an operator. Hooyah.

"Not your call." Ghost motioned Reyna toward the door. "We need her on site to help the victims."

Holding Riot's lead, which Danger had passed her so he could gear up, Reyna tried to move past the men but the Dutchie refused to go on. Only when Danger gave him a signal did he plod inside. Man, they had a lot of work to do.

"What's the plan?" The familiar pre-op buzz kicked in as Danger donned gloves. Felt good to be back in the game.

"She'll be in a surveillance van two klicks out."

"What if things go south and the Guerreros attack the van?" He gritted his teeth. "You know what they do to women, right?"

Ghost gave his plate carrier a tug, then looked him square in the eye. "*She* knows, and that's what matters."

"Hold up. What do you mean?"

"A Guerrero used her to climb the cartel's hierarchy."

The words made Danger sick. The Guerreros were notorious for their violent treatment of women and girls. The kind that gave even a seasoned operator like him, one used to looking evil in the eye, sleepless nights.

Conscience tweaked, he sliced a glance to where Reyna had disappeared—and spotted her heading his way with Riot, fire in her eyes and determination in her posture. A wisp of vanilla filled Danger's nostrils when she planted herself in front of him, one fist pressed on her hip.

The scent threw him back to the field. The softness of her hand beneath his, the curve of her thigh . . . Hadn't planned to get that close.

"I appreciate your concern," she said, her eyes piercing him, "but I breathed Guerrero air for two years. I know what we're dealing with."

Either she possessed the hearing ability of a dog or she could read lips, because there was no other explanation for how she knew what they were talking about.

When Danger didn't say anything, she turned to Ghost. "I need to be with those girls as soon as possible. You get that, right?"

Smart woman—establishing that she was an asset.

The way she was willing to put her life on the line for the girls was warrior ethos and shifted something inside Danger.

Ward Gaines exited the training facility. The sheriff of Blanco County and former Navy commander was in charge of tonight's mission. "Daniels, it's time."

Ghost gave a nod, then looked at Reyna. "You don't have to convince me. We need you in that van. But you are under the authority of Sheriff Gaines, so you stay put until he says otherwise."

Her face brightened. "Yes, sir. Thank you."

After flashing Danger a look, she led Riot back inside. He slipped in behind them.

The training obstacles and bite gear were shoved against the wall, making room for four rows of folding chairs occupied by LEOs. Danger gave Mick a nod, glad he was on scene and would be working this too. Laughter from a bunch of dudes lounging in the first row punctured the gathering tension in the building. At the front, Gaines planted himself next to a screen that displayed an area map.

Since the chairs were all occupied, Danger took up position on the back wall and hooked his thumbs into his plate carrier. Ghost, Reyna, and Riot made their way to Gaines. The front-row clowns quieted and eyeballed Reyna, elbowing each other with grins he wanted to rip off their faces.

One gave a catcall. "Did someone turn up the heat or is that you?"

Hands falling to his side, ready for action, Danger shifted off the wall to deal with Blowhard.

But Reyna beat him to it—turned to the guy with a smile. "I hope your combat skills aren't as lousy as your flirting, or you'd better stay here."

The guys burst into laughter while Blowhard gaped at her.

Satisfaction curled through Danger. She could handle herself alright.

"Okay," Gaines boomed, shutting everyone up. The middle-aged sheriff glanced at his timepiece. "We're tight, so I'm going to keep this brief. Half an hour ago, the DEA was tipped off by an informant that the Guerrero Cartel is taking up quarters at an old ranch house about twenty klicks north of here. Intel shows they're using young girls as mules. The cartel made changes to the location last second, meaning DEA is too far south to interdict in time. Since we're close and have the equipment necessary, it's on us to crash the party. We have to move on this now, or it's a major loss of life and operational hours." He turned to Reyna. "We have an expert on this cartel to get us up to speed on what we could be dealing with." He stepped back and nodded at her. "Miss Reyna?"

Still holding Riot's lead, she stepped forward. "Thank you, Sheriff." Her expression was sober, head erect, and shoulders square. Confident. Professional. She met the crowd. "The Guerrero Cartel is Venezuela's most lethal cartel and competes with Mexico when it comes to smuggling narcotics across the border. The Guerreros are high on money and power—the perfect recipe for human trafficking. They are smart and ruthless. They use all sorts of methods to stay under the radar. I'm sure I don't have to explain to you that the girls are sold with the drugs."

What she lacked in dealing with dogs, she possessed in abundance in communicating with the two-legged species. But her confidence now had Riot's attention too.

"The cartel occupies this old farmhouse located about twenty klicks out." Gaines used the laser pointer at the remote control and drew a circle around a compound outlined on the map. "Numbers aren't confirmed, but guessed at eight cartel and nineteen civilians. The number of buyers is unknown." He took each one of them in. "I know not all of you are acquainted with each other, but if everyone does their job and follows orders, it shouldn't be a problem. We'll have Heath Daniels with the rest of the operators breaching the primary entry point here"—he pointed at one of the Xs—"and Mick Caffrey with the force infil from the south. A third team led by Emil Hansen will serve as quick reaction force and step in if needed. Pierce, I want you to peel off once we arrive and set up overwatch on the east side."

"What's our ROE?" Cathal McGowan asked as he reached his tattoo-sleeved arm toward his fiancée, Rio, who was here with Chaos, her beautiful maligator trained in patrol and combat tracking.

Danger wished he hadn't asked about rules of engagement—because he legit wanted to take the kid gloves off when he caught up with these thugs.

"Capture or kill."

Sweet.

"In light of that," Reyna chimed in, "when you're shooting, please remember there are innocent girls caught up in this."

Gaines nodded. "We don't want any civilian casualties."

"How do we get there?" a female LEO asked. "Choppers?"

"Too much noise. We don't want to spook them, so you'll

wheel in"—Gaines pointed at a spot on the map about two klicks out—"and hoof it to the ranch house." He turned to Ghost. "Daniels, who's handling the narcotics dog?"

Ghost jerked his chin at Danger. "Beau Maddox."

Planting his hands on his tactical belt, Danger straightened. Gave a nod.

"Alright, Maddox," the sheriff said. "I'll need you and the dog to search the compound after the raid. The cartel might have some drugs or mules hidden for later deliveries."

Danger gave another nod. "Copy."

"Good, then let's get going. Team commanders will provide details and answer questions en route."

The LEOs and operators rose and made for the exit. Others in command gathered around a table with maps, screens, and radios. Danger hung back to catch Reyna and get Riot from her. When Blowhard lumbered past, he couldn't help himself. He cut him off.

"I see you glance her way one more time, I'll make sure you never look at a woman again."

Gawking at Danger's damaged eye, Blowhard slowly raised his hands. "Relax, man. It was a joke."

Danger crowded his face some more.

The clown backtracked until he was out of reach. Muttering something under his breath, he turned and paraded to the exit.

Punk.

Danger wrenched his glare from him and found Reyna watching from across the rows of chairs. Either he was delusional or her expression had softened.

"No need for casualties before the op," Ghost said drily.

Danger pulled his attention from her. "Then I'll wait till after."

His boss grunted, then sobered. "You and Riot will infil once all targets are neutralized."

Danger balked but remembered his pay grade. He had no say in this.

"Hey," Ghost said quietly. "I know you've been waiting for this a long time, and the target is your personal jackpot. But you aren't ready, man. Not after what I saw last night."

No, the jackpot would be Osorio, who wasn't here. The coward would never leave the safety of his home country. Still, Ghost wasn't all wrong. Every hit against the Guerreros silenced another one of Danger's demons.

Ghost ran a hand through his hair. "Wasn't even sure if I should let you go at all. But Riot's the only narcotics detection dog we got, and you work best with him."

If it weren't for Riot, he'd be at home sitting on his couch? Holy Hades. Hopefully Reyna hadn't changed her mind about handing him over.

5

A BREED APART RANCH, TEXAS HILL COUNTRY

CLUTCHING RIOT'S LEASH A LITTLE TIGHTER, PAISLEY MADE HER WAY over to Beau, who stood off to the side. The training building had emptied, leaving the three of them. She suppressed a shudder. *Do I really have to do this, Lord? Hand Riot over to a man I don't fully trust and who takes him right into the crosshairs of the Guerreros?*

"Ready to stick it to the cartel?" He had his hands planted on his belt, confidence oozing out of every pore as if he were born to be a warrior—the man was capable, fierce, and no doubt lethal.

Seeing him like that extinguished nearly all her doubts.

She watched the interaction as Riot sniffed him, his tail wagging hard as Beau bent down to give him an extensive ear rub. Tried to steady her drumming heart. "More than ready," she answered.

Not so much when it came to giving up Riot. But she'd made a deal with Heath. She held out the leash to Beau, and he straightened. When he reached for it, his fingers brushed past it. He grasped again, and this time caught it.

It happened so fast Paisley almost didn't notice. What was

that about? Wait, was that because of his vision? If he was blind in his right eye, then did he have problems with depth perception?

When he avoided her gaze, Paisley's heart squeezed at his obvious self-consciousness. As an operator, he depended on his sight more than anything else. It had to be hard for him to be limited like that.

"So, you've been an asset before?" he asked as they made their way outside.

"Yeah." She watched the teams filter down the road to the floodlight-illuminated parking lot, where they piled into sturdy vans, sheriff's Suburbans, and trucks. "But nothing like this—this . . . feels big."

When she glanced over at Beau, she found him watching. He cleared his throat. "Impressive."

The way his gaze kept resting on her made her self-conscious. "Not really. What you guys do is impressive."

He grunted but didn't say anything.

They walked in silence until Paisley nearly burst with curiosity. "What did you say to that guy?" she blurted out.

His focus remained trained to the front, his rugged profile illuminated by the floodlights. "That I liked his haircut."

Paisley harrumphed. That's why his fists had been curled, his eyes shooting daggers? *"He's only a danger to those who pose a threat to his loved ones."*

She pursed her lips remembering Rachel's words. She wasn't a "loved one." Still, she was pretty sure she'd read his confrontation with the smart-mouth correctly. So, did he do that for every woman he knew? Or . . . was there more to it?

They reached the parking lot, and Beau and Riot escorted her to the surveillance van. She was about to climb into the back when a hand on her shoulder stopped her. She turned to Beau standing right behind her.

"I'll do whatever necessary to keep Riot safe, you hear me?"

His gaze and intensity drilled into her, finding the anxiety lodged deep in her belly and soothing it. "I know you will," she whispered. "I trust you." Weirdly, she did.

She stole a second to ruffle Riot's ears and caught the door. Surprise leapt through her when Beau extended a helping hand. Again, she met his gaze, belly awhirl, then accepted his offer and climbed in. Like earlier, his grip was strong. Reassuring. She longed to hold on just a little longer, but he let go and shut the doors. Rapped twice against the hull. The vehicle set into motion. She watched the two heroes—one on two legs, the other with four—shrinking as the van lumbered off the ranch.

"We appreciate your support, Miss Reyna," Sheriff Gaines said as she settled into the bench seat and buckled in. He occupied one of the three seats facing a bank of surveillance monitors. Another officer of the Harmonia PD sat next to him, wearing headphones and watching the screens.

Paisley shifted, realizing just then how dark and cramped the van was. She sniffed, the air stuffy. "My pleasure. Thank you for confronting this cartel."

The next twenty minutes she spent in silent prayer asking God to protect the teams, listening to the chatter coming from a stationary radio and Sheriff Gaines's occasional explanations. According to him, the screens showed the live feed of a thermal camera attached to a drone. For a long time, the images remained a dark purple, until three yellow-and-orange figures and a vehicle appeared.

"Yeah, I see them." Gaines spoke into what looked like a phone receiver straight out of the '60s as he leaned in and stared at an aerial shot. He turned to Paisley. "That's the outpost a half klick outside the ranch. They're guarding the road leading up to it."

The drone moved on until a large structure glared into view. A chill ran down Paisley's spine. This was where the Guerreros were about to sell the girls and drugs. The heat signatures weren't visible through the walls and roof, so they didn't know what was going on inside. Not that seeing was necessary—she could imagine it without visuals.

Lyonel clawed his way into her mind. And made her shudder a second time. She had long forgiven him—only with God's help—and found a measure of healing, but that didn't mean she ever wanted to cross paths with him again.

What if he was here?

Chatter from the radio and Gaines's response snagged her attention. The van slowed to a stop and fell ominously quiet.

"Guards are neutralized," a voice said over the radio. "Moving in."

Two clusters of white figures approached the ranch house: one from the front, the other—that looked like a dog, so must be Riot and Beau—from the back. With every step the men took, the boulder in Paisley's stomach grew heavier. Given the chance, the Guerreros would wipe out the entire team, including Riot. No mercy whatsoever.

She inhaled a lungful of musty van air. *Oh Lord, please hold Your protecting hand over them. Be their shield and fortress. Keep them and the girls safe.*

"Hawk," the radio crackled, "this is Delta Four."

"Go for Hawk," Gaines responded, then angled toward her. "Our sniper holed up east of the property." He tapped a spot on the map. "Here." He shifted his attention back to the op.

"In position," the sniper reported. "Got eyes on nine hostages. Repeat, nine hostages."

Clutching the receiver in his big hand, Gaines pressed a fist to his lips. "S'posed to be more," he muttered, then keyed it. "Copy. Keep eyes out for more."

The radio traffic died down when the teams reached the house. Paisley held her breath, not daring to blink, imagining the convergence of the teams flanking the house. The nerves, the tension as they entered.

A flash lit up the screen, and the figures disappeared into the building, one after the other, in fluid motion. What was happening? The only heat signatures were the sniper's and Beau with Riot waiting by the back entrance.

She kneaded her lower lip, her nerves buzzing.

Chatter revived, shots cracking in the background, but Paisley didn't understand what they were saying. Not because of the military lingo—Jordi had taught her plenty—but because it was deafening and chaotic. The image on the screen hadn't changed for several minutes now, Beau and Riot still waiting in the same spot. Had it frozen?

Wait! What was that?

She jumped up, pointing at the screen. "There!" Whoops, didn't mean to shout, but four figures had popped up out of nowhere at the back of the building, not far from Beau and Riot. How'd the four get there?

"Four squirters—"

"Three," Paisley whispered, her thoughts ricocheting back to her own escape and seeing on the screen how one figure was ahead of the others. "One is the victim. The three are chasing her." She'd bet her life.

Gaines faltered, eyeing her, then the array of monitors. He uttered an oath. "You're right." He keyed the mic. "Make that—"

"Hawk, this is Delta Eight." Beau! "Good copy. Got eyes on one friendly and *three* hostiles in pursuit. Came out of a tunnel."

Even as he said it, his and Riot's glowing figures started moving. Wait, they couldn't go alone. Even if one of them was a hostage, there were still three Guerreros.

"Echo One, this is Hawk," Gaines said. "Back up Delta Eight outside."

"Who's that?" She probably shouldn't ask, but she wanted to know that someone good was backing up her dog and Danger.

"Echo is Mick Caffrey—Maddox's friend."

"Hawk, we are securing the situation. Will move to support in two mikes. Over."

Two minutes? Heart crashing against her ribs, Paisley watched the glowing forms of Beau and Riot pursue the four figures through what had to be trees and underbrush. All of a sudden, the Guerreros scattered, then stopped.

Paisley's blood turned cold. Beau and Riot were walking straight into an ambush.

The two bullets zipped past Danger's head at the same time Gaines's ambush warning carried through comms.

"Little late," he growled as he dove behind a nearby rock, shielding Riot while running a hand over him to make sure he hadn't been hit.

More shots rang through the night, chipping away rock on the other side of their cover. Gunfire ceased only to be replaced by muffled screaming coming from uphill. The hostage. They had to get to her before it was too late.

Riot had announced the presence of bad guys shortly before Danger heard a hatch squeaking open not far from their position outside the ranch house. Through his helmet-mounted night vision monocular—binoculars didn't work any longer with his damaged eye—he'd spotted a slender figure with long hair pop out of the ground, followed by three hostiles. The three had caught up with her quickly, then used her as a shield until they could take cover behind a cluster of rocks and trees. Now they were picking their way up the rocky incline.

Cowards.

Tucking his M4A1 into his shoulder, Danger eased to the other side of the rock, Riot belly-crawling with him. Overhead, the crescent moon cast a glimmer of light onto the rugged terrain of limestone, ash junipers, and underbrush—perfect conditions for night vision.

"Delta Eight, this is Echo One," Mick's voice sounded in Danger's ear. "En route to your position now."

Just now? It'd take a while till they reached him. Long

enough for the Guerreros to get away if they started moving again.

Danger pressed the talk button twice to transmit he'd understood as he hustled Riot to the next cluster of rocks. Couldn't speak or he'd give away his location. He slowed and eased the muzzle of the M4 around the corner, now behind Guerrero number one's position. No movement near the bushes where the bad guy had taken shelter.

Riot's rumbling growl indicated he was still there.

"Hawk to Delta Eight," Gaines comm'd. "Tango number two is heading away from you toward the east, number three uphill with the hostage."

This was his chance to engage target number one.

Shifting his M4 to his back on the sling, Danger adjusted his position. Reached down and unclipped Riot's lead, then held on to his vest.

Anticipating the action, Riot strained against the grip, his snarling increasing.

Danger let go. "Go get 'em."

Agile beauty leapt into action, chasing his prey. Riot bolted off into the brush.

Danger rushed behind him, swinging his M4 to the ready. Sweat trickled from under his helmet and down his temples. Navigating the rocky terrain, he gritted at his lower back throwing a tantrum. Not wanting impaired thinking or reaction, he'd steered clear of oxy before the op and instead gritted through pain. Didn't want to be responsible for casualties.

A shout punctured the humid night air followed by a spate of Spanish curses. Riot had hit his target.

Danger rounded another rock. The Guerrero lay prostrate in the dirt, clutching a gun while desperately trying to crawl away from Riot. Good luck, because the Dutchie had his canines anchored in his leg and kept yanking as if wanting to severe it from the upper body.

The Guerrero whipped around, gun aimed at Danger.

Danger neutralized him with a single round. Keeping his M4 raised, he moved up to the body and kicked the gun under a nearby bush. "Riot, out."

Unlike Cutter, who'd sometimes had to be hauled off the insurgents, the Dutchie released immediately.

Danger took a knee next to him and smoothed a hand over his body, once again checking for injuries. All good. "Good boy," he said softly, then clipped him back to the lead. "If we get the other two guys, you've earned some extra KONG time."

As if understanding, Riot drenched Danger's gloves in slobber.

He smirked. "I said *if.*" Rising, he keyed his mic. "Hawk, this is Delta Eight. One target neutralized. Do you have eyes on the other tangos and the hostage?"

"Affirmative. Tango with the hostage approximately ninety yards north. Second tango east, two hundred yards."

Had to secure the hostage first, then go after the last Guerrero. If the guy wasn't all over the hills by then.

Not on his watch.

As they climbed uphill, snaking around scrub, trees, and rocks, Riot had his snout to the ground, dragging in huge draughts, then puffing them out. He suddenly halted, his nose coming up and ears swiveling forward.

Energy buzzed under Danger's skin. The Guerrero and hostage couldn't be far.

"Let's get 'im," he said, amping Riot, who surged ahead. Up, around rocky ledges.

A moment later, Danger thought he saw something ahead. There, a broomstick of a man dragging the girl backward up the hill by her hair while cowering behind her. Though a pistol was pressed to her temple, the girl made no noise.

Danger stalked closer, the IR laser mounted on his M4—only visible for anyone wearing NODs—gathering in a glowing dot on the fraction of the Guerrero's head not shielded by the hostage. Couldn't risk a shot because their movements were too jerky. Sending Riot wasn't an option either. He could hurt the girl.

The Dutchie's growl lifted over the haunting hoot of an owl.

"Drop the gun and let her go," Danger hollered over the twenty-yard distance.

A string of Spanish curses sailed through the night as the pair came to a halt.

No need to get personal, buddy. Danger had learned plenty of insults during captivity. "Last warning," he barked. "Drop the weapon and let her go."

The sudden fog funneling his brain broke his focus. His vision blurred, the ringing in his ears crowding out any other noise. *What . . .*

He tightened his hold on the M4's forward handgrip, fighting the urge to shake his head to clear it. Any uncontrolled move could tip the bad guy off. And the last thing Danger needed was a dead hostage. Or dog.

Pull it together, man.

Focus returned with his sight, the surroundings rushing over him—Riot's bloodcurdling snarling. The Guerrero's finger on the trigger. The terror etched into the girl's face. Slowing his breathing, Danger lasered in on the glowing dot at the side of the tango's head. He really did not want to take this guy out in front of—

The Guerrero swung his weapon toward him, his own movement fully exposing his head.

Danger squeezed off a round. *Wrong choice, man.*

Blood splattered the girl's face. She screeched and arched away from the guy, who dropped to the ground. Number two neutralized, one to go.

Danger trailed Riot to the body, then again commanded him down. He was about to secure the Guerrero's gun when the girl flung herself at him, digging her fingers into his plate carrier like he was her lifeline. He faltered backward, but caught himself—and her. Sobs ripped through her slender frame.

Her cries undid something in him. "Easy. It's alright." He reluctantly lifted his free arm and cupped her head against his chest.

It's alright? He tilted his head back. Suppressed a groan. What a dumb thing to say to a girl who couldn't be more than sixteen and likely had been through her worst nightmare.

Which reminded him he needed to find the final target. "Delta Eight to Hawk. One tango down, hostage secure." And one punk still on the run. If he acted fast, he could still get him. "Any word on the third?"

"Negative, no visual. Thermals have nothing. Looks like he got away. Support will meet you."

Biting back a curse, Danger shook his head. "Copy." He gently tried to unhook the girl's fingers. "Listen, someone's gonna come—"

Her wails grew louder and her grip tightened.

Mick materialized from the shadows in tac gear and cradling a rifle. A frown built on his face as he ran the flashlight over the girl. He eyed Danger, then reached for her.

Black curls flew as she frantically shook her head. *"¡No, no te vayas!"* She pressed her face back to Danger's chest, the sobbing starting anew.

Mick straightened and gave him a long look.

Danger shrugged. Why the girl sought solace from him, he couldn't fathom. "We have to get her down to Reyna."

With a lot of coercion, soft words, and negotiation of the terrain, they made it back down the hill. Floodlights had been set up around the ranch house, the place buzzing with activity. But one figure stood out.

Reyna came forward with a blanket and tenderness in her gaze.

In his arms, Danger felt the girl tense. "I'll stay close by. Promise."

As Reyna carefully eased closer, she started speaking in Spanish. Her tone was gentle yet firm. Soon, the girl let Danger go, although reluctantly and never taking her eyes off him, especially when he stepped back.

Clucking his tongue, Danger pulled out a KONG. Riot's focus zeroed in on his beloved rubber toy, and when Danger popped it to him, he surged up and snagged it out of the air. The girl laughed, her eyes now lit with surprise instead of terror.

The tension in Danger's shoulders subsided. Seeing something like this reminded him why he did what he did. Why it was sometimes necessary to kill the bad guys. To keep innocents like this girl safe.

Reyna wrapped the girl in the blanket, talking quietly as she rubbed her arms the way a mother would her child. As she gently turned her and guided her away, she glanced over her shoulder at Danger. There was a lot in that simple look—thanks, concern, relief.

He gave an acknowledging nod. It'd been the right decision to let her come.

"You did good up there," Mick said as he watched LEOs lead a coroner up the hillside. "Sorry I wasn't faster."

"No worries. Anyone track that third Guerrero?"

"Nah, lost him."

The burly sheriff joined them. "His heat signature disappeared from the drone images like he was swallowed up by the earth."

"Caves," Danger muttered.

"The only logical explanation." Gaines heaved a sigh. "They chose this ranch house because there is an entire tunnel network in this area. The perfect escape route if the main road is blocked or monitored. No way to find the right tunnel or which way he went."

Danger let out a curse.

"The important thing is that the girls are okay," Mick said.

"Agreed, but now everyone with a daughter or wife needs to double up on security." Gaines spat to the side. "Never thought I'd be fighting these cowards on my own turf."

The sheriff's words burned through Danger. Lyric and Rachel. He had to get home. Make sure they were okay. "What happens next?" He eyed Riot sniffing around a patch of scrub. He'd let him keep the KONG. Darn well deserved it with that exceptional performance.

"I sent the search party up."

Rio Silva and her maligator Chaos were part of that team.

"Choppers are en route," Gaines continued. "Medical examiner is retrieving the bodies. Communications are reviewing the feeds to see if we can find the third." His attention shifted to a LEO jogging toward them. "I'll be right back."

Too little, too late. The Guerrero was probably long gone.

Danger glanced at the rescued girls, all wrapped in blankets, huddled on benches. They each wore an anxious, exhausted, or blank expression, one crying silently. Reyna knelt in front her.

An officer tossed Danger a water bottle. He made Riot surrender his KONG, then squirted some of the liquid at him. The Dutchie inhaled it.

"Maddox." Gaines stalked back to him with several LEOs in tow. The sheriff held up an old cellphone, likely a burner. "One of the Guerreros had this on him. Someone's asking for you. Won't identify himself."

Frowning, Danger took the device and put the call on speaker. "Who is this?"

"Good evening, Beau Maddox."

A dark wave seized Danger as he instantly recognized the tinny voice. "Osorio."

6

TEXAS HILL COUNTRY

IT WAS HIM. LYONEL WAS ON THE PHONE WITH BEAU.

Paisley's stomach churned. She'd been tending the girls—nineteen of them—when Gaines approached Beau with a cell.

Beau's face darkened like the sky before a storm. Then she heard the name come off his lips: *Osorio*. The blood in her veins iced. Why would he call Beau? What did he want?

Paisley asked one of the female officers helping with the girls to excuse her for a moment, then she told Flor—the young girl Beau had rescued—she'd be right back. The girls had been mentally and physically abused and most were barely sixteen! She didn't want to leave them, but she *needed* to hear that call.

Silently praying for them, Paisley weaved past a group of operators and let two officers pass who carried a body bag out of the ranch house.

"Cut the games, Osorio," Beau growled just as she slipped up to the men clustered around him and spotted Riot at his feet, body pressing into his leg.

"Very well," Lyonel replied, his familiar voice tightening the cord around Paisley's lungs. Strangely, he was speaking English, albeit with a strong accent. "Although I think you should be a bit more grateful since I spared your life tonight."

Paisley's breath caught the same time Beau stiffened, his gaze snapping to Sheriff Gaines. Lyonel had been *here*?

A chuckle came through. "Are you surprised that I did not shoot you when I had the chance?"

Wait—*he* was the Guerrero who'd gotten away? Frustration building—they had been so close to ending him!—Paisley scanned the hill rising into the ominous night sky behind the ranch house. Flashlights danced over the limestone, bushes, and trees. Her mind spun with the effort of trying to process the information. *How can this be, Jesus? Why did he come here?*

"What do you want, Osorio?" Beau ground out.

"To tell you to keep watching, Beau Maddox. It would be a shame if something happened to your loved ones."

Beau's free hand curled into a fist. His eyes were wild with fury.

She swallowed hard as realization hit her—Beau's scars. Was that Lyonel's handiwork? Had to be. How else would they know each other so well?

"This is the price you pay for killing the boss's brother so you could escape." Lyonel's voice was no longer mocking. "Next time I will not spare your life, Beau Maddox."

The line went dead.

"I couldn't track the ca—"

"I want someone at my sister's house. Now!" Beau shoved out of the crowd, taking Riot with him toward the ranch house.

Paisley scrambled after them. "Beau, wait."

He stalked on while bringing his phone to his ear. Listened. Cursed. "Rachel, when you get this, lock yourself and Lyric in the house and stay away from the windows. Don't open unless it's the police. You hear me?" He huffed and shoved a hand through his sweaty, spiky hair. "Call me back."

Paisley's stomach revolted. Lyonel *always* carried out his

threats. *Jesus, please let Rachel get this message soon and follow the instructions. Protect them from any harm.*

Ahead, Beau stomped into the house. It was run-down, shutters weathered and crooked, and there was a big hole in one of the walls.

Paisley followed them into the illuminated hallway. The smell of mold, body odor, and blood nearly knocked her over. "Beau?"

He whipped around.

Involuntarily, she recoiled, tasting her heartbeat as his eyes—so dark—impaled her. Her inner alarm system screamed to leave it. To run. It was the same look Lyonel always had before lashing out. Sometimes he'd beat her up so bad she couldn't move for days.

Stop. He's not Lyonel. This was her old friend, Anxiety, whispering lies in her ear. Yes, Beau was an intense man, but he'd never given her a reason to be afraid. The opposite. He'd stood up for her during the pre-mission briefing and now rescued Flor.

"Don't let him get to you." She held Beau's glower. "That's exactly what he wants."

Riot started sniffing her pants, then her fingers. Warm puffs tickled her skin. When his tail started wagging, her heart leapt. It wasn't the exciting kind of wagging he did when he saw Beau, but it was progress.

"You did amazing tonight," she whispered, scratching the top of his head between the ears. "Jordi would be so proud." The thought choked her, and she quieted so Beau wouldn't hear the anguish in her voice. It took her a moment to compose herself. "Thank you for taking care of Riot," she finally said as she straightened.

His expression remained hard. "Riot has to search the compound." With that, he told Riot to "seek-seek" and started working their way down the hall.

RONIE KENDIG & JJ SAMIE MYLES

Pursing her lips, Paisley watched their systematic method. "Wait. Can I do it? Search the compound with Riot?"

Beau stopped with his back to her. Then shot her a glance over his shoulder. "It's carnage in here."

"You mean because of the bodies? I can handle it." As long as she didn't look too closely, she'd be fine. "I lived two years with the Guerreros, remember?"

Never taking his eyes off her, Beau unhooked Riot's leash from his tactical belt and passed it to her.

"Thank you." Elation flooded her as she took it. "Riot. Seek-seek."

To her excitement, the Dutch shepherd jumped right in, his nose hovering over the creaking floorboards like a vacuum cleaner. Tail wagging, he zig-zagged his way into the first room. A fireplace hinted that it once had been used as a living room. She had lived in a home like this for a short while when a family took her in after she'd been rescued from the Guerreros. It'd been her happiest year.

Her heart squeezed, and she let the memories ebb away. "What was the dog you had before like?" she asked Beau as Riot led them into the next room. So far, they hadn't come across any bodies. "Was he anything like Riot?"

"Work the room with him," Danger said gruffly.

Right. She shifted her focus back to the four-legged hero. There were a hundred other questions she'd rather have asked. Like his connection to Lyonel. And she wanted to know what he was concocting, because he wasn't the kind of guy to let someone threaten his family and get away with it.

The silence stretched between them, filled with voices filtering in from the other rooms and outside, and Riot's eager sniffing.

"Name was Cutter," Beau muttered as they moved on to the other side of the room. "Belgian Malinois. Explosives detector dog." Beau's gaze was pinned to Riot. "Loved people, disliked other dogs. Riot's the opposite. Picky with the two-legged species, chill with his kind."

Yes, she was one of the two-legged species he didn't like. Though they were making progress.

"They're both driven," Beau continued. "Dutchies are usually less intense in their drive than maligators. Riot's an exception." He sniffed, pointing to a chest and trailing his hand over it, urging Riot to sniff it. "Both suckers for attention."

Strike me pink. Was that a *smirk*? Just like earlier, the right side of his mouth had kicked up. Only a little, but Lord have mercy! Good thing he didn't do this more often.

Good grief, what is wrong with you, woman? "What happened to Cutter?" When his grin froze, Paisley instantly regretted the question.

Beau clenched his jaw. "He starved."

"How?" Not what she had expected at all. Shot or blown up, yes. But starved?

"They tied us up inches apart. Just enough so I couldn't reach him. Wouldn't give him food, and he wouldn't take the rations I shoved over with my foot." Although his voice was void of emotion, his rigid posture gave away that he'd just bared a part of his broken soul.

And the pain festering there was so strong Paisley could feel it in her own heart. "That's awful," she whispered. "I'm so sorry, Beau."

"Did you see his tail flag?" He jutted his chin at Riot. "He's on to something."

And just like that, the walls were back up.

Riot's tail picked up speed, faster than before. His muzzle vigorously examined one of the floorboards. He stopped, sniffed around the same place, the sniffs turning longer, more examining. Then he sat.

Taking a knee next to him, Beau pulled a knife from his vest and stuck it in the crack between the floorboards. The one he leveraged came up effortlessly. He shoved it aside and stuck his gloved hand into a roughly three-foot-long gap. His arm disappeared up to his shoulder, then he eased back, drawing out a package with white powder.

Oh, she knew those bricks well.

"You found the stash," he said to Riot as he ruffled the Dutchie's ears. "Good boy." It was a heart-warming tone that didn't at all match his raw exterior and behavior.

He rose, unearthed the KONG, and pitched it to Riot, who snagged it from the air. The Dutchie darted to the other side of the room, dragging Paisley along. Gasping, she tried to stop him, but he was too strong.

"Let the lead go," Beau said. "He won't go anywhere. Just likes to have his KONG to himself."

Paisley dropped the leash with a breath. "There is so much more I have to learn."

"Patience. He'll come around eventually."

The way his gaze lingered on her had her mind in a tangle. Was it possible that he was talking about himself instead of Riot? That she shouldn't let his stoic manner keep her away?

He keyed his mic. "Hawk, this is Delta Eight. Found a stash in the second room to the left. Not sure what it is." He listened. "Copy."

"That's snow," Paisley said. "Cocaine."

Riot's head snapped up at the word, and Beau arched a shredded brow at her.

"The color is pure white, and I bet it smells sweet and floral with a note of gasoline. That's what the Guerreros use to manufacture it." She was tempted to cut a package open for further inspection but knew better than to tamper with evidence.

"They made you work in their labs?" His blue gaze drilled her as if its destination were her soul.

"That too, but I learned a lot from my mom." Paisley dropped her gaze to the package in his hand. "She was an addict." When she looked up, she found an indecipherable expression on his face. Pensive, maybe. Or . . . pained?

Footsteps advanced from the hallway seconds before Sheriff Gaines appeared, followed by two officers. "Well done. Team will take it from here. Finish up and go home."

Going home was not an option for Paisley until she knew the girls were in a safe place. "I should get back to the girls. I promised I'd go to the shelter with them."

"Anything new on Osorio?" Beau asked, angling aside for her to pass.

Gaines shook his head. "Nada. The guy vanished into thin air. You'd better get home to your sister."

Mouth in a hard line, Beau gave a curt nod. And oh, Paisley knew heading home wasn't the only thing on his mind.

He was going to take matters into his own hands.

HARMONIA, TEXAS

Danger shot up, greedily gulping oxygen. "Augh!" His heart pounded in his chest, his whole body shaking. Wan light pressed through the window, giving him an idea where he was. In his living room, not a bunker smelling of gore and death.

Rachel and Lyric. A quick glance through the window showed his sister's house beneath the squat trees. Dawn was cracking, blue bleeding into the black night sky. The security app installed on his phone showing no alarm triggers slowed his raging pulse. No intrusion on their property.

Planting his feet on the floor in front of the sofa, he buried his head in his hands and let out a groan. Hadn't meant to fall asleep, but apparently his body had needed it after the op. Sleep deprivation impaired his reflexes and situational awareness, so the two hours he'd gotten had done him good.

Except for the nightmares. Hadn't been that real in a long time. Or ever. It'd felt more like a flashback, the taste of metal and smell of burnt flesh way too real. And Rudy's scream . . . it'd been right here.

His memories of captivity were hazy . . . vague, with revelations popping up slowly, over time. But that dream . . . felt like his gray matter was playing tricks on him, conjuring images after last night's hostage rescue. As much as he hated to admit it, the op had to be the trigger.

Ghost had been right. He wasn't ready. He might've suppressed the flashback that'd struck in the middle of the hunt, but what if he failed next time? People could get killed.

Images of Charlie Team and Cutter ghosted through his head. Like them. He'd killed them all.

Danger dug his fingers into his scalp to drown the pain suddenly searing his chest, making it hard to breathe. His sweat-drenched T-shirt scorched his skin. Gone. They were all gone. Why did he get to live when they were dead? *Why, God?*

As if he'd get an answer from the man upstairs. With a growl, he grabbed his SIG P226 9mm and punched to his feet. He was alone in this and needed to focus on keeping this torturing emptiness from eating his insides. All it did was paralyze him, make him weak. Anger was better. Anger kept him going, kept him fighting for justice. Kept him looking for Osorio until he'd found and deep-sixed him. Now that he was threatening Danger's family . . . Did he know about Rachel and Lyric? And how'd he gotten into the States?

Danger hooked a shaking forearm against the window frame and again visually traced the front perimeter of Rachel's home. Was his vision playing tricks on him or did that tree have a weird shape? SIG in hand, he eased open the storm door and stuck his head out.

A blur from his yard made him jerk back. A large, dark mass vaulted into his house. Smacked into him, punching him back onto the floorboards.

Danger wrestled against the weight on top of him. Brought up the SIG. *Soft. This is fur.* He saw the brindled face like a derpy teddy bear. "Riot, what the—" He slumped back and stared at the ceiling, expelling a ragged breath. "What're you doing here?"

Claws dug into his chest as the Dutchie worked his way up until he reached Danger's face with his tongue. Dragged it over Danger's mouth.

"We ain't that close." Danger scratched the Dutchie's favorite spot behind the ears. How had he gotten out? "Did you run off?" He rubbed a little firmer.

The tongue disappeared and Riot moaned with pleasure, leaning into the massage.

"Don't tell me Reyna didn't notice your jailbreak."

"Uh, yes, she most certainly did." Her voice carried through the open door. "I'm so sorry, Beau."

How many times did he have to tell her his name was Danger? A flare of temper brought him into a sitting position, and Riot huffed his disapproval over being shoved away.

Reyna's silhouette shifted. "Can I come in?"

Clenching his teeth, he tossed a glance at the shirt plastered to his torso. "I'll be out in a sec." He let Riot out the door, went to his bedroom to don a clean T-shirt, then headed outside.

Reyna sat on the stairs leading to the scarcely dawn-lit porch, smoothing her fingers over Riot's head who was curled up next to her. She wore an oversized tank top and yoga pants, her hair spilling down her back. "I'm sorry." Her eyes followed Danger as he leaned a shoulder against the post on the other side of the stairs. "Riot scratched at the door, and I thought he had to do a job, so I let him out the back. He cleared the fence and dashed right to your house."

Still looking for his handler. Or maybe he'd sensed the nightmares.

"He should've let you rest," Reyna said. "I'm sorry he woke you."

"He didn't wake me." Danger scanned the neighborhood. The houses sat in semidarkness, the air charged with humidity.

"You couldn't sleep?" She let out a huff. "Me either."

And now she'd launch right into grilling, then psychoanalyzing him. As if resurrecting his demons would help. What he needed was a drink.

Hold on, he wasn't that guy anymore. A long, hard workout—that's what he needed.

"Rachel texted—said she isn't going to stay with your parents," Reyna said, her gaze fixed on his sister's home. She looked back at him. "Can't you do anything?"

He grunted. "Tried, trust me. She wouldn't even let me pull security at her house. Doesn't want Lyric scared." He could strangle her for being so bullheaded. At least she'd given him access to her security system.

"Does she know you're the target of a lethal cartel because you . . . ended the boss's brother?"

"She knows I'm not messing around when it comes to her and Lyric's safety."

"Fair enough . . . The girls from the ranch are in a secure location. Again, thank you for rescuing them."

Feeling her eyes on him, Danger flared his nostrils. Had she forgotten that he'd let Osorio slip? "This wasn't even a scrape in the Guerreros' organization. You of all people should know that."

"You guys saved nineteen precious lives. This might feel small in comparison to Guerreros's organization, but every life counts," she said. "An entire team risked their lives to get me out. If they hadn't, I wouldn't be here. Probably wouldn't even be alive."

Danger looked down at her.

She absentmindedly stroked Riot's side as he savored the attention with closed eyes.

Making sure he didn't squash the Dutchie, Danger settled next to them on the top step. "How'd you get caught up in that?"

Riot got up and spun ninety degrees. With a huff, he sprawled his upper body on Danger's legs, hind paws pressing into Reyna's outer thigh.

She laughed. "Of course I get the feet."

"At least he doesn't drool on you," Danger said, smirking. When the Dutchie jerked his head up in protest, he smoothed a hand over the dog's nose. "I'm joking, bud."

With a huff, Riot lowered his head back down.

"I was sixteen when Abuela—my grandmother—died." Reyna ran her fingers down the Dutchie's brindle fur. "Mama wanted to move back to Venezuela, so she took me out of high school in the States. The problem was that she was an addict and didn't care about getting a job. So instead of continuing school in Venezuela, I waitressed. I could barely keep us afloat, but then I met this guy. He was so . . . kind and generous. He was always there for me and even helped me pay rent."

Yeah, Danger knew where this was going, and he didn't like it. At all.

"I didn't know he was a Guerrero recruiting girls to traffic. He isolated me from the few friends I'd made and used my vulnerability to make me dependent on him. Then Mama overdosed, and I had no one. He said he'd take care of me, but I had to help pay for living expenses." Reyna lifted a shoulder. "That's when he started selling me to other men. The cartel pocketed ninety percent of the income, he got ten and moved up the hierarchy."

All at her expense.

Danger clenched a fist. One of the things that got him most worked up was someone with power exploiting the weak. The way Reyna had talked about it, so matter-of-factly, said she was long past the pain, but it didn't change the fact that she'd walked through Gehenna. "You said a team rescued you . . ."

Smooth one, Danger. Act like you don't care about her pain.

A small smile played on her lips. "Yes. Jordi tried to find me for two years, and when he finally did, he used his connections to gather a team. Six brave men rescued me while I was on a job in Caracas. Even back then that city was a Guerrero stronghold, and I always had guards with me. But God worked miracles, and they managed to rescue me and bring me back to the States." She pursed her lips. "Living with Jordi would've been too dangerous because we knew the Guerreros would come looking for me, so one of the guys let me stay with his family in North Carolina. I caught up with high school, then went to Duke University."

"That's where you met Rachel."

"Mm-hmm. In my free time I took self-defense classes at a gym close to the university, and that's where we met. I didn't want to make friends, because I knew if the Guerreros found me, they'd kill my friends too. But your sister . . ." Reyna laughed. "She wouldn't back off. After a year I moved in with her."

Danger snorted. "Sounds like her. She's a pit bull." He smoothed a hand down Riot's sturdy chest, and the Dutchie squiggled until he was on his back, belly exposed. "What's the guy's name whose family you lived with?"

"Jude Payne."

He started. "You're kidding."

"You know him?"

"Did some ops together."

Reyna beamed. "After rescuing me, he moved to Venezuela to keep fighting the Guerreros. He's my contact." She tipped her head back, watching the dawning sky swallow the stars.

For a moment, they said nothing, and Danger realized how calm he was without having gone on a bender or working out. How on earth did she do it? The same had happened at the ranch house after Osorio's call.

He glanced at her. There was something about her that sucked him into her vortex. She was probably the bravest woman he'd ever met. Not many people ran back into the proverbial burning house to save others after they themselves had been burned.

Her head came back down, the corner of her mouth tugging into a smile as her eyes met his. "What?"

Forcing himself to maintain a lock on those pretty eyes and

not drop to her lips, he cleared his throat. Couldn't drag a woman into his darkness. Not even if she was a counselor. "What's the name of your trafficker?"

Her smile fell, and she scrutinized him as if assessing what he was going to do with that information. "Why do you want to—"

"Osorio. It was him, wasn't it?" Her hesitation gave it away, and man, he wanted to send his fist into something. That guy didn't stop giving him reasons to shred him to pieces.

"Yes," she said quietly. "But it was a long time ago. God helped me forgive him."

"Forgive—" Danger shifted, causing Riot to squirm and flip to his belly. "How can you forgive a guy like that, huh?"

Her hand found his lower arm. Squeezed. "By God's grace. He set me free and helped me move on. He can do the same for you, Beau."

The peace she radiated felt like a sucker punch. There was no denying this was God's doing. How else could someone forgive scum like Osorio?

If only he could have that peace too. Maybe if he tried praying again—

Are you really that delusional? He clenched his jaw so hard it throbbed. God wasn't on his side. He didn't even need to try. What was he without his anger? Anger he'd dealt out against the deserving. Like Osorio.

"What's your plan, Beau?"

"What plan?" He knew exactly what she meant, and that made his gut cinch.

"With Lyonel. I know you want revenge." She tilted her head to look at him. "What are you going to do?"

The pleading in her voice gave him pause. "Not sure." It was true. He'd asked everyone he knew with ties to the Guerreros to keep their eyes out and alert him if anything came up. Apart from that there was nothing he could do except keep Rachel and Lyric safe.

"Whatever you're planning," Reyna said, "I pray God is with you."

Good luck with that.

He'd rather she prayed for him to find Osorio before the thug escaped back to Venezuela. Once there, getting to him would be impossible. The entire country was a Guerrero stronghold.

7

AUSTIN, TEXAS

A WEEK HAD GONE BY WITHOUT NEWS ON LYONEL'S WHEREABOUTS, and Paisley could tell Beau was more restless by the minute. While he showed up to train her and Riot every day—they were making slow, albeit steady progress—he radiated a growing intensity.

She knew better than to try to rescue someone, but when he'd invited her to one of Lyric's soccer games, she'd jumped at the chance. She guessed he wanted to keep an eye on his niece and Rachel, and he'd said she could practice being in a public setting with Riot. She prayed it took his mind off Lyonel. Frankly, she was on edge too, although she knew better. The Guerreros' MO was letting their victims squirm in the dark.

At the athletic fields, Beau had insisted on watching the game from afar because of Riot, so they stood a good thirty yards away under a live oak. Thank God for the shade—the afternoon heat was no joke. What she wouldn't give for Chicago weather.

"Where's Lyric?" she asked Beau as she watched the six-year-old girls chasing the soccer ball down the field. Too sweet how none of them stuck to their assigned position because all wanted to score a goal.

"Number eleven. A head shorter than the rest." He wore tan cargos—was that a gun holstered at his back?—and a dark gray T-shirt, his hands tucked into his armpits. Behind the ever-present Oakleys, he monitored the small crowd lined up along the field and their surroundings like a hawk.

"Ah, I see her." Lyric *was* shorter than the rest, but what she lacked in height, she made up for in speed and tenacity. The ball was passed to her, and she dribbled around an opponent, then another. "Wow, she's good!"

"She's the best." Beau's chest puffed a little, and Paisley had to smile. The way he adored Lyric like she was his own daughter warmed her heart.

Lyric scored.

"That's my princess," Beau muttered, clapping, then folded his arms again.

At the sideline, Rachel cheered, and when Lyric ran to her, she caught her in a hug. Beau's buddy Mick was there—*well, that's interesting*—and high-fived Lyric.

"See?" Beau smirked. "She's got Maddox blood running through her veins."

"Does anyone else play soccer in your family?"

"Dad did. He was a goalie. So that's what I did too."

Riot's whining brought her attention down. He was lying at their feet in the grass, muzzled, his attentive eyes fixed to the soccer ball the goalie fished out of the net.

"Sorry, boy," she said gently. "That's not for you. You can have your KONG later."

At the K-word, his head swiveled in her direction, drool dripping from the muzzle.

Beau snorted. "She said later, bud."

As they continued watching the game, Paisley couldn't stop thinking about Beau's father. Rachel had mentioned how his death had affected Beau the most. He'd copied his dad in soccer.

Did it end there? "Did your dad inspire you to become a SEAL? Rachel told me he was one too."

Staring ahead at girls kicking the ball down the field again, Beau sniffed. "Yeah. As a kid, I copied everything he did. There's a picture of us in the bathroom, both with shaving cream on our faces as we look into the mirror. I was five."

The image he painted made Paisley smile. It sounded like his dad had been very important to him. His superhero. "That's sweet," she said quietly, her heart all of a sudden heavy.

She'd never had that kind of experience. No dad to look up to. No possibility of mirroring her daddy—or being daddy's little princess—because she'd never known who he was, not even his name. Mama had always said it was better that way, but sometimes Paisley doubted her mother knew anything about him. The way the woman had torn through man after man . . . Doubtful.

"When I found out he was a frogman and what that meant, I wanted to be one too. Enlisted right after high school."

"I'm sure he would be very proud of you."

Grunting, Beau turned away, obviously not sharing her opinion. Was being a decorated SEAL not good enough?

"I can't imagine how challenging the years after his accident were," she said quietly.

"Pretty sure Rachel told you."

Oh, sore spot. Paisley shook her head. "She's never talked much about you. All I know is that you were with your dad in that accident and that you hit something."

"Power pole." His mouth pulled into a grim line. "We were visiting our grandparents—Dad's parents—in Colorado. It was a winter evening, and Dad had to go into town to pick up a part for his 1978 Ford Thunderbird. He was obsessed with that thing. Worked on it for hours when he wasn't deployed." He ran a hand behind his neck. "I went with him. On the way home, our Jeep swerved. Probably ice or something on the road. Hit a power pole. Dad's side got crushed, trapping him. I was unharmed, and he told me to get help. This was the time with no cell phones, but we'd just passed a small town, and he wanted me to run back." Beau's Adam's apple jerked as he swallowed hard. "I didn't. Just couldn't leave him alone."

Paisley closed her eyes, her heart aching at the thought of eight-year-old Beau afraid to leave his injured dad behind. He must've been terrified.

"We had this thing, you know, where he'd say, 'If knocked down . . .' and I'd continue, 'I will get back up.' Then we'd fist-bump and end with 'Every time.' So when he finally convinced me to leave . . ." Beau clenched his jaw, the muscles going rigid. "He held out his fist and said his part, but I . . . I didn't. I just ran off. By the time I came back with help, he was dead."

Paisley drew in a breath. "I can't imagine how difficult that must've been for you." Heart-wrenching stories were her daily bread, and she'd learned to distance herself from the heaviness that otherwise would crush her. But for some reason, Beau's story reached her on a completely different level. The way he'd told it sounded as if a part of him, his eight-year-old self, was still grieving. Even regretted that he hadn't finished their ritual.

Arms folded again, Beau sniffed. Kept watching the game.

A low growl pulled their attention to Riot, who slowly rose to all fours, his gaze pinned to a lanky teenager wearing a red hat, strolling their way.

Unease seeped into Paisley's stomach, and she tightened her grip around the leash. "Riot, no. Out."

The snarling deepened.

"Beau?" Paisley looked to him for help, the confidence she'd built up in training vanished.

His arms were no longer crossed but at his sides. "Red trucker hat, stay where you are," he said loudly, his tone cool.

"Hey, it's okay. I like dogs." The teenager kept closing in. "Just wondering why your dog wears this thing."

"Are you deaf? I said back off!"

Paisley nudged Beau's arm. "I don't think he understands the graveness of the situation."

Beau took a solid step forward. "This dog is trained to kill. If you don't want him to eat your face off, take a hike." Although his voice was controlled, he clearly fought to keep his temper in check.

The teen jutted his chin, arrogance oozing from him. "You can't tell me what to do."

Beau reached for the lead and she handed it off—but in that split second, Riot lunged. The nylon ripped between their hands.

"No!" Paisley shouted.

"Riot, heel. Out!" Beau's command was lost amid cheering from the game.

Riot bridged the gap to his target with three big leaps and, snarling, full-on muzzle-punched the teenager in the stomach.

The teen was thrown back and went down hard, Riot on top of him.

It all happened so fast, and by the time Paisley reacted, Beau had already sprinted over and seized Riot's collar, hauling him off the kid. "Stupid punk! I warned you to back off."

Aghast at the entire encounter, Paisley rushed to the teen and crouched next to him. "Are you alright?"

His face was pale and contorted, one hand pressed into his stomach. Dirt and grass stained his T-shirt, and there was a tear in the fabric surrounded by a sprinkle of blood from Riot's claws.

"Hey!" A man in an expensive-looking suit hurried from the crowd at the soccer game and came sprinting over. "What're you doing to my son?"

The teen suddenly wheezed—like, fake wheezed. Whimpered. "Dad, her beast of a dog attacked me!" He wailed and yanked away from her.

Paisley bit down the retort about to bubble up. Riot was *not* a beast, and if this boy had listened, nothing would've happened.

But she knew better than to start a debate. It'd only make matters worse.

The businessman now loomed over Paisley. "You stay right here. I'm calling the authorities."

"Sir, this was an accident. My dog—"

"Save that for the officials. I don't want to hear it."

Paisley blinked. Wow, no surprise the boy had no manners.

"Again, I'm sorry." With a last glance at the teenager, who seemed somewhat okay, she turned and strode to the parking lot. The feeling of having done something terribly wrong clawed at her. Why hadn't she held on to the leash longer?

Riot's aggressive barking resounded in her ear. She shuddered. Never before had she witnessed him act so savagely. It gave her a whole new awareness of what he was capable of.

When she reached the parking lot, she saw Beau standing at the open backdoor of his running Tacoma, his broad shoulders rigid.

She walked up to him. "I'm sorry."

"Not your fault." He didn't turn.

"Yes, I thought you had it and let go—"

"I said, not your fault."

The way he stressed every single word twisted Paisley's already churning gut into a knot. Beau wasn't just ticked—something was wrong. "Is Riot okay?"

Forearm resting against the top of the vehicle's frame, Beau turned slightly, but said nothing.

"Beau?"

He pushed off and faced her, and although the shades obscured his eyes, the hard line his mouth built said enough. "He's the one who has to pay for it."

Frowning, Paisley's heart hiccupped. "What do you mean?"

When Beau nodded at something behind her, she turned and scanned the parking lot for what he indicated. She saw cars, a van pulling in—

"No!" She stumbled back at the logo on the side of that van—animal control.

Riot. They were here to take him. Panic seized her. *No, no, no! Don't let them take him from me!*

The vehicle stopped, and a young officer climbed out.

"Beau?" Paisley reached behind her and clutched his arm. "You can't let them take him."

She could feel Beau stir—maybe wave, because the officer came right for them.

"Sir. Ma'am." He tipped his hat. "My name is Officer Ted Kowalski. Did you report the dog attack?"

Paisley wanted to make clear that it wasn't an attack, but the words wouldn't form. The tendril of panic cording her chest tightened.

"No, but it's our dog." Beau shoved Paisley aside, granting the officer unrestricted view of Riot.

Incredulity sloshed through her. How could he offer them Riot on a silver platter?

"Okay," the officer huffed. "Give me a minute." The officer walked over to the rude man and his son, talked to them for a minute, then started back. His head hung low and he rubbed the back of his neck. "I'm going to need your name and contact information." He recorded the information Beau provided. "Kinda hoped you'd tell me he was one of Crew's dogs."

Beau's lips flattened. "No, but we work him."

"Well"—the officer sighed again—"please get him out. He has to come with me."

Again, Paisley watched in disbelief as Beau opened the crate, clipped the lead on Riot, and lured him out. He wasn't even *trying* to do something.

"Beautiful dog." Officer Kowalski took the leash Beau handed him. Again, just like that.

"Wait, you can't take him!" Both Beau's and the officer's gaze snapped to her. She schooled her voice. "He did nothing wrong. Please."

Officer Kowalski glanced at Riot, then back at her. "I'm afraid I have to, ma'am."

"But he was muzzled and felt threatened!"

"Sorry, ma'am, that's the law. We'll take good care of him."

Paisley's stomach convulsed as she groped for Beau's arm again. "Do something. Please."

He looked down at her hand clutching his arm. "Let them take him."

Paisley's mind scrambled to get ahold of his words, somehow make sense of them. But they didn't make sense. How could he say something like that? Did he not care about Riot?

She dropped her hand and stumbled back, all of a sudden not able to be far enough away from Beau.

Officer Kowalski guided Riot into one of the stalls of his air-conditioned vehicle. The *click* of the door latch reverberated through Paisley and made her twitch.

"No . . ." Why did this have to happen? Things finally had started to get better, and now this.

Officer Kowalski climbed into his vehicle and drove off, taking Riot . . .

The van wasn't yet out of sight when a shout echoed over the parking lot. "You!" The businessman came charging at them, crimson-faced, stabbing his finger at Beau. "You need to learn how to control your dog!"

Something happened with Beau that she couldn't quite comprehend. It was like a dark storm moved over him. And when he grabbed her elbow and shoved her to the passenger side of his Tacoma, she knew things were about to get serious.

He opened the door. "Get in and don't come out until I give you the all clear."

His tone left no room for argument. When a soldier switched into operator mode, the only smart thing to do was comply. She climbed in, her eyes glued to the side mirror, where she saw Beau plant himself in front of the man. To hear the conversation, she turned off the AC Beau must've left running for Riot. Thanks to the cracked windows in the back and her lip-reading skills, she could piece it together.

"And you need to learn to control your kid." Beau's voice was low and lethal. If Paisley were that guy, she'd have beat it the second Beau stepped up.

Instead, the man offered a mocking laugh. "Say what you want, but I will sue you. And make sure that beast gets euthanized."

Euthanized?! The word sliced through Paisley, pitching her into a black pool of horror. The man was dead serious!

Beau looked like he'd grown a few inches. "Do that and I'll give you a real reason to sue me." With that, he stalked past the businessman back to the soccer field.

Wait, where was he going? Paisley twisted in her seat to see what he was doing. What about going to the animal control center to sort things out? They couldn't just leave Riot to his fate.

"You'll hear from my lawyer, tough guy!" the businessman yelled. When Beau kept walking, he ranted as he climbed in his convertible and sped away with squealing tires.

Slumping in her seat, Paisley whispered a prayer of thanks that Beau hadn't hurt the man. Still, the dread of Riot possibly being euthanized . . . Worry pushed her out of the truck. She retraced her steps to the soccer field.

The game was still going, parents cheering and shouting like nothing had happened. Beau stood next to an older woman, both their phones out. Just as Paisley reached them, the woman returned to the game.

Beau stalked right past Paisley. "I told you to stay in the Tacoma." His tone was hard.

She fell in step beside him. Nearly had to run to keep up. "I'm really worried about Riot. I couldn't sit still . . ."

"Get in. We're going to the animal control center."

"Oh. Good. Thank you." She eyed him as she buckled in, relieved he was focused on Riot too.

But what if his expertise wasn't enough?

Oh, Jordi, I'm so sorry. All she'd wanted was to honor his will by giving Riot the best life. And more, Riot had somehow snuck right into her heart. She couldn't imagine a life without him anymore.

Instead, she might have just signed his death warrant.

Riot's life was on the line because of his idiocy.

Danger gripped the steering wheel of his Tacoma. Muttered an oath that made Reyna shift on her seat. He gritted his teeth, combating the urge to gun it. Feeling like every second that passed was the one that Riot ceased to exist. But the last thing they needed was to be pulled over for speeding.

Shouldn't have unleashed his aggravation over that punk kid and father. No, shouldn't have brought Riot to a public place with lots of distractions and unpredictable kids in the first place. Yeah, harebrained idea, solely because he'd wanted to keep an eye on Rachel and Lyric. And because he'd wanted more time with Reyna. He was man enough to admit he liked her. Had the crazy urge to get to know her better.

See, that's why he didn't let women into his life. They were a distraction. Now Riot might get euthanized simply for responding the way he'd been trained. Another life going on his account.

Loosening his death grip on the wheel, Danger focused on the road. *Get your head straight.* Dissecting his mistakes didn't do any good. It'd happened. He couldn't change that. Now was all about saving Riot.

"Wasn't your fault," he said, unable to take Reyna's silence any longer.

"I let the leash go." Emotion thickened her voice.

"Negative. He would've dragged you along. It was on me. I should've commanded him to stand down."

Quiet held them hostage in their own guilt. "What triggered him?"

"Trigger is negative. He's trained. Disciplined." Danger hit the brake to avoid the white sedan creeping in front of them. He bit back a curse. *C'mon, granny.* "He's trained to protect his handler at all times, without commands. That's what he did—that kid aggressed toward me, and Riot dealt with it as he was trained." He flared his nostrils. "My own anger at the boy didn't help the situation. In fact, it fueled Riot."

"Emotions travel down the lead?"

Surprise lit through him. He shot a glance her way and found a sad smile on her lips. "Yeah . . ." Impressive. "Riot executed perfectly. Can't say the same for his handler."

"That lady you were talking to at the field—what was that about?"

"Evidence. Earlier, I'd seen her recording the game on her phone. Took a chance and, sure enough—she unwittingly caught the whole encounter. She sent me the file."

"Oh. That's . . . smart."

"I also called Ghost. He'll meet us at the AC center. He knows the officers there. Not the first time he's had to deal with something like this." Still, this whole situation could get Danger sacked. Couldn't even blame Ghost—ABA had a reputation to protect, and an incident like this could put them in a bad spot.

"Oh, good."

The relief in Reyna's words seared into his skin like tiny pieces of shrapnel. She didn't trust him. "Mick's coming too. Said that guy and his son are known boat-rockers."

For the rest of the short drive, Reyna kept quiet. At the AC center, Danger pulled into the parking lot and killed the engine. He climbed out and started for the run-down building, but noticed he was alone. Turning, he found Reyna still sitting in the Tacoma, staring down at her lap.

He doubled back and opened the passenger door. "You coming?"

She said nothing. Looked so fragile, so lost—nothing like the spitfire PTS shrink he'd met two weeks ago.

"I can't lose him, Beau," she whispered. "Riot's the only thing I have left of Jordi."

There it was, the thousand-pound anchor around his throat and the reason she didn't want to hand Riot over to ABA—sentimental value. Same reason he'd held on to Dad's Bible, though he'd never cracked it open. No intentions to, either.

"I don't understand why Jordi didn't reach out." She looked at him. "I could've helped him."

He steeled himself against the vulnerability in her eyes. "Kept him from blowing his brains out? Fat chance."

She sucked in a breath, her eyes piercing him. "You don't understand. We talked about everything, and I mean *everything*. I knew he was down and discouraged, but never suicidal. He *promised* he'd never do that." She turned her head away, a strand of hair falling into her unusually pale face. Her small frame heaved with a sigh as if the weight of the world was crushing her. "He even seemed happy when I talked to him last—the day before he died. Like he had a plan . . . I'm a trauma counselor, for pity's sake! How did I miss that?"

Danger gripped the door handle. How messed up was that? Happiness apparently came with a suicide plan. Guess he understood—finally seeing an escape from the black and never-ending tunnel . . .

"You're not alone—he was my neighbor for two weeks, and I never saw it coming either. Some people are good at burying their pain. Not everybody wants to be helped. You said it yourself, he had it planned. Last will written, stuff sold. Heck, you can consider yourself lucky he didn't call. Imagine having him on the phone saying goodbye while you're far away, not able to intervene."

A single tear broke free and rolled down her cheek as she looked up at him. "I know there are people who can't be saved because they don't want to be. I just can't believe Jordi was one of them."

"Maybe, but now . . ." Danger glanced at the AC center building. "There's someone else who needs saving, and he's not making a call either." Bad joke, man. "I swear I'll do whatever it takes to get him out."

Reyna's chin quivered. "But what if—"

"Hey." Danger leaned in, holding her gaze. "I promise."

She jolted out of the seat, her arms cording around his torso. "Thank you!"

The sudden embrace, her body crushed against his, cut off Danger's oxygen. He snapped straight, trying to regain control over his derailing thoughts. *Are you just gonna stand there like an idiot or what?*

Driven by his inner voice, he started to move his arms around her. Hesitated. Hugging her back felt so final, like firing a weapon—once the trigger was pulled, the projectile was unstoppable. She was a counselor, and he didn't need his brain picked or his soul x-rayed—or what was left of it, for that matter. And if he let his guard down . . . Her quiet sniffles reaching his ears had him peering down. Her forehead was pressed into his shoulder, her face buried in his T-shirt.

Something broke loose inside him. His arms coiled around her shoulders and pulled her closer. Her body shook as she clung to him. It was weird, holding her. He hadn't been hugged in ages. Not like that, and not by a woman like Paisley.

Resting his chin on top of her head, he closed his eyes. Took in her subtle vanilla scent. *Paisley.* There it was, breaching one of his security barriers. Maybe this was the problem—that it wasn't so much about mistrusting her but himself. That he allowed her to play havoc with his mind, even *liked* it. So much that he was willing to compromise his initial mission to keep her out of his life.

Maybe he was digging his very own grave. But as of right now, he couldn't care less.

8

ANIMAL CONTROL CENTER, AUSTIN, TEXAS

Heart full, Paisley crouched in the hall of the animal control center with spread arms. "Come here, you goofball."

Riot strained against the leash, paws slicking over the tile floor and tail rotating as he fought his way toward her, dragging the twiggy officer behind him.

After two hours—thanks to Ghost and Beau, who'd kept true to his word and presented the evidence he'd gathered in a way that made animal control hand Riot over without fuss—he was finally free to go home.

"It's okay, you can let him go," she said to the officer, who dropped the leash immediately, obviously relieved.

Seizing the newfound freedom, Riot darted to Paisley, excitedly sniffing her hands while prancing. Before she could pet him, he bounded off, farther down the hall, to where Beau stood, phone to his ear.

A chuckle bubbled out of Paisley as she watched Riot rear on his hind legs, his front paws clawing Beau's chest and face. Way more eager to see Beau than her, as always. She didn't care. All that mattered was that he was free.

She rose, thanked the officer, then joined Beau and Riot.

"Thanks, man. I owe you." Beau tucked his phone in his pocket and seized Riot's head with both hands, then proceeded to give him a vigorous rub. "Freedom smells pretty sweet, huh, bud?"

Riot's tongue darted out and brushed across Beau's face.

"Okay, okay. Message received." A rare smirk pulled at Beau's lips. "Off."

Huffing his dislike, Riot obeyed and backed down.

"Good news." Beau's blue gaze found hers. "Mick said the suit backed off."

Paisley gasped. "No euthanasia?" When he shook his head, she flung her arms around his neck. "Thank you!"

This time he didn't stiffen, those strong arms cording around her without hesitation. In a heartbeat, Riot joined the celebration, barking, his paws on Paisley's back. Beau laughed, roughing the dog's head, then told him to get off, but Riot was intent on being part of it—and she appreciated the excuse to stay in Beau's arms, memorize this moment. Like before, the heat radiating from his solid body infused a feeling of safety and comfort. Soothed the aching places in her heart. Once Riot finally complied, Paisley drew back. Beau didn't need any more of her snot caking his T-shirt. Besides, the way he avoided people made it obvious that, unlike her, physical touch wasn't his favorite love language. Feeling suddenly shy, Paisley peeked up at him. "This won't become a thing, I promise."

Beau's intense gaze locked with hers. Pinned her. "Shame."

Her breath hitched, and she held his gaze, wondering what was happening here. Knowing she would absolutely love to be in his arms again . . . and again . . . Oh boy, she was putty in this man's oh-so-capable hands.

A bark snapped her back to reality. Riot danced around them, clearly impatient.

"A'ight, let's head home, bud." Beau caught his leash and made for the door.

"I'd like to take you out to dinner," Paisley blurted.

Door handle in his grip, Beau stilled.

"In return for everything you've done for Riot," she rushed on. He'd done so much for her. The least she could do was buy him dinner.

Beau turned. "You know it's the dude who invites the lady, right?"

"Why, does your manhood feel threatened?" She flashed a smile. "No need. I'd never doubt you're a man."

His shredded eyebrow rose, then his lips twitched. Whatever had crossed his mind, he kept it to himself.

An hour later they sat on a platform obstacle in one of the training yards at the ABA ranch, a rare treat and time for Riot to be off lead and run off some of his energy while they watched the sunset and ate Chinese takeout. Regular barking came from the kennels, making Riot's ears swivel.

Her dog loped across the yard, probably digesting the chicken he'd scrounged off Beau.

"I never thought I'd enjoy suburbia so much." Paisley dropped the chopsticks into the empty box of her sweet-and-sour shrimp.

Hands propped on the platform behind him and ankles crossed, Beau watched Riot. For once he wasn't wearing his Oakleys and ball cap, and his tan hair was slightly mussed. "You a city kid?"

"Grew up in Pilsen, Chicago," she said with a nod. "Our apartment walls were paper thin, so there was constant background noise. Traffic, sirens, fighting neighbors . . . Silence makes me anxious."

"I get that."

She eyed him. "You do?"

Grunting, he stood. "When you constantly have a team around you—and I mean constantly—and are always combat ready, it's hard to come home and sit in an empty house. That's when the demons find you." He ambled across the green, Riot diverting toward him. He turned on water for a water obstacle and let the small pool fill.

Paisley rose and followed. "Demons?" She dipped her fingers into the cool water.

"You know, regrets over things I did. Didn't do. Wrong calls." A shadow darkened his features as if he was thinking about a certain event.

"How long have you been wrestling your demons on your own?" When he didn't say anything, she dried off her hand. "Is not reaching out for help worth all the suffering?"

The veins in his corded forearm protruded as his fingers curled into a fist. "It's my battle. No one else needs to get involved."

"Problem is, by not getting help you inadvertently involve others." She shrugged. "Your pride isn't hurting just you, Beau." Oh, she was skating on thin ice, but the man needed to face those demons. Acknowledging he had them was a start. The next step was to filter out the lies they whispered into his ear and defy them.

He kept staring at the water.

"What if God wants to fight for you?"

This brought his glare up to her. "He doesn't."

The pain lacing his growl was unexpected and stabbed Paisley's heart. She'd wondered about his stance on God—apparently, a relationship that lay in shards.

Not trusting her voice, Paisley focused on her fingers as she dipped them back into the water. *Father, You see his pain and know better than anyone else what he needs. Please soften his heart toward You and let him accept Your help. And show me what I can do.*

Water splashed her arms, legs, and T-shirt. Gasping, she drew back. "Riot!"

Her dog thrashed around in the shallow pool, exuberant and exhilarated. He slammed his forelegs into the water, backside sticking up, then whirled around again.

Beau snickered. Snickered! The smug expression on his face nearly undid her.

Wait, how come there wasn't a single drop on his clothes?

She stabbed a finger at him. "You!"

His hands shot up. "Not my doing. I swear." But he eased back a step.

Feigning a scowl, Paisley whipped at the water. Thrust a handful at Beau, only a few feet away. It hit him full on.

Oops, that was way more than she'd intended. It dripped from his hair and chin onto his drenched T-shirt.

Their eyes met. Fire ignited in his, revenge sparking.

Oh no! Paisley whirled around with a shriek and started running at the same time Beau lunged.

A strong arm shot around her waist and pulled her into a wet wall of muscles. "You asked for it."

His voice low in her ear sent goosebumps all over her skin. Funny, considering he was getting *under* her skin. Oh, she could stay in his arms forever.

Riot spun circles around them, clearly picking up on the excitement.

Shoving the fuzzy feeling Beau's proximity evoked aside, Paisley tried to wrestle out of his grip. Not a chance.

His arms held her like a vise. "Show me how you get out of this." His words husked along her ear and jaw.

"I'd stomp on your foot." Paisley demonstrated the move she had learned in self-defense.

"And if I lift you?" Beau's grip tightened, and her feet abandoned the lawn.

She kicked, tried to somehow slam her elbows back. Nope. Helplessness morphed into panic—and rage. "Stop." What were the self-defense classes good for if he could immobilize her with one simple move? "Stop-stop-stop."

Beau set her down and considered her, concern in his gaze. "You alright?"

Letting out a trembling breath, she nodded. "Yeah." Had to

conquer that seizing fear. She drew up her courage. "Do it again." She wanted to know how to extract herself from a hold like that. So it never happened again. "Go. Do it."

"Whoa, easy there." He fetched a water bottle from their dinner and extended it to her. "Drink."

"I—"

"Drink," he insisted. "Then we train."

Anger bottoming out, Paisley accepted it. "Thank you." She gulped the water, realizing the adrenaline dumping from her body.

Beau turned his back to her and wiped his face with the hem of his T-shirt. He let it down and faced her again.

It struck her as weird, but she capped the water bottle and tossed it aside. "Ready."

He stepped behind her and loosely brought his arms around her, his familiar scent rushing over her. Um, how was she supposed to focus?

"Okay," he said at her ear, "snake your right leg around mine from the outside."

She set aside the awareness of being body-to-body with him and honed her full attention on mastering this. When she complied, he hoisted her backward. Or tried—her leg around his worked like a lock, stopping him halfway.

"See?" he grunted, the word rumbling through his chest into her back. "Can't lift you when you do that, and my grip slips, giving your arms room to move." He let her back down. "Okay, again."

They repeated the process, Paisley not just hearing what he said but understanding it. Experiencing it.

"Notice how your body slightly shifts to the right. This leaves me unshielded, and you can ram your left fist back into my groin." He huffed. "But, uh, no demonstration there, please."

Laughing, Paisley slowly simulated the move.

"It's okay to be a savage and do it several times. Once might not be enough because of adrenaline in the attacker." Beau eased her on to the grass again. "When he lets go"—he doubled over—"kick the side of his knee. It'll damage it enough so he can't come after you."

She did as said, then repeated the steps, combining the first two, then all three. Until they were moving fluidly a third time.

"Hey." Heath strode into the yard, Riot greeting him with a wagging tail. "You guys got a sec?"

Feeling awkward that Heath could see them flush against one another, Paisley shifted aside. Tucked her hair behind her ear.

Beau let her go. "Good job." He turned to Heath. "Yeah—"

"I have a great instructor."

The smile he gave her warmed her chest.

Heath cleared his throat, drawing their attention to him. His expression was grave. "Got a break—assets on the ground in Venezuela spotted Osorio."

The words coldcocked Danger. Not that Osorio's exfil came unexpected. The guy was too cunning to get caught. Still . . .

A phone went off. "Gotta take this," Ghost said.

Watching him stalk off, Danger fought to keep his breathing controlled. This was his fault, but he might have a chance to redeem himself.

But what would make this jaunt to Venezuela any different from the last? Or from the joint effort with the sheriff's department? The guy won. Always won.

Cursing, Danger pivoted, met Paisley's concern-crowded eyes, and muscled past her. With Riot glued to his side, he made his way to the back of the training building, where he braced against the metal corrugated wall. Closed his eyes. *THE ABILITY TO CONTROL MY EMOTIONS AND MY ACTIONS, REGARDLESS OF CIRCUMSTANCE, SETS ME APART FROM OTHERS.*

"It's not your fault he got away."

He gritted his teeth at Paisley's quiet words. Why was she always up in his business? He pivoted to her. "In case you didn't get the memo—I'm not one of your clients who needs fixing."

Her gaze held his, unflinching. "That's not how I see you."

"That right?" he scoffed. "Then how *do* you see me? Huh?" When she didn't answer, something inside him snapped. "It *is* my screw-up that let Osorio get away. As long as that piece of work is loose, he'll break people." He ripped off his T-shirt, baring the scars. "Like this!"

"I-I know." Her eyelids fluttered as she took in his torso. "I'm sorry he did this to you."

Danger flared his nostrils. "I got what I deserved, but this isn't about me. It's about the innocents out there, vulnerable to his sadism."

"What?" Paisley frowned and shook her head. "How would you deserve *any* of this?"

Wadding the damp T-shirt into a ball, Danger looked away. "Got my entire team killed."

Paisley shifted closer. "I don't believe that."

He leveled a stare at her. "Didn't know you were there."

"You're right, I wasn't." Like a flip had switched, her tone suddenly went solid. Adamant. "If you tell me what happened, I might understand."

"Your pride isn't just hurting you, Beau." Her earlier statement had been a bull's-eye. It *was* his pride that had kept him from reaching out. Asking for help was weak. *Frogman* and *weak* didn't mesh.

But if she wanted to have this can of worms opened, she could have it.

Forcing his shoulders to relax, he pinned her with a glare. "Cutter and I were sweeping the exfil route for explosives when a dog came at us. Cutter broke behavior and pulled in his direction. He's not supposed to get distracted by other animals, but he hated his kind, and we'd just left a warehouse reeking of chemicals. That stuff messes with a dog's senses. Behind us, the enemy was closing in. The team counted on *my*"—he stabbed a finger at his chest— "call." Rising shame made him look away. "I trusted my own instincts more than Cutter's and let the dog pass. It'd been rigged with explosives. The blast caused the jet fuel of our extraction helo to spew like lava. Burned most of the team."

Paisley drew in a breath. "But you, Cutter, and another team member survived," she whispered. "And the Guerreros took you captive."

He ran his tongue along his teeth, steeling himself. "I woke up chained to a wall."

"You survived the unthinkable."

A wet snout nudged Danger's hand, and he reached down to run his fingers over Riot's head. Drew comfort from him, because the memory sliced through him like a freshly sharpened Mark I trench knife.

There was another feeling, though. A weird sense of peace chipping away at the pain—the doing of the woman standing in front of him. He eyed her. She didn't just cool his jets; she also spoke to his demons.

"I understand your anger," she said, taking another step. No more than four feet separated them. "That you want to go to Venezuela and end everything. Me too. But we both know this isn't how it works. The Guerreros are too big, too well organized, and even if we manage to defeat them, another cartel will take their place."

Chop the serpent's head off and another one popped up. Story of his life.

"As long as we live in this world there will always be evil, Beau. But one day Jesus will come, and there'll be no more pain, no more injustice. Until then we do what we can to make the world a better place, however small the impact."

He wanted to believe it, that one day everything'd be okay. And maybe he did. But as an operator, he didn't wait for opportunities to attack the enemy. He created them. Tip of the spear.

"Why do I feel like no amount of words will change your mind?" Paisley pursed her lips. "At least promise me that if there's any way I can help, you'll come to me."

Danger took her in. All of her. He might not know her entire story, but what he'd seen was enough to tell she was brave and tough and selfless. And so beautiful it freaking hurt to look at her. "Deal."

Not that he had any intentions of involving her.

Her gaze dropped back to his torso. "Why did you hide your scars from me earlier?"

Because I didn't want to send you running. Which reminded him that maybe he should don his T-shirt. Never should've ripped it off in the first place. He snapped it out, a sudden need to put it back on making him struggle to sort the back from the front. Riot watched him with a tilted head. A seam popped. Son of a—

A hand gently gripped his lower arm, stopping his uncoordinated moves. A softness appeared in Paisley's expression that he'd never seen before. "Here." She took the shirt, turned it the right way, and held it up.

"What am I? Two years old?"

"Just let me help you," she said with more of that softness that called to him.

Huffing, he stuffed his arms in and hiked it over his head, but she was still there, helping. Stopped at his ribcage, her eyes fixed on his scars. Her hand trembled as she let her fingertips whisper over the burns across his right ribs.

Danger sucked in a breath. Although her touch was gentle and cool, it scorched. Apart from the doctors, no one had ever touched his scars.

"Acid," she murmured as she moved on to the thick scar plowing from below his ribs across his abdomen. "And they took one of your kidneys."

"How on earth do you know?"

"They made me watch. Never in my life have I heard grown men scream like that." She shuddered. "I had to stitch them up and force antibiotics down their throats so they wouldn't die from an infection."

All Danger could muster was a grunt, way too aware of her fingers still on his skin. He was about to grab her hand to end her little discovery trip when she let the T-shirt down.

Her gaze lifted to his. "You have nothing to hide."

He barely perceived the words. Her heady scent of vanilla mixed with a hint of body odor from their sparring session messed with his sanity. His gaze caught on her lips. *Don't do it, man. Bad idea.*

"I've got something for you." She dug in her jeans pocket, then pulled a chain out.

A small stuffed animal fell into the grass, and Riot lunged.

"Riot, no. Leave it." Paisley's command was firm.

The Dutchie's snout hovered inches from the monkey, his eyes lifted to hers. Pleading.

"No, you already shredded her twice."

More begging, but he maintained his position.

Look at that, the two were making progress.

Chest puffing a little, Danger dug out the KONG and tossed it to Riot, who snatched it from the air and trotted to the side, where he plopped down and chewed the toy.

The monkey was no longer of interest, and Paisley plucked it from the lawn. "Actually, this is for Lyric. I, uh . . . make these in my free time. Crocheting calms me." She flapped a hand. "Anyway, Lyric wanted one. Can you give it to her?"

Danger took it. It had tiny ears, black button eyes, and a long tail. The best part was the banana it held. Looked like hard work. "I'll give it to her when I take her to soccer practice tomorrow."

"Thanks." She extended something else. A dog tag. "And this is what I wanted to give you."

Curious whose name he'd find on it, he accepted the tag.

The Lord is with you, mighty warrior. Judges 6:12

A Bible verse?

"It was Jordi's," she said. "I don't know why, but God put it on my heart to give it to you."

Not wanting to hurt her feelings, Danger pocketed it. "Thanks."

"Oh, the monkey's name is Kala. Of course, Lyric can name it however she wants."

"Kala as in Tarzan's adoptive mother?"

Paisley nodded. "Growing up, I always hoped a mother like her would adopt me." She lifted a shoulder. "The name stuck." Her brows furrowed, then a smile tugged at her lips. "Wait. You've watched Tarzan?"

Danger smirked. "More times than I can count."

"Oh?" That smile widened.

"I watch a lot of Disney movies in my spare time."

Understanding replaced the amused expression. "Ah, Lyric."

"Tarzan's her favorite."

"And yours?"

"Rapunzel."

Paisley's laugh made her eyes glow. "I've never seen it, but I heard it's good."

And now his attention was on her lips. He felt the crazy urge to claim them. Definitely would've if there hadn't been this lingering feeling to go easy on her. After everything she'd gone through at Osorio's hand, he shouldn't push it.

Unless she gave him an invitation.

He leaned against the cool metal wall, hoping it would keep him from morphing into a phoenix. Watched Riot enjoying way too much KONG time.

The little buffer he'd crated vanished when Paisley took another step forward, her leg brushing against his. "Your name," she said, reaching up and placing her hand on his face. "Beau. It means 'beautiful' in French."

He gave a wry chuckle. "Appropriate, eh?"

"Yes, you're beautiful in your own way." She ran her thumb

over his shredded eyebrow, caressing the scar where the Guerreros had slashed his eye. "Is this what rendered you blind?"

"No, it was the acid."

Her gaze searched his, then dropped to his mouth.

Talk about an invitation . . . He slipped his hand around the back of her neck and pulled her close. Captured her lips with his—

"Holy Moses."

The muttered oath snapped Danger out of the moment and turned him toward the intruding voice.

Crew Gatlin stood at the corner of the building, brows nearly disappearing under his ball cap. He pivoted and headed away, waving a hand in the air as he went. "As you were."

Stellar. Hopefully his buddy didn't tell the entire ABA team. Last thing he wanted was them—or Ghost—on his back.

Biting her lip, Paisley drew away. "Riot and I, uh, should head home. It's getting late."

"Yeah." Man, he could strangle Crew.

Or . . . not. Starting something with Paisley wasn't fair to her. Not when he was going to Venezuela to end Osorio.

Chances that he made it out alive equaled zero.

9

HARMONIA, TEXAS

OH BOY, LAST NIGHT SHE HAD CROSSED A LINE SHE SHOULDN'T HAVE. Paisley threw the blanket back and rose from her bed. She had to talk to Beau. Tell him that the only intention she had was a serious relationship. Nothing else was an option. But . . . if a relationship was on the table, she wanted to take it slow.

It was still dark out and another hour until they were supposed to drive up to the ABA ranch for training, so Paisley let Riot into the fenced yard. She still didn't dare take him on a walk through the neighborhood, especially after yesterday.

Feeding him breakfast was the usual struggle, but making him sit and wait—making him work for it as she'd learned—bought her some obedience and time not to get her hand bitten by the velociraptor part of him. Even getting him to "hup" into the Bronco went well. Who knew? Maybe they'd survive each other after all. She drove to the local bakery with him to pick up coffee, the warm morning breeze carrying through the broken window and caressing her face.

Over and over, Beau's scar-covered torso popped into her mind. It was a massacre of melted skin and red-and-white lines in all sizes. The most remarkable scar—crimson and thick—ran from right below the ribs across his abs, so far down it disappeared beneath the waistband of his cargo pants. She didn't dare to imagine how much pain he must have been in when the Guerreros' "doctor" removed the kidney.

Memories shoved aside, Paisley fetched the coffee and drove back home. By the time she pulled into Beau's drive, the sun had climbed over the horizon and the neighborhood had come alive. A woman walked her dachshund, another neighbor watered his flowerbeds. A plumbing van parked at the curb farther down the street.

Arms crossed over his chest, Beau stood on the porch, watching. He wore tan cargos and a black T-shirt. Was he still worried about Lyric and Rachel? Lyonel was gone . . .

Cutting the engine, she noticed her shaking hands. She and Beau had made so much progress in their relationship, and she didn't want to destroy it. She quickly prayed for the right words, then got out. "Morning." She waved and headed to the back to let Riot out.

Free of his crate, he darted across the lawn straight up to Beau and greeted him in his usual climbing-all-over-you-to-give-you-a-face-wash manner. For some reason, Beau always allowed it.

"Mornin'." Beau slapped Riot's side, then gave him a good rub.

Smiling to herself, Paisley retrieved the to-go cups from the middle console and joined them. "Thought maybe you could use this?"

Beau commanded Riot to heel and plodded down the steps. Reached for it.

"Black," she said as he lifted it to his lips, pleased with herself that she'd learned that's how he drank it.

"Thanks."

His fingers brushed hers, bringing back the sensation of his uneven skin under her touch. Despite all the scars, she couldn't help but notice his lean muscles. It showed that he channeled his anger and grief into hard workouts.

Ahem, definitely crossed a line.

He readjusted his black ball cap. "Sorry 'bout the Incredible Hulk show yesterday."

Paisley laughed. "I've had some strange encounters with clients, but I don't recall any of them tearing their shirt off." She quickly held out her free hand. "Not that I think of you as a client. I would've never kissed you if I had."

Stop rambling! She was supposed to clarify things, not make them worse.

Eyes on the neighborhood, Beau took another sip of his coffee. He seemed . . . distant.

The plumbing van tore away from the curb, the engine revving.

"Can we—" Paisley's attention was drawn to the other side of the road, where Lyric came skipping down the boardwalk. "What is she doing out here all alone?"

Beau glanced in that direction, then back down the road. He pitched his coffee cup to the ground and sprinted in Lyric's direction.

What . . . why—

The van roared up the road way too fast, right . . .

Toward Lyric!

Danger reached for his SIG. The SIG he wasn't carrying. "Lyric!"

His niece waved, then cringed, pulling away from the van that whipped up next to her. Her face furrowed in fear and confusion at the man lunging from the already open door.

As he snatched her from the sidewalk, she screamed, a shrill, pealing sound that scored Danger's heart and unleashed a nightmare.

No! "Riot, attack!" He heard the Dutchie barking up a storm, and a blur shot past him.

Too late. In the blink of an eye, Lyric and her cries were swallowed by the pealing tires of the accelerating van. Danger threw himself into the vehicle's path. No freaking way were they taking Lyric. He pushed himself, pulse and rage pounding in his ears. Tucked his chin, determined to make them stop or divert. Only as the van barreled down on him did he realize he faced an adversary just as determined. Oh sh—

Thud!

"Augh!" The impact vaulted him over the sloped hood of the vehicle, over the windshield, the world whipping into a frenzy as he rolled. He groped for a grip, traction to stop his fall. To save the precious cargo inside the van. He caught the wiper and grabbed tight. His trajectory slowed . . . *Crack!* Gravity snatched him backward. He hit the concrete hard, flipping several times.

The van skidded around the corner with a scream of its tires.

No—

He scrambled to his feet and sprinted to his Tacoma. In his periphery he registered Rachel running out of her house. "Call 911!" he hollered to Paisley. Rachel's screams echoing down the street fueled him as he jumped into his Tacoma. Whipped the truck out of the drive and slammed it into Drive. Gunning it, he speed-dialed Mick.

His buddy picked up on the second ring. "Hey, man. What's up?"

"Lyric just got snatched. White van." He rattled off what he remembered of the license plate. "Last seen headed east on Pecan Street."

"That intersects 35."

"My thoughts exactly. I'm heading to the interstate."

"I'm scrambling response units now. If you find them, report in and let us know where. Don't engage. Hear me?" Mick knew him well enough not to tell him to stop tailing them.

Danger hung up and kept driving. He'd do whatever was

necessary to get Lyric back. He took the road leading to the highway. Cars honked when he bombed past them.

Each mile amped his anger. He had to find her before it was too late and those thugs took her out of country. Because they weren't just any thugs. They were Guerreros. He'd noticed that van parked, a guy with his arm dangling out the window—obviously not doing any work—the distinctive G inked on his bicep leaving no doubt.

Danger's pulse spiked when he spotted a white van parked on the side of the road. He stopped behind it, dug his Glock 19 from the glove compartment, and approached the vehicle. "Get out of the van!" he called over the highway noise and zipping vehicles. "Get. Out!" He edged up, saw no movement in the back windows. Took as wide of an arc as he could to reach the front, and snapped his weapon at the driver's window. Empty. He opened the door and traced the interior with his gun. Empty.

Muttering an oath, he rushed to the other side, peering out across the open terrain of the Texas Hill Country. Gone.

He pivoted and sent his fist into the side of the van. "Augh!" The only reason he'd moved back to Texas was to make good on his promise to Tyron to keep Rachel and Lyric safe. Instead, he'd let Lyric get kidnapped in broad daylight with one of the oldest tricks in the book. Why hadn't he noticed the driver's tattoo sooner?

He yanked out his phone and relayed what had happened to Mick. Barely got the words past the anger and frustration jamming his throat.

"Hang tight," Mick said. "We'll find her."

Danger swallowed. "You better."

But he doubted it. The Guerreros were too smart, too fast, and too well connected to succumb to normal LEO traps. They'd drag Lyric back to Venezuela and . . .

God, You can't allow this. She's . . . Clenching his teeth, he slid behind the wheel of his Tacoma. Why even pray? God didn't listen, especially since it was—once again—his screw-up. He started the engine, now feeling the throbbing in his side and arm where the van had hit him.

The only reason the Guerreros had taken Lyric was because of him. He'd dragged her into a personal vendetta, and it was up to him to get her out.

And he would. No matter the cost.

"I should've listened to Danger." Diluted mascara trickled down Rachel's cheeks, her blonde bangs sticking to her forehead. "I just couldn't believe anyone would do something so terrible to a child. But *why* would they take my baby girl? What did Danger do to them?"

Sitting next to her, Paisley quietly rubbed her friend's back. Telling her that Lyric had fallen victim to an act of revenge on Beau would only make matters worse. And until there was confirmation, it was best not said. Best not to breed panic. Especially since it'd taken a good ten minutes to get Rachel to stop scream-crying and agree to return to her home, where she'd collapsed on her living room sofa.

So Paisley simply listened and comforted her friend while they waited for the police to arrive. She glanced at Beau's empty coffee cup sitting on the couch table. No idea why she'd brought it with her, but somehow it felt . . . symbolic. Things had been normal and right one second, then in one espresso-dumping moment—everything was wrong. Terrible.

The way Beau had stared down that van, raced right into it as if he could take on a two-ton vehicle . . . It both stirred and haunted her. She needed to know he was okay. That he hadn't died from internal injuries in that collision or that he hadn't been shot by whoever had taken Lyric. Though she had no proof, she didn't have a sliver of doubt this was related to the Guerreros.

Riot paced and panted, stopping every few seconds to look

out a large floor-length window, as if looking for Beau. As if he knew . . . And he probably did.

Lead dangling on the floor, he plodded over to her, nudged her hand, let her pet him, drool hitting her jeans.

Yes, it was the Guerreros. Had to be. She recalled too well Lyonel's threat against Beau after the raid, that he had to pay for killing the boss's brother.

Riot's head swiveled to the window, then he darted to it, stuffing his nose against the sheer curtains.

Peering out, Paisley spotted Beau's truck pulling up. "Oh, thank goodness."

Rachel vaulted to her feet and stormed out the door.

Grabbing Riot's lead, Paisley hurried after her.

Beau had barely gotten out of the pickup when Rachel reached him and pounded his chest. "Why?" she screamed. "First Tyron, now Lyric! Why is God doing this to me? Why didn't you stop them?"

Color drained from Beau's face. His jaw muscle tightened, but he let Rachel beat his chest. "I'll get her back," he said low and evenly as he wrapped his arms around her. "I swear it."

With a strangled choke, Rachel stopped her attack. "My baby. They took my baby."

Her wrecked sobs made Paisley's eyes and chest burn. She scrambled for something comforting to say—anything—but had no words. She cast a glance at Beau.

Torment tightened his mouth. Clearly, he blamed himself.

A police cruiser eased into the drive, and Detective Mick Caffrey got out. He hurried up to them.

"What're you doing here?" Beau barked. "Why aren't you—"

"She's gone, Mick." Rachel shuddered as she turned to him. Covering her mouth, she suppressed a sob. "She was right here, eating breakfast and watching TV. Next thing . . ." She shook her head.

"I know. I'm sorry."

Beau shouldered in. "Shouldn't you be looking for her, not—"

Holding up a hand, Mick nodded to him. "I . . . have news."

Paisley's stomach squeezed at his tone.

"We got a call from an executive airport outside Austin. Have an arrangement with them, considering trafficking running is so hot near the border, to contact us if they see anything out of the ordinary. They reported two Hispanic males with a small child boarding a Leer that's registered to *Logística de Cazadores*."

"Hunter Logistics," Paisley murmured, shifting her gaze to Beau. "Osorio means 'hunter of wolves.'"

Fists balled, Beau shot his friend a look. "Stay with her." He stalked off, Riot trotting with him.

Torn between following them and staying for her friend, Paisley shot Mick a questioning look.

He gave her a nod, then walked Rachel inside her house, quietly talking to her.

Grateful her friend was in good hands, Paisley went in search of Beau. The door to his house stood open, and she went inside. Followed the rustling coming from his bedroom and found him moving around and stuffing clothes into a backpack on his bed.

Riot gnawed his KONG as he sprawled out on the covers. He paused, his gaze flicking to hers, then went back to chewing.

"What're you doing?" Paisley asked from the threshold.

Beau grabbed several boxes of ammunition and put them in the bag. "Getting her back." A long graze stretched across his forearm, probably road burn from being hit by the van.

"From?"

He flashed a glare. "Don't kid yourself—we both know who did this."

She did. "Now what? You just go to Venezuela?"

He kept packing.

"You can't just walk in there, guns blazing. We're talking about the Guerrero Cartel, Beau!" Oh, she didn't mean to raise her voice, but he was scaring her.

Riot's ears twitched back. Well, she didn't like fighting either, but she wasn't going to let a man she cared about—and yes, she did care about Beau . . . a lot—run into the clutches of a lethal cartel.

"You have to know this is a trap." Stepping up behind him, Paisley—too aware of the way Riot stilled again—gently set her hands on Beau's. "They're just waiting for you to come get her. And they won't let you walk out alive."

He glanced down at their hands. Then to her. "I got her into this mess, I'll get her out." He pulled away and dug something from his pack. Held it up. Kala. "I need to bring her this." The words emerged hoarse, and his eyes glistened.

His pain, the guilt—so palpable—snagged Paisley's breath. Her arguments.

Expression darkening again, he picked up the gun on his bed. Ejected the magazine and checked it. Popped it back in and racked the slide. "I already survived them once."

"Yes, because God saved you."

"For whatever reason."

"Because He's not done with you. As long as you're breathing, it's because He has a reason to keep you on this side of heaven."

"Yes, getting Lyric out of there."

As much as she didn't want him to face them again, she knew that without Beau, Lyric wouldn't stand a chance. "A-at least take someone with you. A team."

Beau tucked the gun into a holster at his back and pulled his T-shirt over it. "I'm not gonna drag anyone else into this." He slung the backpack over a shoulder. Paused. "But I need Riot."

At his name, her dog jumped up with a bark, his tail wagging.

Paisley folded her arms and stuck her hip out so Beau couldn't get past her. "No."

His eyes hardened. "It wasn't a question."

"Riot is my dog. You can't just take him."

129

Beau shifted the ruck on his shoulder. Clearly, he hadn't expected a no. But she wasn't going to let him go down there alone, even with Riot. He needed someone watching his back. She lifted her chin. "If Riot comes along, I do too."

"Not happening."

"Do you know where they are?"

He faltered. Glared at her.

"I do. And if they're not there, I know the right people to find out where they are." She jutted her chin. "Also, we had a deal. You promised you'd come to me if there was any way I could help."

Mouth tight, he looked from her to Riot, then back to her. He dug out his phone and thumbed the screen. Set it to his ear while pinning her with a glower. "You better not make me regret this."

10

OUTSIDE ALBUQUERQUE, NEW MEXICO

TWENTY-NINE HOURS HAD PASSED SINCE LYRIC'S ABDUCTION—THE longest hours of Danger's life. In that time, he'd called his former master chief, Pete "Deke" Deacon, and asked him to vet a team. Then Danger had packed Riot and Paisley into his Tacoma and driven up to Albuquerque, where Deke had all the resources necessary for the op, including transport.

Now assembled in an old hangar on an abandoned airstrip, they waited for the last team member to show. Once they were briefed on the op plan, they would load up on a private cargo plane and jet straight to Venezuela.

"You ready for this?" Hands on his tac belt, Deke scrutinized Danger with those all-knowing brown eyes. While on SEAL Team 3, he hadn't only been Danger's team leader but also a father figure.

"I'm good."

"Not what I asked, but I'll let it slide." Deke nodded to the three operators sitting around the table in the otherwise empty hall. "It's a good team. We'll get it done."

No doubt. While Danger didn't recognize a single mug, he

RONIE KENDIG & JJ SAMIE MYLES

knew they were solid if Deke had vetted them. The chief had read him in on them: Abel Logan was the demolitions expert, Cyprus Vu comms specialist, and Anna Mara Freud the medic. They were waiting on Stallion—the sniper who'd also been Danger's former teammate and swim buddy.

Danger sliced his gaze to Paisley, who was wandering the length of the hangar, phone to her ear. She wore a determined expression, deep in thought, and navigated around Riot, who hugged her side as if they were tracking on patrol.

What if I fail them too?

She was right though—he stood no chance of finding Lyric without her intel, even with Riot's help. Venezuela was a big country, and the Guerreros had strongholds in many of its states. Lyric could be in any of them. Riot could track her scent for months without success.

Thanks to Paisley's connections—who didn't easily cough up intel to outsiders for security reasons—the odds of finding Lyric improved dramatically. Having her along *would* help.

As long as she stayed out of the way.

"She important to you?"

The too-perceptive question tightened his gut. "Her intel is."

Deke smoothed his fingers over his mustache. "I need you to stay sharp. Clear?"

"Yes, sir."

The door behind them slammed open, and a tall figure carrying a bag over the shoulder sauntered in, dust swirling in the daylight flooding the grimy floor.

"What's up, party people?" Rafiq "Stallion" Khalil grinned like the Joker as he kicked the door shut with his heel and dropped his gear. "If that ain't my favorite battle boo and daddy."

"Waiting till the last possible moment so you can make a big entrance." Deke received him with a bro hug. "Drop the 'daddy,' Khalil."

Stallion let him go and snapped straight. "Yessir." His gaze landed on Danger. "Holy smokes, babe. You look like a lawnmower made a U-turn on your face."

That was a first. And probably the most accurate description yet. Grinning, Danger pulled his former teammate in. Slapped his back a little harder than necessary. "Keep talking and I'm happy to give you a copy."

Stallion chuckled. "Long time no see, brother."

Indeed. After Danger had left Team 3 for DEVGRU, they'd barely been in touch.

"Group up," Deke called to the team from the table where he stood next to Paisley, who was pocketing her phone. "We've got good news." His eyes struck Danger. "Your niece has been spotted."

A jolt went through Danger. "Where?" He pulled a chair up, Riot parking his rear at his feet.

"Caracas." Deke turned the laptop sitting in front of him so the team could see the screen.

The black-and-white picture was grainy, yet left no doubt it was Lyric. She wore the same clothes from yesterday, and a man hauled her by the arm.

"This," Deke said, using his master chief voice as he brought up a school photo of Lyric, "is our objective: six-year-old Lyric Moore—niece of one of our own. She was abducted in broad daylight from the street in front of her home yesterday morning." He clicked back to the surveillance image. "This is from a bank security camera outside Caracas, Venezuela, taken nine hours ago. The man with the kid is confirmed as part of the Guerrero Cartel. Footage showed them heading south out of Caracas. Assets on the ground believe there was another sighting two hours ago of her in a mountain village farther east."

Danger dug his fingers into Riot's fur, settling into operator mode. Couldn't look Rachel in the eye ever again if he failed to find Lyric.

"How are we sure it's the Guerrero Cartel?" Stallion asked.

Deke retrieved the next photo of a man wearing shades and

an expensive watch. "The man in the photo is Lyonel Osorio. He took over as enforcer and right hand to Carlos Ronal Querales Mendoza after Miguel, Querales's younger brother, was killed seven months ago."

Memories ghosted through Danger's mind. Fighting for his life. His hands around the punk's throat, squeezing hard. More struggling until he managed to neutralize the threat.

Danger rubbed Riot's ear. No regrets—Miguel Querales had abused and brutally murdered too many to count, including women and children. The guy had gotten what he'd deserved.

But Danger had killed him, and because of that, Lyric was in mortal danger.

"Although Carlos Querales and Lyonel Osorio are both high-value targets, our primary objective is Lyric." Deke drew up a map of Venezuela. "The village I mentioned earlier is our target location. Population five hundred, adjacent to Guerrero territory. Just like the FARC, ELN, Sinaloa, and Hezbollah, the Guerreros work with the government—we can't just stroll into the country, or they'll know we're coming. Since we don't want to worsen the already strained relationship between Uncle Sam and Venezuela, we'll jump to an LZ fifteen klicks outside the village. Because of the dog, we'll stay below fifteen thousand feet. We'll rendezvous with our asset and hole up in a bunker at the village." He looked at Paisley. "Ever jumped out of a plane before?"

Her eyes bulged. "No, sir."

"Okay, you'll go with Rafiq, then."

Danger fisted a hand under the table. He would've objected, but his tandem partner was Riot. Why did Stallion of all people have to be the most seasoned jumper? There were two reasons for his call sign—one was because his snoring could drown out a CH-53E Super Stallion. The other because he had a way with the ladies.

Leaning back in his chair, the sniper gave Paisley a lazy grin. "Don't worry. I'll make sure you'll have the experience of a lifetime. All safe and secure, of course." He winked at her, and Paisley flashed him a grateful smile.

It took everything inside Danger not to lunge over the table at his buddy. The primal instinct to protect her no longer had anything to do with her being his kid sister's friend. Or her past. Now it was because of *her*. That moment behind the training building at the ABA ranch. The grip she had on him was tighter than a torniquet.

And he wasn't mad about it.

Deke shut the laptop. "Alright, let's roll. Further details will be discussed on the way."

The team stood and headed out. Danger didn't miss that Stallion had a trajectory to intercept Paisley.

Not happening, man.

"Paisley," he called. "Hold up."

Having stepped into the scorching afternoon sun, she slowed and turned toward him—away from Stallion. She shielded her eyes and squinted.

He touched her elbow, sending Stallion a "stand down" look. His buddy smirked and started for the two black Jeep Wagoneers parked on the tarmac.

"Hey, listen," Danger said, not sure why he felt so coiled inside. "We both know the type of people we're going up against here, so . . . uh"—he glanced at the vehicles again and saw Stallion standing at the first Jeep, grinning at him—"just do what we tell you. If we say move, then move. If we say down—"

"I'm not really that dense, you know."

He frowned. "Nobody said that. I just want to be clear, because when the action starts, we won't have time to repeat orders, and I don't want you getting hurt."

"You assume I'm the one who will get hurt."

Why was she making this so difficult? "No, I—"

"Problem here?" Head cocked, Stallion ambled closer.

"No." Even Danger heard the bark in his word. "Back off."

He refocused on Paisley. "Look, I don't want to bring body pieces home in my ruck because you didn't listen."

She shrugged. "Then leave my *body pieces* in Venezuela." She smiled at Stallion and started toward him.

"Wait." Danger caught her by the shoulder. Felt Riot press into his leg as if reminding him to cool his jets.

When she turned, the smile was gone. "I don't have issues with following orders, but I have issues with people who can't communicate them in a civilized way."

"If you want civilized, stay here. Won't be any of that in Guerrero territory." Realizing he was shoveling a lot of harsh, Danger held up a hand. Knew he was butchering this. "I—"

"Hey, Paisley." Stallion was there again. "Can I get your pack for you?"

She smiled at him. "Sure." Stepping away from Danger, she handed her gear off, then fell into an easy conversation with his buddy. Slid into the Wagoneer.

Danger cursed himself. That wasn't how he'd seen this going at all. He moved to enter the vehicle, only then realizing it was full.

"Sorry," Stallion said with a smirk. "No room at the inn." He pulled the door shut.

Now he cursed his buddy. His gaze connected with Paisley's for a second, but she firmed her lips and looked away.

Okay, yeah, he might've been rough, but they were heading into trouble. She had to be protected.

He escorted Riot to the other Jeep and tossed his gear in the back, then claimed the free backseat next to Abel, Riot settling between his boots. Danger stared out the window. He'd intended to convey that he cared—and instead made her hate his guts. Stellar.

"We good?" The driver wearing a 'Nam Veteran ball cap met Danger's gaze over the rearview mirror, and Danger confirmed with a nod.

But if he paid a listen to the sense of foreboding rising in his gut, then no—they weren't good.

15,000 FEET ABOVE BOLÍVAR, VENEZUELA

She was going to die.

How could she have ever thought that talking Beau into letting her tag along was a smart idea?

"You'll be fine." Behind her, their harnesses connected at her shoulders and hips, Rafiq—or Stallion, as they called him— shouted over the wind whipping in from the open rear ramp of the midsized cargo plane. He gave Paisley's harness a hard yank. "See? Holds just fine. If something goes wrong, you won't die alone."

All she could come up with was a strangled grunt. Seeing nothing but black of night, she felt her stomach revolt. A faint red light illuminated the plane's hull and the team geared up in black suits, helmets, and backpacks attached to the front. She sought out Riot, strapped to Beau and wearing a muzzle and doggles, acting so chill as he waited with his tandem partner. How was he so calm?

The fear of this jump hadn't allowed her to get a wink of sleep on the ten-hour flight. Meanwhile, the team had snoozed in hammocks or on the benches lining the hull like they were at home in their beds. She should've accepted the Ambien the team medic, Anna Mara, had offered.

The red light flicked to green. Standing closest to the opening, Deke held up a thumb. The team followed his example, each member giving a thumbs-up to the person behind them. Abel and Cyprus shoved a box with gear down the ramp. When—*swoop*—it got sucked out, Paisley's breath caught. She watched it plummet, the chute flapping behind it.

Just like that.

Next, Abel bellyflopped into the dark with spread arms and legs, and was tightly followed by Cyprus.

Rafiq shuffled Paisley farther down the ramp, right at the looming black hole. The wind grabbed at her pants, and she feared her legs might get ripped out from under her. She dug her nails into the straps of her harness. *God-oh-God-oh-God.*

Her pulse spasmed when Beau and Riot jumped next.

Now it was her and Rafiq's turn.

Heart racing, she stood frozen when—without warning—Rafiq shoved them out. The shriek got stuck in her throat as her stomach heaved with the sensation of freefall.

Oh God, I don't want to die!

The feeling disappeared as quickly as it had come. Wait. What? Now they were . . . floating. Had Rafiq deployed the chute already?

No, still falling. Frigid wind roared in her ears, tearing at her clothing, limbs, and cheeks. Paisley dared cracking open an eye behind her goggles. Complete darkness. Unlike the rest of the team, she wasn't equipped with night vision.

When Rafiq patted her shoulders twice, she released the harness and spread her arms and arched her back like he'd instructed. *"Think a banana."*

More like *going* bananas.

They fell for what felt like forever before they were yanked upward—first slightly, then forcefully. The harness cut into Paisley's skin before it slacked and they glided through the night, now in a vertical position. The air was warmer. Far out she could make out a cluster of twinkling lights. A city? Stars overhead.

Behind her, Rafiq operated the toggles. With the terror gone, she was acutely aware of his well-muscled body plastered to her back. Awkward, but she was glad to have someone so experienced bringing her down. So far, he'd been nothing but a gentleman, and admittedly, he was easy on the eyes—tall with dark hair and a white smile, maybe of Middle Eastern descent. Still, she would've preferred it to be Beau.

Although, after that "obey orders" performance of his, she wasn't sure where they stood right now. She'd thought she'd seen something in his gaze, heard concern . . . but then he'd been irritable and sharp. What had happened? Why had he gotten uptight? She'd hoped to talk to him on the plane, but as soon as they were in the air he'd stretched out on the bench, ball cap tugged over his eyes and Riot crated beneath him.

Dark shapes below caught Paisley's attention. Trees. Were they that far down already? A moment later they were so close to the treetops she feared they'd crash into them. A clearing opened up and what Paisley guessed to be a grassy patch rushed at them.

Slow down. Slow down!

Pulling the toggles, Rafiq halted them. They were lifted back up, then their feet hit the ground and they ended up in a butt-slide, dragged by the chute, which he worked to release. Seconds later, he freed her, extricated himself from behind her, and turned to secure the chute.

Sweet mercy, solid ground! She fought the urge to drop and kiss the grass. Nothing could ever make her repeat this madness. The adrenaline rush she'd gotten out of it would last a lifetime.

Chute secured, Rafiq shifted his rifle to the front, hooked her arm, and hurried to the tree line rimming the small clearing. There, he guided her down and took a knee, weapon trained out. Like the others, who were nothing but silent shadows in the night. They were strategic, swift, focused. A silhouette crouched in the grass near them, his night-vision device casting a feeble glow around the eyes.

Rafiq straightened. "C'mon." He pulled her to her feet and set her hand on a nylon band on his ruck. "Hold that, stay low and on me." Over his shoulder, he met her gaze. Nodded.

Paisley's knees still trembled from the jump as they moved through the tall grass, deeper into the jungle. A chorus of birds and bugs, along with the familiar, earthy smell, evoked a flood of memories. She was really back in Venezuela, and this time not tucked away in a safe house.

A shudder seized her. *Father, please keep the team safe. And Lyric. Don't let Lyonel—or anyone else—lay hands on her.* A request she couldn't bring before God often enough.

How was Beau dealing with being back here? Wouldn't be surprising if he struggled too. Trauma did that. It lurked in the dark recesses of the mind—sometimes for years—and all it took was a trigger to plunge a person right back into that horrible experience.

Protect his mind, Jesus.

In the quasi-safety—no place in Venezuela was safe from the Guerreros—of the trees and brush, they waited as Riot and Beau made it to them.

She started toward them, but Rafiq ushered her on. Oh, she just wanted a moment to find out how they were doing.

Rafiq kept her near as they crept deeper into the jungle. Not having the advantage of his NVGs, and with the thickening canopy plunging them into near blackness, Paisley tightly gripped that strap he'd put her hand on. Placed her other hand on his pack. Did her best not to trip over his boots or random roots.

Ahead, a light grew brighter with every pace. This had to be Jude Payne, aka Pita, her contact. His call sign had nothing to do with the flatbread and everything with his last name.

The team slowed to a stop and went to a knee. Scouting what was ahead. A moment later, they were moving again. Straight up to the two pickups, whose headlights made the area glow. The team split into the two vehicles, Riot and Beau settling in the bed of the second. The mix of humidity, the stench of sweat, and the winding path made Paisley nauseous, and she was glad when they reached the mountain village. Their driver—Raúl, as he'd introduced himself—passed a gate and pulled into a dirt courtyard, the headlights illuminating a run-down two-story concrete building. Once the second vehicle pulled inside, the gate whirred closed.

Paisley climbed out into the much cooler air—how high were they?—and looked for Riot and Beau.

"This way." Raúl whisked them into the stingily furnished house and down concrete steps that ended at a massive door. He jerked back the heavy bolt. The bunker behind it mirrored the somber scene upstairs. Neon lights displayed a large metal table in the center holding two laptops and other electronic equipment. Apart from four chairs, there was nothing else. Clearly the idea of this place was safety, not comfort.

"Pais."

She spun to the door. Grinned. "Pita."

Jude Payne came strolling over, a smirk on his tan face. His inked arms came around her, and he scooped her up. "Good to see you, kiddo."

"Ditto," she mumbled on his shoulder. It'd been two years since she'd last seen him.

When he set her down, he sobered. "Sorry about Jordi. He was a solid man."

Paisley managed a small smile past the pain squeezing her heart. "He was."

Riot plodded up to them, tail swishing back and forth. He briefly stopped by her—she barely could brush a hand over his back—then circled Jude and pressed his shoulder into his leg.

"Long time no see, boy." When Riot licked his fingers, Jude smiled and gave him a good rub behind the ears. "Can't get over how beautiful you are. Almost as beautiful as your handler."

"You talking about me?"

Paisley stilled at Beau's low voice behind her.

Straightening, Jude took him in. Huffed. "Good night. What did they do to you?"

Beau dropped his gear. "Free plastic surgery."

"I think you should sue that surgeon." Grinning from one ear to the other, Jude pulled him into a hug and pounded his back.

141

"Intend to address the issue one-on-one." The thirst for vengeance spiking in Beau's tone warned he was heading down a dangerous path.

Jude laughed. "Still the same bonehead. Glad the damage is only skin deep."

"Now his mug finally matches his personality," Rafiq tossed over his shoulder. He stood next to Abel and watched Cyprus operate one of the laptops.

Deke was quietly conversing with Raúl at the other end of the room, Anna Mara checking her AFAK, or Advanced First Aid Kit.

"New call signs: Beauty"—Jude pointed at Riot, then to Beau—"and Beast."

Beau sniffed. "You guys just crushed my dreams of becoming sexiest man alive."

"Seriously, though," Abel said. "How much can you see with that eye?"

"Enough to tell you could pass as a woman with that haircut."

Snickers filtered through the room.

"Okay, people." Deke got the team's attention, including Riot's, as he stalked to the table. "Jude and Raúl here are our support while in country. We'll start in the village and try to track our objective from where she was last seen. If the dog picks up her scent, we follow. If not, we'll conduct recon." He ran his fingers over his mustache. Despite being shorter than the other men, his bearing demanded attention and respect. "There's a festival today starting at noon. We'll blend in, see what we find. Our story is that we're missionaries. A buddy of mine owns a gym in Albuquerque, Iron Sharpens Iron, and they run missions each year. That's us."

Paisley smiled to herself. Not a bad cover story. Who else was crazy enough to enter Guerrero territory besides missionaries?

"Dawn's cracking. Get packing and change into this garb." He pointed to a plastic bag by the door. "These are *ruanas.*

They're worn only in the Andes, but they'll perfectly camouflage our armor. If you get laughed at—which you will—say that we just came from there and like them a lot."

Accepting Rafiq's help, Paisley packed her ruck with the equipment the team had hauled into the bunker. The only weapon she accepted was a knife. While Jordi had taught her to shoot handguns and rifles, she wasn't willing to take anyone's life. Not even a Guerrero's.

An hour later, the team left the bunker and spread out around the village, wearing ruanas over their standard tac gear. At least now they somewhat fit in.

Except Beau. The ruana did nothing to hide the intensity he radiated. Everything about him screamed operator.

The sun rose, warming the crisp air and spreading its power over the nearby peaks covered by lush jungle. Paisley watched Beau slide on his Oakleys, then pull out a ziplock bag holding one of Lyric's shirts from his pocket. He opened it and held the fabric to Riot's snout.

Sniffing it, her dog wagged his tail harder and harder.

"Seek-seek," Beau commanded, and the Dutch shepherd immediately dropped his nose to the ground, hauling in scents. Tracking in a zigzag pattern of the scent cone, he led them down a maze of pressed dirt roads, past simple concrete buildings, palm trees, and random patches of grass. The occasional motorbike clattered by, villagers eyeing them.

Paisley's gut clenched with every step. They were completely unprotected out here, and the way the guys inconspicuously scanned rooftops and windows confirmed they were sharply aware of it too.

"She was definitely here," Beau said as Riot focused on a spot, sniffed around, then returned and set off again.

Here . . . but gone now.

Completely in his element, Riot kept tracking, his tail high. Sometimes he lost the scent, circled back, and picked it up again. The serpentine sweep narrowed until he stopped in front of a baby-blue building on the outskirts of the village. Sat, his tongue lolling out the side as he squinted up at Beau.

Paisley's heart sped—sitting meant he'd found something! That was good, right? Yet . . . bad because it meant their only lead was gone.

Brows drawn low, Beau unearthed Lyric's shirt and once again held it to Riot's nose. "Seek-seek."

Riot took it in, then eagerly swept the floor around him. Sat again. Beau led him a block down the road and tried again. They ended up back at the exact same spot.

Beau spat out a string of hair-raising curses. Running a hand over his mouth, he turned away, then back to them. "They took her someplace else in a vehicle. Riot can't track that."

11

BOLÍVAR, VENEZUELA

LYRIC HAD BEEN AT THIS VERY SPOT AND WAS NOW GONE, NOT A shred of a scent for Riot to trace.

How many more times would God hammer it home that He didn't have Danger's six?

Message received.

"Good boy." Danger roughed Riot's head, using the comforting presence of his furry partner to dial back his frustration.

"Maddox." Deke's boots appeared in Danger's range of vision on the dusty road that reminded him too much of Afghanistan.

Straightening, Danger tossed Riot his hard-earned KONG. Watched him snag it from the air, then looked at Deke.

"It's not over. We'll conduct recon. Ask the villagers if they saw anything." The chief's brown eyes projected understanding and reprimand alike. "Don't give up."

Danger sniffed. "Throwin' in the towel was never an option." He'd tear the place apart if he had to. Wasn't leaving this country without her.

145

Deke gave a nod. "Let's grab some grub, then head back to the bunker."

They spent the rest of the morning poring over local intel and maps. When Riot got antsy, Danger took him topside. They were about to step into the walled yard when the Dutchie doubled back into the living room. "Dude, what are you even doing?" he laughed as he let the retired MWD have some fun.

Riot hauled in heavy draughts around the sofa. Sat and looked at Danger.

"Seriously?" Danger stalked to him, glanced at the cushions. He stuffed his hand between them and touched plastic. Pulled the bag out. Pills.

"What's that?" Deke asked, stepping into the room.

"Oxy." Danger bounced it in his hand. "Could use a few of these for tracking." This combined with Lyric's scent . . . it could lead them straight to the Guerreros.

Deke scrutinized him for a second, no doubt thinking about Danger's fight with substance abuse. "Take ten. And I expect them returned when this is over."

"Understood."

"We're heading to the festival."

Twenty mikes later, Danger positioned himself at an outdoor bar bordering the jungle, ticked with the way things had developed. Riot was posted at Danger's feet, watching the raging festival a good thirty yards away.

The villagers filled the spacious dirt square amid the concrete homes, eating and chatting at picnic tables or dancing to the fast-paced music a quartet played—which, according to Paisley, was *joropo*, Venezuela's national music and dance.

The smell of fried food wafting through the air had Riot licking his chops and drooling. He nudged Danger's thigh with his nose.

"Don't give me that Bambi look. You already ate." He'd fed and hydrated him—besides, no way would he put greasy food on this guy's stomach in the middle of an op.

With a dissatisfied groan, Riot slumped to the hardpacked ground and rested his snout on his forelegs.

"What can I get you, *guapo*?" the young bartender asked with a strong accent. Didn't even try Spanish.

Like a heat-seeking missile going for its target, Danger's focus zeroed in on the amber liquids lining the counter behind the bar. That rum begged to be downed.

Don't be an idiot.

He cleared his throat. "Water."

A bar wasn't the wisest spot for a guy who'd gotten too fond of amber liquid, but this was the best position near enough to maintain visual on the dance floor, without being so close that someone could inadvertently elicit a defensive attack from Riot.

The bartender returned with a plastic bottle and slid it over the counter. Winked. "Here you go."

"Thanks." Taking a sip, Danger kept watching the revelry.

A native to the area, Raúl took lead and was making his way around the festivities, surreptitiously gleaning intel while Jude, Cyprus, and Anna Mara were having lunch with a Latino and his wife, who owned several food stands. Abel had found a petite woman to swing around the dance floor.

Danger's gaze rammed into a sight that made his gut clench—Stallion and Paisley were dancing too. Should've seen it coming. The guy couldn't pass up a chance like this. Got the moves covered too. Didn't help that Paisley was glowing like a Christmas tree.

The urge to wrap his hands around Stallion's throat and squeeze hard was overwhelming. The plastic bottle crinkled in Danger's grip.

Deke settled on the stool next to Danger. Resting his arms on the counter, he leaned in. "You need to loosen up," he muttered. "You're sticking out like a guy wearing a tutu in a sea of grunts."

"Loosen up? When Lyric's somewhere out there, probably being . . ." Danger almost choked on the word. "It's killing me—

147

we sit here, eating and dancing, and she's out there . . . every breath I take could be when she breathes her last."

Riot sat up and pressed his warm body against Danger's leg, earning himself a solid ear rubbing.

"I hear you, okay?" Deke looked Danger square in the eye. "But if you keep acting like that, you'll get us burned. Remember what that'd mean for Lyric." He glanced at the crowd. "Raúl knows what he's doing."

Didn't matter. The villagers wouldn't talk, even to their own. Too afraid of the Guerreros—for a good reason.

Yet Deke was right. Getting them burned wouldn't help. Duly chastised, Danger turned his focus back to the dancing.

Paisley's feet tapped the floor, her ponytail bouncing. Shouldn't bother him so much that she was enjoying herself in another man's arms.

But it did. A lot.

"Why her?"

The question startled, but there was no use arguing—the chief had known back in Albuquerque that Danger cared about her. But being called out made him reach for Riot again, and the Dutchie nudged Danger's palm. "She isn't scared of my demons. Heck, knows how to muzzle them." Didn't run from his temper or foul moods, his booze problem or the scars.

For a second, he allowed the feeling of her fingertips brushing over his skin to consume his mind. When had she gone from being someone he liked hanging out with to someone he couldn't imagine being without?

Deke guzzled some water. "Then take it from an old man," he said and pointed to where Stallion held Paisley a little too close. "Let your girl dance with another guy, and you'll regret it the rest of your life."

Your girl.

Those two words had a blast radius measured not in distance but in years—a lifetime's worth. Danger found Paisley again and met her eyes over the dancing couples.

She smiled.

Clamping Deke's shoulder, Danger stood. "Hate it when you're right." He handed the lead to the chief, who'd once been a handler. "You know the drill. Upset him and he'll turn you into a bite suit."

Deke eyed the Dutchie. "I have scars that won't let me forget."

Brown eyes flicked to Danger as if saying, *You're ditching me for her?*

"You get some KONG time later, bud." Mustering his courage, Danger stalked to the dirt plaza. Snaked through the crowd. Stallion was about to whirl Paisley around when Danger seized the ambush opportunity, caught her wrist, and pulled her to him.

She sucked in a breath, huge hazel eyes gaping up at him. Then she smiled. Looked over her shoulder at Stallion with an apologetic shrug.

The guy smirked. "About time, tiger." He pivoted and offered his hand to a little girl. Giggling, the maybe-six-year-old accepted, and man, she could dance!

Lyric loved to dance too.

The fist around Danger's heart squeezed. What if he didn't find her? Or found her too late?

"I thought you made such a big entrance because you wanted to dance with me."

The light teasing drew his attention back to Paisley. Dance? Hold up. What on God's green earth had he been thinking?

"Relax, *tiger*. I'll guide you." Suppressing a smile, she took his right hand and moved his left to the middle of her back. "It's a one-two-three beat."

"That helps."

She laughed. "Move the right foot back, tap the left where it is, bring the right foot to the front. Then the same thing moving forward, starting with the left foot."

Embarrassing, considering the guy was supposed to lead.

And his teammates grinning like idiots didn't help. But he tried. Messed up. Tried again. Did better.

"There you go." Paisley picked up speed.

Despite her encouragement, he was distracted, trying to maintain focus to recon while her soft curves were in his arms. When the music slowed, the tension in his shoulders waned. Easier to keep eyes out. He copied the other men dancing and drew Paisley against him.

"You're way too tense, Beau. Stop looking around and loosen up. Move to the rhythm."

See, this was where things got tricky. He didn't *move to the rhythm*. Ever. His body was made for taking hits and stalking prey. Not for dancing.

But he focused on the feeling of Paisley in his arms. Her intoxicating scent. The way her body was pressed against his, despite the plate carriers . . .

Easy there, man.

Right. Not the smartest thing to focus on. His blood was already running a little hotter, and it had nothing to do with the stifling ruana.

"Tell me about your favorite childhood memory."

Paisley's question was so out of context that Danger needed a second to catch up. He scoured memory lane until he found himself at a festival in Boulder, surrounded by people, laughter, and the smell of cotton candy. "Right before Dad's accident, he took Collin and me to a festival. They had this challenge for families going—tug-of-war, sack race, an obstacle course, and shooting gallery. We were super competitive, loved to push our boundaries." He had to smirk. "Not to brag, but we smoked the other families."

"Sounds like a wonderful time." The smile was audible in her voice.

"It wasn't the winning, you know. It was that sharing of a bond with someone. Knowing they had your six, and you had theirs. Being part of a tribe." Danger looked away, feeling awkward. Somehow, this woman always got him talking.

"That makes so much sense. I get it." She nodded. "We all have a desire to feel connected, to belong. I think when God said it's not good for man to be alone, He didn't necessarily mean that everyone needs a significant other, but that we have people in our lives to support us—as you would say, to have our six." The longing in her voice suggested she desired something similar, possibly the same.

Danger grunted, relieved she understood him.

"You found that bond in the SEALs again, didn't you."

It wasn't a question, and yes, she definitely got it. "After Dad died, I felt disconnected from everyone. The Teams—the brotherhood—changed that."

"And now you've lost them again."

Undone that she read him like a book, he said nothing. Just hugged her a little closer. Breathed in her scent.

"Growing up, I'd always longed for a family," she said at his chest. "I mean, Mama and Abuela were family, but I wanted a dad. Most of Mama's boyfriends ignored me, except for one. He was good for her, managed to get her off drugs. Took us to church. We'd have barbecues, and she did all the things a mother does. We were a real family . . ."

When she shifted, Danger looked down at her, and his warrior instinct to protect rose to the fore at the pain swimming in her eyes. He ran his thumb over her cheek. "What happened?"

"Mama relapsed. He couldn't take it and left."

Danger drew her back to himself and wrapped his arms tight around her narrow shoulders. Couldn't imagine how hard it must've been to grow up with such a selfish mother. If that woman had done her job, her daughter wouldn't have ended up at the mercy of the Guerreros. "I won't let Osorio hurt you again." He was going to find that scum and put him six feet under, funeral costs on him.

Paisley sucked in a breath and pushed away.

Danger tensed, cursing himself for bringing Osorio up. But that's when he noticed she stood staring at something to his three. He followed her gaze and spotted an earlier-twenties woman wearing tan pants, a pink T-shirt, and a satchel slung over a shoulder start down a path into the jungle behind the bar. He'd noticed her earlier, sitting next to Deke and chatting with the bartender.

"You know her?" Danger asked, maintaining visual on the girl.

"Let's go!" Paisley grabbed his hand and pulled him past the dancing couples toward Deke. "She'll lead us to Lyric!"

"How do you know she'll lead us to Lyric?" Beau asked beside Paisley as they dodged locals.

Her heart pounded in her chest. They had to stay on the young woman before she vanished, but running after her would not only spook her but also draw suspicion from the villagers. "Because this used to be my job. She's an ambassador—her duty is to report back to the enforcer."

"Osorio," Beau muttered.

The name slithered like ice down her back. They were running right into the beast's cave.

"What's up?" Deke asked quietly when they reached him.

Beau grabbed a crumpled napkin from the bar. "The girl who sat next to you might lead us to the package."

"She definitely will," Paisley put in.

Some kind of taciturn conversation happened between Beau and Deke, then the team leader nodded. "Alright, I'll summon the team and—"

"No time," Beau said as he angled the napkin to Riot and let him sniff it. "I saw her using this to wipe her mouth, but if the scent isn't strong enough for Riot to pick up, we'll have to keep eyes on her." He lifted his gaze to Deke. "We can't lose her."

Lips tight, the team leader considered him. Nodded. "Don't go in too far."

Upon Beau's command, Riot lowered his snout to the ground and started sniffing around the bar. He zigzagged his way toward the village, then veered toward the jungle.

As soon as they made it past the tree line, Beau shed his ruana, a signal to Paisley to do the same. She had to grin when Beau pulled out his beloved ball cap and donned it.

With Riot in the lead—his harness-attached leash was tethered to Beau's tac belt—they hiked deeper into the jungle. Beau drew a handgun from his side holster and held it in front of his chest as he moved with lethal stealth.

The cacophony of birds and chirping insects combined with the petrichor of wet earth brought dread and calm alike over Paisley. Dread because they had officially moved into Guerrero territory. Calm because, back then, the jungle had been her safe place, since the Guerreros had been too lazy to accompany her on the long hikes necessary for the ambassador's job. She had relished the precious hours without abuse.

I sought the Lord, and he answered me; he delivered me from all my fears.

That verse reminded her that God had given her one of the best protectors she could've asked for. *"I won't let Osorio hurt you again."* Beau's words had sunk right in, a balm to the tender places of her soul. Being cocooned in his strong arms had felt like coming home and letting go.

Fist up, Beau halted, and Paisley nearly bumped into him. There, between the trees about twenty yards away, strolled the young woman. The satchel whipped with her steps as she followed the narrowing trail.

Cupping Paisley's elbow, Beau drew her behind a tree, Riot with them. "We're good—Riot's got her scent."

Her dog's ears swiveled at his name, drool dripping off his tongue as he panted heavily.

Beau unearthed a satellite phone from his pants pocket and typed something, then tucked it away. "Team's about two klicks behind us." He took a step toward Paisley and grabbed her chin. Tilted it up.

Her heart stumbled. What was he doing?

He held up a small pallet with face paint. "Camouflage."

Oh. For some reason she'd thought he'd kiss her. Silly.

He started applying the paint above her brows with a finger. He'd removed his shades, his expression focused as he worked. "What's the girl's job?"

Paisley shoved aside the fluttering feeling that his touch and rugged smell evoked. He was so close she could make out every detail of his scars and damaged eye. Job—he asked about the job. "The term *ambassador* is misleading. She goes around the villages to collect taxes. Sometimes has to perform other . . . services."

Beau's hand froze, his blue gaze finding hers. "Did you have to—"

"Yes."

A muscle in his jaw popped. He looked like he wanted to shred someone to pieces. Namely Lyonel. But he refocused on her nose, working his finger down it with an efficiency that proved he'd done this a thousand times. "Why's nobody watching her? She could just run off."

"They would kill her entire family and everyone she knows. Then kill her too."

"Of course," he growled, running his finger repeatedly along one of her cheek bones, then the other. As he continued applying the paint, his eyes kept dropping to her lips, then refocusing on the part of her face he was working on—including her ears and neck. "A bandana."

"What?"

"Use it to keep the sweat out of yours eyes. Should be one in your ruck." Once done, he painted his own face, and within two minutes, every bit of skin had disappeared behind a perfect blend of two different shades of green.

Riot snapped to attention, ears swiveling toward the underbrush.

"Team's coming," Beau said.

Sure enough, they popped out of nowhere wearing tac gear, faces painted and weapons slung across their chests.

As Paisley found the bandana and tied it around her head, she once again became aware of how heavy the tac vest was and the heat trapped beneath it. But it was an absolute must. Few made it out of Guerrero territory alive.

"Where's Raúl?" she asked Jude.

"He'll pick us up with a helo once we're ready to get out of here."

"You know the rules," Deke said quietly. "Fifteen-foot intervals, no chatter or abrupt movements."

Beau and a way-too-eager Riot took the lead, and the team trailed them in the requisite every-fifteen-feet formation. Rafiq, however, stayed closer to Paisley, covering her since she didn't have a weapon.

For the next half hour, Riot led them deeper into the jungle. The vegetation grew denser as the trail sloped down the mountain, the canopy thickening until no sunlight could penetrate. Roots turned into trip hazards, vines snaking around and hanging from trees as if reaching for them. Paisley shuddered despite the increasing humidity. What they were doing was crazy. How would they ever make it out alive?

She was immersed in prayer when their train suddenly stopped and the team crouched, Rafiq pushing down on Paisley's shoulder. She took the cue. Ahead, Riot's body was rigid as he strained against the lead.

Blood rushed in Paisley's ears. Why had Riot alerted? Was there a Guerrero checkpoint?

At Beau's hand signal, they moved on, although slower. All team members had their rifles tucked into their shoulders, scanning and sweeping—careful not to cross their lines of fire on each other.

Looking at something to his left, Beau spoke into comms.

Paisley noticed the tension pressing down on the team flake away. Though tempted to ask Rafiq what was going on, she remained quiet and trudged on.

Holy moly, what was that stench? Rotten meat, or eggs, or—

She swallowed a gasp at the scene before her. Five bodies, dangling upside down from a massive branch. As they moved past them, she saw maggots and bugs crawling in and out of their hollow eye sockets. Flies buzzed around. All men wore shorts but no shirts. The word *rata* was carved into their torsos. *Traitor.* These men were Guerreros.

The pungent odor of death pressed the contents of Paisley's stomach up her throat. She swallowed it and refocused on the path ahead.

They kept going, still downhill. Her calves burned, sweat trickled down her back and gathered under her armpits, and mosquitos whined into her ears. An entire hour had passed when Riot alerted again. This time, Jude slipped past Beau and disappeared into the thicket.

A hair-raising chill swept over her. Waiting for him to return, her gaze drifted to Beau, who gave a slight nod as if to say it was okay.

It felt like forever but had only been fifteen minutes at most when Jude reappeared. "It's an outpost. Wooden hut, six unfriendlies armed to the teeth. The girl just left it."

"Copy," Deke said. "Let's cloverleaf around it."

Veering farther from the path turned out to be a real challenge. The vegetation was so dense with vines, bushes, and tree limbs that they had to squeeze through. Branches grabbed at Paisley's body and scratched her face. Finally, the density loosened, and they could move more freely again. No wonder the Guerreros had set up a checkpoint here. It was nearly impossible to go around it. Which meant they had to be past it now.

Riot barked.

Crack-crack.

A yell punctured the humid air and was accompanied by more gunfire.

Amid the crack of weapons firing, Paisley ducked, and as she did a blur came out of nowhere. She braced as a solid mass drove her back behind a tree.

"Stay down!" Beau barked as he pivoted around, shoulder braced against the trunk, his body shielding her. Where had he come from? And where was Rafiq?

Tremors raced up and down her body, her heartbeat clogging her throat.

Beau stepped around the trunk to return fire. Wood spat at him beneath the power of bullets.

The acrid odor of gunpowder filled Paisley's nostrils, and shells dropped to the leaf-covered floor as Beau squeezed off shots. She eyed a seemingly unaffected Riot, standing guard at Beau's side, shoulder to the operator's leg. Paisley lifted more prayers heavenward. The report of the rifles and the shouting were deafening. She wanted to curl up with her hands pressed over her ears.

"Gotta move." Changing out magazines with jaw-dropping speed, Beau shifted back and squatted next to her, attention ever forward. "Let's go."

Movement in Paisley's periphery nearly stopped her heart.

Two Guerreros stepped from behind a tree fifty feet away, rifles aimed at them.

Her pulse rapid-fired, seeing the collision of circumstances. The Guerreros aiming at an unaware—"Beau!"

12

PAISLEY'S SCREAM TORE THROUGH DANGER THE SAME TIME BULLETS sprayed the tree behind them. "Contact!" he yelled as he whipped his M4 to his two. Squeezed the trigger. Shifted. Squeezed again. Both Guerreros dropped, hitting the ground a split second apart. He keyed his mic. "Two hostiles neutralized."

His heart jackhammered against his ribs as he scanned the underbrush for more unfriendlies. It was eerily quiet; the shots had scared away the birds and monkeys.

A chorus of *all clears* carried through the comms. But it meant exactly nothing. More Guerreros could pop out of nowhere at any time. This was jungle warfare. Dense vegetation made it extremely difficult to spot the enemy. One could be hiding literally three feet away.

He dropped a quick gaze to Paisley and Riot. Paisley huddled against the tree, saucer-eyed and shaking. Didn't respond to the Dutchie, who nosed her neck, licked her face.

"She okay?" Stallion asked, standing at a spitting distance.

"Pais." Eyes out, Danger took a knee next to her. Touched her shoulder. "You hit?"

158

She slowly shook her head.

Just to make sure, Danger scanned her body. No blood. Riot was fine too. "You did amazing," he said, meaning it. "Obeyed orders like a champ. Heck, you saved our lives. I didn't see them because of . . . my damaged eye." Humiliation heated his neck. But being open kinda felt good, especially when Paisley turned to him with a faint smile.

Her gaze stayed on him for several long seconds, and it seemed she understood the significance of what he'd just admitted. "Hey, I can scream anytime you need me to."

He sniffed.

"Carry each other's burdens," she murmured quietly, "and in this way you will fulfill the law of Christ."

Danger cocked a brow. "What?"

"We carry each other's burdens—complement each other." She reached out to Riot and smoothed her hand down his brindled neck. "You too, boy."

Riot leaned into the affection and praise. Squinted in pleasure.

Apparently, he and Paisley weren't the only ones bonding. The moment when he'd painted her face flashed through his mind. Her lips, her exposed neck . . . He'd been so close to kissing her.

"Danger, SITREP," Deke said over comms.

Danger rose. Did a visual 360-degree sweep. "All clear. Hoofing it your way." He extended his hand to Paisley. "C'mon."

They found the rest of the team by a spartan wooden hut in a small clearing. They'd secured the perimeter with Anna Mara, Deke, Cyprus, and Abel on guard while Jude and Stallion frisked the six bodies sprawled all over the place. This outpost had been crawling with trouble.

"This wasn't the amateur hour I'd expected," Stallion growled. "Check out the equipment." He booted a rifle on the ground—an FN SCAR-H.

Jude plucked a radio from a Guerrero's belt. "They pretty

much have unlimited funds, and it's rumored Querales hired a bunch of *Fuerzas de Acciones Especiales*—the special operations unit within the Bolivarian National Police—to train them. They have the reputation of a death squad. The kind that dumps a mag into a crowd just for the sake of it."

Cyprus took the radio from Jude. "This is an MMR."

"What's an MMR?" Paisley asked.

"A multimode radio. It provides line-of-sight communication over wideband, but also satellite. And they're waterproof." He fidgeted with it. "Too bad it's broken."

"Alright," Deke said to the team, "let's keep tracking the girl. It won't take long till the Guerreros know we're here."

If they didn't already.

"C'mon, bud." Danger resumed point with Riot. As the hours progressed and darkness lengthened beneath the thick canopy, the ground slowly grew wetter. Thick fronds surrendered their power to more rugged terrain—including rocks. Bugs buzzed and dive-bombed them, earning more than one growl of frustration. Steps turned into suctioning sloshes that promised blisters. Only positive was that the darkness progressively lost its power, light beckoning to them.

Ahead, a glimmer on glass snagged Danger's attention. What—

Splash!

Hearing the Dutchie yelp, Danger rounded a towering rock. Found not only Riot scrambling back onto the swampy ground—and shaking out his brindle fur—but light spearing down between cliffs that formed a ravine. "Holy . . ."

On the left, an orange residue lined the shelf-like rock formation that rose easily a hundred meters up. The right was a collage of moss, vines, and wet rock. High overhead, the two clefts converged, and from it a blanket of vines and thickets dangled like some elaborate chandelier. The entire mouth of the ravine was steeped in at least three feet of water all the way to where it banked to the right eighty yards ahead.

"You've *got* to be kidding me," Stallion groused.

Jude snickered. "Forgot your swim trunks?"

"I ain't going in there." Stallion balked. "If you wanna end up as piranha snack, fine. Not me."

"Wait, are there really piranhas in there?" Anna Mara asked, eying the water.

Jude shrugged. "I'd say no, but then . . ." His mug split into a grin. "Whoever has an open wound goes last."

"Need me to hold your hand?" Danger asked Stallion. "Lookin' a little green there."

"Shut up."

Smirking, Danger eyed Deke, whose expression was tight as he considered the area. "Reeks of ambush."

With another splash, Riot was in the water again, swimming.

"Not a problem now." Danger hated to admit it. "He's got a scent."

"Of course he does," Stallion growled.

Deke nodded. "Let's do this. Head on a swivel."

Not wanting Riot to tire and drown, Danger hiked him onto his shoulders. And in they went. Six feet wide, the ravine welcomed them into its chilled water and hauntingly eerie cliffs flanking the small river. Holding Riot's forelegs and hind legs, Danger trudged in a heavy-legged pattern as he pushed himself through the water. His boots hit slick rock, and he worked to keep himself steady with the dog panting a hundred miles an hour in his ear.

"Stop!"

Danger froze. What had Paisley seen?

"Don't move." Water splashing, she appeared in his peripheral vision. Pointed skyward. "Look."

Angling his gaze up, the back of his skull pushing into Riot's soft belly, Danger squinted. Bit back a curse. Amid the tangle of vines and roots snaking overhead hung a giant wrecking ball with punji sticks—wooden spikes—jutting out in a dozen directions. The contraption was tethered to a support that, when triggered, would vault the ball into the unsuspecting.

AKA: Riot and me.

Holy Gehenna. What was this? Vietnam?

"Swinging mace," he called to the others.

"There's the tripwire." Paisley pointed to a vine he could barely see in the water. It stretched across the path and wound up the cliffs to a square support. "They plant explosives in the mace."

Wouldn't surprise him if the punji sticks were covered in human feces too—a great accelerant that would also increase chances of infection if the victim survived the impact.

Danger shifted to the side and let Riot hop onto one of the orange ledges while they sorted this.

"Move back." Paisley made a shooing gesture at the team. Shoved against Danger's plate carrier. "You too."

He sloshed back, his boots slipping on the mossy rocks below the surface. "What're you doing?" Didn't like that determination on her face.

"Defusing it."

"No freaking way!"

She dropped her pack on a ledge and scrutinized the rock wall. "I've helped set these up in the past and know how they need to be handled."

Danger grunted. "We'll just climb over the trigger—it's safer."

"You might bypass this one, but there's likely more than one trigger."

"So we backtrack. Find another way."

"Riot has a hit—we can't leave this path. Besides, no way am I going to leave it for some unsuspecting migrant or local to die from. Now let me do this. I know what I'm doing." Her hazel eyes softened. "*Trust me,* Beau."

Whoa. Those three words skewered his objections. He

glanced over his shoulder at the team, who were suddenly and insanely interested in the water. "Deke?"

The chief gave a firm nod. "She knows her stuff and we're out of options."

Danger faced Paisley again. Nearly choked when he realized she was already climbing the cliff on the right. And deftly.

He was going to strangle her if she survived.

Eyes peeled on her, Danger backtracked to Riot. The Dutchie pranced, clearly feeding off Danger's unease.

Paisley clambered over one jutting ledge after another, using vines to haul herself up. She monkeyed all the way up until she was above the spiked ball. Had to be a good sixty feet high. Wrapping a vine around one arm, she let the other hand go. Broke off a branch, leaned out, and stuffed it into the pulley. The wrecking ball swayed.

A curse seared the air from behind Danger—no idea who'd said it, but he agreed. If the vine she was holding on to broke and she fell, she'd be impaled right before exploding to pieces.

"She's nuts," Abel muttered.

Dead. That's what she was if she made it back down alive. "Easy," he called to her, wondering if the words were more for himself.

She pulled out the KA-BAR from her leg strap, caught the rope with the hand with the vine wrapped around it, and started sawing below her grip.

Sweat slipped down Danger's temples. He'd rather stroll through a minefield than watch this. *God, don't let her fall.* The prayer escaped before he realized it. Whatever. Could use some divine help here.

Once the rope was severed, she sheathed the KA-BAR and tied the rope around the vine. Yanked at the knot. Seemingly satisfied, she started her descent. Held on to the thick vines while groping for purchase with a foot. Once found, lowered the rest of her body.

"Nice and slow," Danger encouraged her.

Riot let out a keening whine, his focus on Danger. Smelled and felt every emotion coursing through him.

Paisley made it down to forty feet.

"Doing good." He couldn't help the comments.

A vine ripped away from the cliff. Yanked Paisley out with it. She yelped. Flailed.

Danger's heart jammed into his throat as he heard someone suck in a sharp breath behind him. Fists balled, he watched, breath held. *Please, God . . .*

She reached out for another vine . . . and missed. His heart felt it. She tried again. Another fail.

He muttered an oath.

With a grunt that echoed in the ravine, Paisley surged out and caught hold of another vine. Clung to it. Steadied herself. "All good—"

Snap. Crunch. Crack.

The entire tangle of vines ripped loose, swayed . . .

"No no no."

And lurched free of the cliff, taking Paisley with it.

Paisley's stomach spasmed with the fall. A blur of brown and green rushed before her eyes. Fire seared her arms, legs, and stomach. Then she was yanked up and everything went still.

Her pulse thrummed in her temples. *What is happening?*

Stunned, she glanced down her body. Found it tangled in vines and bushes. She was . . . *sitting.* A laugh bubbled out of her. *Thank You, Jesus.*

"Paisley!" Beau's shout was more a growl than anything.

Riot's barks echoed up to her.

She looked down, finding them fifteen feet below.

Riot had his front paws planted against the rock wall, his tail wagging as he barked excitedly. Brows drawn together, lips tight, Beau looked spitting mad. The team cast her wary glances as they maintained security, keeping watch for Guerreros.

"Coming down." Paisley's hands shook as she started to untangle the mess.

She used the knife to cut herself free and scrambled down the rest of the wall. Dropped with a splash into the water.

Beau caught her shoulder, his grip solid. "You okay?" His intense gaze scanned every inch of her. Locked on her skinned hands. "You're bleeding."

Flushed at his attention, she dropped them. "It's nothing."

A tail-wagging and prancing Riot leaned out over the rock and shoved his furry snout between her face and Beau's. Swiped his tongue up her cheek. Sniffed her ears and hair. Licked her again.

Laughing, she rubbed his sturdy neck. "It's okay, sweet boy." Joy flooded her heart. He finally welcomed her the way he did Beau! Funny that she had to nearly die to earn it, but beggars couldn't be choosers.

Beau's icy glare daggered her as he shouldered in. "*Never* do this again! You hear me?"

His remonstration thundered through her. She swallowed, then pressed her lips together. The laugh—where was this coming from? Adrenaline?—broke out of her anyway.

"You think this is funny?" Roughing a hand over his chin, he turned away. Whipped back around. "I could've lost you!"

Paisley stilled. Blinked. Oh.

Chest heaving raggedly, Beau glowered at her, the muscles around his damaged eye twitching. It seemed to hit even him at that point what he'd just said.

Warmth spread through Paisley as she held his gaze. Breath trembling through her, she tried to fathom what he'd just inferred—to lose her meant he felt like he *had* her . . . like she was his. Belonged to him. Oh, she wanted to wrap her arms around his neck. Kiss him. Because the feeling was mutual. There wasn't anyone else for her.

The realization forced her to draw in a weighted breath.

"Maddox!" Deke's sharp tone burst Paisley's happy bubble. "Need to stay on the girl."

Beau's mouth flattened. "Copy." He jutted his chin at Paisley. "Her hands need bandaging."

Paisley wanted to object, but as she inspected the cuts from the vines and handholds in the ledges, she had to agree—after all, infections happened much faster in the tropical environment of the jungle. Even the smallest cuts could fester or get infested with parasites. Especially in water.

Anna Mara did quick work of cleaning and dressing her cuts while Paisley watched Deke giving Beau a stiff dressing down.

Her stomach knotted. She should be there too. After all, she was one of the reasons Beau was so distracted.

When Deke stepped aside, Rafiq angled up to Beau with a wide grin. "Holy smokes, man. Might as well take a knee and pop the question."

Beau remained stone-faced. What was going on inside him? She didn't want to cause him any more grief, so she'd ask him as soon as they had a moment alone.

They wound their way out of the water and found a small canoe that drew heavy sniffing from Riot. Then he moved away decisively, going from side to side, clearly finding the scent again. In a steady plod they left the ravine behind, crossed a swamp, and found themselves dropped into the semidarkness of the jungle again.

"Take ten," Deke commanded.

After the quick break to wolf down MREs—not as terrible as Paisley had expected—they went on. The scrapes and cuts burned more with every step. Her backpack weighed a ton and made her legs ache and throb from the effort of the rigorous trek. Her wet clothes chafed, the boots so much it felt like her feet were on fire—she looked forward to taking them off. No doubt she had blisters all over her heels and every single one of her toes.

Paisley glanced at the team and sighed. How did they do it? None of them seemed the least bit tired or struggling, even though they were all bearing a way, *way* heavier load while constantly scanning their surroundings. And Jude—he'd scouted ahead, which meant he'd had to jog, not walk, yet he didn't complain. Even Riot showed no signs of exhaustion.

Lord, please give me the strength to keep going. I can't do this much longer.

The sun had to be setting soon, because the darkness under the dense canopy increased slowly.

A low growl from Riot startled her.

The team dispersed to the sides, crouching in the vegetation.

"What—"

"Incoming," Beau muttered a second before Jude jogged into view.

The team stood, and Jude diverted to Deke. They exchanged a few words, then the chief faced them. "There's a village a klick to our ten, where the girl is spending the night. There's also a waterfall nearby with a natural pool. Since we don't know which way the girl will head, we'll bunk down for the night too. We're outside Guerrero territory, but stay frosty."

Thank God! What an answer to her prayers.

As they followed Jude, the impenetrable walls of greenery relented, allowing glimpses of the overcast evening sky through the thinning canopy. The ruckus of monkeys, birds, and insects yielded to the gentle rushing of water. Before them a clearing opened up, and they found themselves atop a waterfall cascading down overgrown rocks into a pool of emerald liquid forty feet below.

"I'm taking a dip," Beau announced. "Got an entire ant colony crawlin' in my shirt."

While half of the team stood guard, he, Riot, and Abel hiked down the path leading to the pool. The Dutch shepherd dove in after his KONG, Beau right behind him.

Smiling to herself, Paisley turned to her backpack and started digging for food. She was famished. After scoring a protein bar, she sat down, her gaze drawn to the pool. Her breath caught in her throat—nearly choking her—when she spotted Beau. Hip deep in the water, he'd taken off his shirt and was washing it, clearly unaware of his audience.

Wrong. He always knew who was watching. Either he felt comfortable enough around his team to show the scars, or he simply didn't care. As if he felt her gaze, he looked in her direction. The man might have scars, but they didn't make her look away; they were her reason to stare. And guiltily, she indulged. The muscles cording his body should be illegal. And that he stood there, not embarrassed that the team saw the mangled flesh, made her proud. He'd come so far. Let her into his dark world and slowly learned to accept help.

She sent him a smile of respect, and he cocked his head at her.

Riot bounded up the path and settled his backside in the dirt next to her, then hiked his hind leg toward his ear and scratched. When he stood, he shook out his fur, showering her with water droplets.

"Beast!" she laughed.

He nudged her fingers with his wet snout and warm breath.

Taking the cue, she ran her hand over his glistening, damp coat. Fur stuck to her fingers, and she shook it off.

Beau materialized before her. "I'm here to relieve watch." He'd donned his T-shirt and ball cap, water dripping from it. His face paint was almost gone. He looked at Paisley. "Mind taking Riot back down to the pool? He needs to cool off some more."

Excited to get some quality time with her dog, she rose. "Sure."

"Put him in a sit-stay, then toss it from up here." Beau handed her the KONG. "He'll love that."

"Really? Jordi said he hated water."

Beau smirked. "Try him."

As instructed, Paisley flung the rubber toy off the forty-foot cliff.

Riot watched it like a hawk, his jaw chattering and his body quivering with anticipation.

"Go, get it!"

He took off like the fur-missile he was, careening down the path. His powerful body stretched as he lunged off a rock and sailed into the water, as if trying to break some dock-diving record. Unbelievable! He wouldn't do that with Jordi, and now he loved the water. Guess they had all changed, hadn't they?

"Is he always like that?" Anna Mara asked.

Beau sniffed. "You mean like the Energizer Bunny on crack? Pretty much."

"Sounds like Abel's spirit animal." Rafiq's comment provoked a chorus of laughter.

As they dove into stories of pranks they'd done to teammates, Paisley strolled down the path to the languid pool where Riot lay on a grassy patch, chomping into his KONG. The lingering anxiety of being in and near Guerrero territory had simmered down to an almost unnoticeable sensation. After constantly being on the lookout for threats, she was glad to finally breathe a little easier.

A droning hum sifted over the rushing of the waterfall. First far away, then closer . . . closer . . . What was that? Shielding her eyes, she looked into the sky. Saw nothing but clouds.

"Down. Everybody down!" Jude's shouts lifted over the rising roar.

Paisley dropped to the jungle floor and rolled into the scrub to her left. Where was Riot? She should've made sure he was down. What if something happened to him? Peering in the direction she'd last seen him, she felt panic edging her. Where had he—

Something brushed her bare forearm. A shriek jammed her throat. She spotted a brindle coat. Riot! KONG secured between his jaws, he belly-crawled in closer until the full length of his body pressed warm against hers.

Wrapping an arm around him, Paisley squeezed her eyes shut. *I sought the Lord, and he answered me; he delivered me from all my fears.*

Her thundering heart competed with the now deafening roar of the engine.

It was coming right at them!

13

BOLÍVAR, VENEZUELA

THE PLANE PASSED SO LOW DANGER'S CHEST VIBRATED. THE TEAM had taken cover in the thicket, and from his position behind a massive trunk, Danger saw the twin-engine light aircraft—probably a Cessna 402—dive and disappear beyond the treetops. The engine noise faded till the rushing of the waterfall and chirping of crickets once more gained the upper hand. Mentally, he worked through what kind of threat that plane could be. Since the village lay north of their location and the Cessna had touched down southeast . . . If it wasn't the villagers, it could only be Guerreros.

Might not be such a safe place to set up camp after all.

The team stayed low a while longer, then Danger eased to the top of the waterfall, M4 at the ready, and peered down at the pool where Paisley and Riot had been. The vise around his chest tightened. Where were they?

He again scanned the water, then the area around it. Rocks, shrubs, roots, trees. Movement snapped his attention to a plant with cordate leaves. Paisley lay under it, prone, with one hand over her head, the other coiled around Riot.

His ticker slowed. Unscathed.

Abel's blond head quietly emerged from the depths of the pool, only his eyes and nose above the water. Danger signaled him to bring Paisley and Riot up, then kept an eye on their surroundings.

"Where'd he go?" Stallion asked.

"No idea." Jude ran a hand over his buzz cut. "A year ago, there wasn't anywhere to land out here. I'd say the Cessna is carrying mining equipment or gold, but there are no mines out here. Has to be a narc plane."

"So, Guerreros," Danger muttered, earning a stiff nod.

"Guess their operation is expanding again. We should go check it out. Could be an important lead."

Down at the pool, Abel and Paisley made for the path. Riot charged ahead.

Danger signaled him to surrender the rubber toy and heel. "Playtime's over, bud. Back to work."

Tail mopping dirt and leaves, Riot gave off a bark. They were forged from the same steel. Rather dodge bullets than loiter like slugs.

Deke nodded. "Alright—"

A splashing sound snapped Danger's attention to Abel, who was hunched over a few feet away. Groaning, face pale, he straightened and leaned against a tree.

"Abel, what's wrong?" Anna Mara was already by his side.

He wiped his mouth with the back of his hand. "A snake got me."

"When? What kind?"

"About thirty mikes ago, and didn't ask."

"Cut the jokes and sit!" Muttering something under her breath, Anna Mara pushed down on his shoulder, and Abel sank to the ground. "Where?"

He pulled up his pant leg, revealing two punctures in his swollen calf. "Looked like a brown water snake. Non-venomous."

"The plants you just watered with your stomach contents beg to differ," Deke said. "Could've been a Venezuelan lancehead—they look similar. Freud, fix him up with antivenom."

The medic grabbed her pack. "On it."

"Why didn't he say something?" Paisley asked quietly next to Danger.

"Because it's no big deal. Mind's on the mission."

"No big deal." She shook her head. "Of course it isn't."

Smoothing his fingers over his mustache, Deke faced Jude. "Hate splitting up the team, but Logan isn't going anywhere. You, Cyprus, Danger, and Riot—conduct recon. See what that plane is about. No engaging. We clear?"

"Yes, sir." Jude looked at Danger and Cyprus. "You guys good to go?"

"Give me a sec." Danger geared Riot up, then pulled Paisley aside. "You okay?"

Nodding, she brushed a raven strand from her camo-painted face. Would have to freshen it up later.

"Stay with the team, alright?"

She grabbed his plate carrier and pulled him down. Pressed her lips to his.

A jolt went through Danger, his mind blanking as if he'd been tasered.

Paisley eased off, her hazel eyes glowing. "Just making sure you're coming back," she whispered.

Holy Hades. Everything in him screamed to cup her nape and pull her in. Kiss her. *Really* kiss her, not that maddening lip brushing. This was the second time, and it was starting to feel a lot like the torture he'd endured at the hands of the Guerreros.

Had to tough it out a little longer. Didn't need another one of Deke's chewing-outs. *Mind on the mission, Maddox. No margin for error.* Clearing his throat, he straightened.

The chief was right. He'd never had issues with emotions during an op. With Lyric and Paisley involved, things were different. He'd never been so distracted.

Double tapping his leg to signal Riot "heel," Danger headed out before he changed his mind.

The Dutchie shot to his left, and together they stalked past a rubbernecking team. Even Abel grinned.

Ignoring them, Danger cocked his head at Jude. "Let's go."

They slipped into the darkening underbrush. It wasn't ten minutes before Riot suddenly stopped, sniffed the air, then lowered his nose to the floor and hauled in draughts as he snaked around trees, bushes, over roots.

"What's he got?" Jude asked.

Danger readjusted his grip around his M4. "Looks like your narc-plane theory was right on the money."

Riot's ears swiveled as he kept going, tail high. He halted, snout back in the air. His nostrils twitched as he worked to sort the direction. A low growl rumbled deep in his chest.

Unfriendlies.

Danger signaled Jude and Cyprus as they stalked on, quiet and stealthy.

Ahead, the jungle started to lighten. They crept closer to the edge.

Signaling Riot "down," Danger flattened to his stomach between the Dutchie and Jude, moving aside a twig of the bush that served as their cover. Luscious vegetation gave way to a manmade clearing the length of four football fields, a dirt airstrip running its length. A good 250 yards from their position, the Cessna was parked by a small shack overgrown with plants and roots. Seven men formed a bucket-brigade line from the shelter to the plane, tossing each other packages, loading the aircraft, their shouts carrying through the sticky evening air.

Jude muttered an oath under his breath. "None of this was here last year."

Using the sights on his M4, Danger checked for threats. Four guards monitoring the area cradled their FN SCARs, while the others had standard fare AR-15s or AK-47s slung to their backs.

With the growing darkness and from this distance, faces were hard to identify.

Danger tried to locate a head honcho but couldn't. "Looks like a transit point."

"Yeah."

A tall man wearing a maroon button-down and black slacks stepped out of the building. Danger's ticker rapid-fired. Osorio. If he was here, Lyric couldn't be far. This op might be over sooner than expected.

Jude grunted, watching the scene unfold through binoculars.

Danger readjusted the rifle butt against his shoulder and fixed the reticle on Osorio's head. Moved his finger into the trigger well. Inhaled and held his breath. One shot, and the world was a better place.

A whine ripped him from his revenge fantasies back to the Dutchie at his side. The four-legged combat hero knew the game. Blowing Osorio's head off would stir up a hornet's nest, causing the Guerreros to go into lockdown. If that happened, they'd never make it out of here alive, and then he'd be responsible for Lyric's death. When they hit, they had to be sure she was there and make a rapid exfil.

Osorio clapped, then moved his hand in a circular motion, indicating for the men to wrap things up.

An older guy joined him. Hiked his pants up over his paunch as he said something.

"That's Querales." Jude sniffed. "Christmas has come early."

Fact. And Danger was ready to rip open the presents.

"Actual, this is Pita," Jude comm'd. "We've got eyes on two HVTs and eleven tangos."

No reply.

Querales slapped Osorio on the back, then made for the plane while Osorio disappeared inside the building. A second later, the enforcer returned, carrying—

Danger sucked in a breath. "Son of a—" Pink T-shirt, dark curls . . . *Lyric.*

"Easy, brother," Jude muttered, then keyed his mic. "Actual, this is Pita. We've got joy. Repeat, we've got joy."

Still nothing.

Cyprus shifted. "Darned foliage absorbs the signal. I'll hoof back till—"

"No time." Adrenaline punched through Danger when Osorio heaved Lyric into the Cessna. "We gotta engage them on our own."

Steel in his expression, Jude gave a tight nod. "Let's do it."

They stood, signaling readiness, and pushed out of their cover into the open. With Riot glued to his side, Danger dispatched the first guard lurking next to the Cessna, then the one to his ten while Jude took care of the other two. Cyprus engaged the remaining Guerreros.

Shouting erupted, the cartel members scrambling for their weapons. Danger, Cyprus, and Jude advanced, squeezing off rounds as dirt spat up around them. In his periphery, Danger saw Osorio pull up the airstair door. "Riot, get 'em!"

The Dutchie propelled forward. Flew through the grass, the muscles rippling beneath his brindle coat.

Danger neutralized the last Guerrero, then diverted to the aircraft.

The propellers started spinning, the exhaust coughing.

Osorio was about to close the top section of the door when Riot lunged with an explosive force. Soared higher and higher. Hit the open space with his upper body.

A scream cut through the din of the Cessna. The aircraft started rolling, Riot's rear hanging in the open.

"Riot, out! Out!" Blood rushing in his ears, Danger tore after them. If the plane took off and the Dutchie fell from a great height . . .

The Cessna gained speed, Riot's hind legs pedaling for purchase on the slick hull.

"RIOT! OUT!" Danger's lungs and throat burned, every step rattling his bones. "OUT!"

Distance grew, the aircraft now peeling down the airstrip.

And then Riot let go. Dropped and hit the hardpacked dirt, the speed making him violently flip several times till he came to an abrupt halt.

"Riot!" Even as Danger ate up the remaining yards separating them, the Dutchie writhed and fought back to his paws. Came limping toward Danger.

"You crazy—"

Riot leapt, nearly knocking Danger over. Slobbered his face.

"Good boy." Danger roughed the Dutchie's sides, the relief dying as he saw the Cessna pull into the air. Almost shave the treetops.

Gone. They'd been *so* close; now Lyric was gone. Again.

And the possibilities of her new location were endless.

Blackness more impenetrable than any Paisley could remember surrounded her. To avoid being spotted from above, they had moved camp deeper into the jungle. The crickets made a lot more ruckus than during the day, and there were other sounds— she didn't want to know what critters they came from. Every now and then she could hear a team member move around but only once saw a faint red light when Anna Mara and Abel relieved Cyprus and Deke from village watch.

The rough bark of the tree Paisley leaned against bit into her back as she shifted into a more comfortable position. Fatigue pressed down on her, but worry about Riot, Beau, and Jude kept her awake. What was taking them so long? They'd been gone for an hour. She would give it another ten minutes, then ask someone.

Crack.

Paisley jumped, heart in her throat. What was that? A snake? Jaguar?

She grabbed the handle of her knife lying in her lap.

"Can't sleep?"

Her brain needed a moment to match the voice with Rafiq. Willing her heart to slow, she let the knife go. "How do you know? I can't see anything, and Beau said night vision doesn't work in complete darkness."

Rustling indicated Rafiq was settling. His arm briefly brushed against hers. "Thermal imaging. The trees are an issue, but it's better than nothing. And the red-lens light is to preserve night vision. Less harsh on the eyes and doesn't cause blinding spots like the white."

Oh. "Do you know what's taking Beau and Jude so long?" She couldn't keep the worry out of her voice.

"They're on the way back. That what's keeping you awake?"

"So they're okay?"

"Yes."

The way Rafiq drew out the answer told her there was more to it, but she let it go. "Yes, they're keeping me awake, but also the idea of venomous critters crawling all over me." Especially after that snake bite. Thank God Abel was okay.

She shuddered. While she'd spent a lot of time in the jungle, it had never been at night and definitely not sitting up against a tree. Apparently that's how operators did it, taking two-hour naps at a time.

Rafiq chuckled. "Not a fan either. I hate the jungle." He cleared his throat. "Danger's a good man, Paisley. He's intense and passionate, but he'd never hurt you."

She stilled. Where had that come from? "I know."

He cared about her—deeply—and made her feel safe. And yes, she wanted to trust him with all of her heart, but a sliver of fear lingered in her bones. Letting him in meant breaking her own rules—which got people, including herself, hurt. Killed.

But what if she put her fear aside for once? What she had witnessed argued her doubts about him. Left her confused, but longing, *willing*, to trust.

Fifty feet ahead, red light danced across the bushes and jungle floor accompanied by silent rustling.

"They're back." Rafiq stood, and Paisley with him.

Her gut clenched as she followed him. She nearly tripped on a root.

The red light hit boots, then disappeared, leaving them in complete darkness.

"What've you got?" Deke's question barely carried above the crickets.

Something wet brushed Paisley's hand. She squatted and ran her hand over Riot's head, the knot in her stomach loosening. "Hi, boy," she whispered, and heard his tail whip against tactical pants. Beau's?

"A clearing with a dirt airstrip, probably a narc transit point," Jude said. "They loaded the plane with cocaine. Querales and Osorio were there with our package."

Package . . . "Lyric?" Paisley's voice pitched. "You saw her?"

"We tried to intervene—Riot even took a bite out of Osorio—but they got away."

"Lyric's alive, that's what matters." Beau shifted to Paisley's side. "They headed east, but no idea their destination." His voice, so dark, sent a shiver clawing up her back.

She felt for his hand. Found it clammy. Interwove their fingers and squeezed. He clung to her as if his life depended on it.

"Our plan remains unchanged," Deke said. "The girl is still in the village—we'll keep tracking her. Maddox, Payne, you'll relieve Freud and Logan in an hour. Khalil, you and I watch the camp, the rest of you rack out. Rotate every two hours."

Again using the red flashlights, the team scattered.

Beau's strong arms came around her and pulled her in. His vest dug into her chest, but she didn't care. She buried her face in his neck and breathed in his familiar scent.

"You should get some rest." His chest rumbled as he spoke.

"Just hold me a little longer." She needed this, and something told her he did too.

With a huff, he cupped her head. "I saw her . . . right there . . . and couldn't save her." Grief lanced his words. "She looked okay, so I have to believe he isn't wanting to harm her. But I'm ticked that he has her."

"We'll find them," she vowed, hugging him tighter. "I know you will. And we'll all help take him down."

He pressed a kiss to the crown of her head. "C'mon, let's grab some rack time." He guided her through the dark, Riot plodding along, then they settled against a tree.

Pillowing her head on Beau's chest, Paisley relished the warmth he radiated. For years she'd wished for a man like him. One who would protect her. Beau was that man.

She knew not being able to extract Lyric bothered him. "We'll find her, Beau. It'll end differently this time." When no answer came, she shifted. "Beau?"

No response. The man was deep asleep.

14

"No!"

At the shout, Paisley startled awake. Blood rushing through her ears drowned the jungle sounds as she hastily scanned the camp in the wan light of dawn. Trees, bushes, vines, a backpack. Was it the Guerreros? Had they found them?

Her gaze struck a slumbering petite form resting against a trunk, arms crossed and head down. Anna Mara. She wouldn't be sleeping if there was an attack.

Grunts and sounds of a struggle combined with barking arose behind Paisley.

"Easy, bro. All secure." Rafiq's voice was low, soothing.

"Riot, quiet. Out!" Jude.

Paisley peeked around the tree she'd been leaning against. Rafiq and Beau wrestled each other on the ground, and Jude restrained Riot, who bared his sharp teeth, snarling and straining against Jude's grip.

Wait, Beau wasn't wrestling . . . he was *thrashing*. Holding Beau from behind, Rafiq had his arms and legs tightly coiled around him, talking calmly in his ear.

What . . . Heart thudding, she pushed to her feet.

Finally, Beau went limp, the only movement the ragged rising and falling of his chest. After a while, he pushed off Rafiq and hiked to his feet. He grabbed something from his ruck and stalked in the direction of the pool. Riot shot to his heels.

Despite the urge to follow them, she forced herself to settle back against the tree. He probably wanted to be alone. But somehow, she knew that was wrong. Knew after the way he'd held her last night, that the way he seemed to anchor her felt the same for him. They found comfort in each other. Just as she'd said before.

She rose and took a step, then hesitated. What if she made him mad? She wet her lips, thinking . . . but then her gaze hit Deke's. He cocked his head in the direction Beau had gone, confirming she'd been right.

With a breath for courage, she followed the path to the pool. She spotted Riot sniffing around a few yards farther down. Slowly, she ambled down the trail and found Beau behind a rock, sitting on a grassy patch at the water's edge. His arms rested on his knees, one hand clutching the other wrist, and a plastic bag with brown liquid dangled from the other hand. What was that?

"Do you mind if I join?"

When he grunted, she made herself comfortable next to him. Knew to let him tell her when he wanted to talk. She whispered a silent prayer that she'd have the right words when he opened the dialogue.

"Coffee?" He offered the bag.

Paisley took it. "Thank you." She sniffed. "What I wouldn't do for a latte or mocha."

A grunt from him.

But hey, this was better than nothing. Right? Expecting something strong enough to launch her out of her boots, she tentatively took a sip. The taste of mild roast surprised her.

"Not bad, huh?" Beau asked.

"Not bad? This is *really* good." She took another sip, then offered it back, but he indicated for her to keep it. Glad for something other than water, she finished it.

The singing of birds and gentle rushing of the waterfall settled over them. Riot trotted around, then slumped onto Beau's boots.

Paisley blinked. "He likes your boots!"

"What?"

"Riot is obsessed with Jordi's boots, now he does the same with yours."

Beau roughed Riot's chest. "It's not about the boots," he said. "He's resource guarding me."

"Re-what?"

"Lying over my boots is his guarding me. It can also be a sign of dominance"—he rustled Riot's head—"but we know better. Right, bud?"

Riot moaned, eating up the attention.

"Do you want to talk about the dream?" Paisley asked gently after a while. She wouldn't push it.

"Not really, but . . ." Beau kept raking a hand over Riot's coat. "It's always that same picture of Lyric. I'm holding her limp body in my arms. She's covered in blood. Unresponsive. No matter what I try, how much I shake her . . . It's that helplessness I felt when Dad died. When Hank abused me. When my team got ambushed." He stared out to the water. "I just can't stop thinking about what they're going to do to her."

Hank had abused him? Whoa, things suddenly made a whole lot of sense.

"These are incredibly challenging experiences you've gone through. Feeling helpless in such situations is absolutely valid." She looped her arm through the gap of his leg and arm, and interlaced her fingers with his. "Thank you for trusting me with that. I know it wasn't easy. And there are no quick remedies, but I'm here for you. The team is too. And God fights for you."

"He really doesn't."

"Sure He does—you just haven't noticed His work." She squeezed his hand. "'My grace is sufficient for you, for my power is made perfect in weakness.'"

"So I *am* weak—that's what you're saying."

"We all are at some point, Beau. The only One who's unwaveringly strong is God. That's why we need Him. But why do you believe He doesn't fight for you?"

He looked out at the water, squinted in silence for a few minutes, then exhaled heavily. "When Hank started beating me, I prayed to God to make it stop. It only got worse." His jaw muscle popped. "Then I begged Him to save Cutter and Rudy. Both died. The image I have of Him isn't a figment. It's born from experience."

"I feel you, I do." And her heart ached for him. "After realizing what kind of man Lyonel was, I thought God was cruel for allowing all those girls to be abused." She nestled her head on his shoulder. "But there was a girl . . . despite everything, she radiated this crazy peace. When I asked her about it, she told me that if my image of God depends on my experiences and feelings, my faith will constantly waver. But if I hold on to who the Bible says He is, nothing can shake my faith. That changed everything for me."

Beau shifted, making Riot ogle up at him. "I can see that peace in you."

"You . . . do?"

"Hard to miss."

A pleasant hum warmed her at the thought that he'd notice something so important to her. A little self-conscious, she decided to move on. "Tell me, how come Rachel speaks so highly of Hank?"

Shaking his head, Beau drew in another breath. "For some reason, Hank was hooked to adopt Collin and Rachel but not me. Turned out I reminded him of my dad—I was his spitting image. He and Hank were best friends in high school, but Mom got in between them. When she chose Dad, Hank hated him for it."

"So he took it out on you." Why didn't his mother step in? What about Rachel? Oh, wait . . . "Do they know that Hank abused you?" She leaned forward to catch his gaze, and when his lips flattened, she had the answer. "Why didn't you tell them?"

"Dad's death destroyed Mom. It wasn't until Hank that she started living again instead of just vegetating. Even at ten I understood that if I talked, it would shatter her newfound happiness."

The pain slicing into Paisley's heart wrenched away her breath. "You kept quiet for eight years? Oh, Beau!"

His head jerked around, intense eyes pinning her. "You can't tell Rachel, you hear me?"

Even after all that, his concern was not for himself but his sister. That touched something deep in her. "I won't. Promise." She was about to rest her cheek on his shoulder again, but his lingering gaze made her hesitate. "What?"

"You're a brave one, Reyna."

She blinked. Frowned. "Hardly. I . . ." Not sure where this was going, she clamped her mouth shut.

"After everything that happened, you're right here, sticking it to the Guerreros. Bravery isn't being fearless. It's being scared and doing it anyway."

"Maybe." She jutted her chin. "But I don't always feel that peace I told you about. Since childhood I've had this fear of breaking rules and causing someone else or myself pain. One of Mama's boyfriends freaked out every time I left dishes in the sink. I tried to remember but sometimes forgot." She shrugged. "He let his anger out on Mama and me."

Mouth in a grim line, Beau said nothing.

"Then Lyonel happened, and there was this nice young guy who always had pity on me. Andres tried to help me escape, and

Lyonel killed him." She swallowed hard. "I broke the rules and he got killed. Then Jordi died."

"But he wasn't your fault."

She faltered. "I . . . broke a cardinal therapy rule—hear what they *don't* say as much as or more than what they do say." She shrugged. "I break the rules, people get hurt. A faulty belief, but I—I can't seem to break the lie." Not able to look at Beau any longer, she turned away.

His hand cupped her chin. "Hey." He urged her to face him. "I can't undo what happened, but I promise I'll do whatever is necessary to keep you safe."

His words—their meaning—sank into her. He was willing to die for her. *Oh, what a gift You have given me with this man.*

"You scared the spit out of me in that ravine."

At his low, husky voice rippling through her, her mind wandered back to the booby trap. *I could've lost you!* Had anyone ever cared so much?

Beau brushed his thumb over her lips, leaving a tingle in its wake and her heart thundering in her chest. His eyes darkened. Mirrored her longing when he moved in slowly, monitoring her as if making sure she was okay with his intentions.

She was. She wanted that kiss he was withholding. Eyes closing and silently giving him consent, she angled in.

His lips were warm when they met hers, the kiss so unlike him. Gentle, almost cautious.

There it was again—him making her feel cherished. Safe.

The last sliver of doubt melted away. She slid her fingers into his hair, like she'd wanted to do so many times, and deepened the kiss.

A groan came from the back of his throat, and just like that, all caution was gone. His strong arm came around her back, and he pulled her to himself. In response, she locked her arms around his neck. Couldn't be close enough either.

His stubble scraped her skin as he deepened the kiss, and he tasted of coffee and desperation—

He broke off, breathing hard. "That's all I got for now."

The way he slurred the words made Paisley giggle. She wasn't feeling any different. Besotted.

"Hey, lovers. Girl's on the move."

Paisley jumped at Rafiq's loud bark.

A wide grin split the sniper's face. "We're bugging out. Storm's coming too." He saluted, then retreated up the path.

Only now did Paisley notice the surface of the pool rippling, and the waterfall had gained in intensity. She turned to Beau. "Can water wash the scent away? I'm asking because during wet season, the lower parts of the jungle can be flooded within minutes."

"Yeah." The grim expression on Beau's face told her he'd been thinking the same. He stood, Riot with him. "C'mon."

Accepting his hand, Paisley rose, and they scrambled up the already muddy path.

And then the sky opened up and rain poured down, morphing their dread into reality.

The downpour was fast and hard, causing the already swollen river along their route to flood and turn the jungle into swamp. The waist-deep water not only forced Danger to take Riot into a fireman's carry but caused the Dutchie to lose the girl's scent. So for the past twenty mikes, they'd kept heading in the general direction, hoping they were still on to her.

Fire seared Danger's lower back. Teeth gritted, he readjusted Riot's weight across his shoulders. Hiking against the current of the river exhausted him. Unsettled him. If the terrain didn't rise above swamp level any time soon, where they could resume tracking, they'd lose the girl for good, and with her, Lyric.

"... if my image of God depends on my experiences and feelings, my faith will constantly waver. But if I hold on to who the Bible says He is, nothing can shake my faith."

Paisley's words had stirred something in him. A hope, maybe, that God had his six after all.

Either way, he wouldn't lose Lyric. Not on his watch. Osorio might've relocated her, but he'd find her. Couldn't live with himself if he didn't.

Riot panted in his ear. Licked his face.

Nothing like wet fur against his cheek.

Ahead of them, Jude sloshed through the water, M4 at the ready, the rest of the team at their six.

They kept climbing a steady slope, and then, *finally*, Danger spotted jungle floor. As if to congratulate them on their endurance and the blisters from their boots and rucks rubbing their skin raw, the rain surrendered.

"About time," Danger muttered. Once out of the swamp, he took a knee, and Riot lurched off his back. Pain spiked as he straightened, then died down. He let out a relieved groan. Time to move on. "C'mon, bud." He got Riot focused back on tracking, his insides churning as he walked an eager Dutchie around the thickets and fronds. Hoped the lessening rain and better terrain wouldn't thwart them longer.

"How's that work?" Paisley asked from behind them. "He just automatically tracks what you give him the scent for? Does he ever forget?"

"The training is specialized," he said as they hiked. "He will always respond to narcotics." He tugged the pills Riot had found at the village. "Test us."

Her eyes brightened. "What?"

"Hide one of these on the guys as we track, and then watch him get the hit."

Tentatively, she took the pills. Her gaze bounced to his. "Oxy . . ."

"Not mine," he reassured her. "Found them at the village. I asked Deke for some to help us cue Riot into the drugs to track."

"Okay."

"Look, he's got something, I think." He indicated to his brindled warrior.

Tail down, snout hovering over the mud and slick jungle litter, Riot veered to the left, then banked right. Spun. His ears twitched. Tail rose. He broke into a zigzagging trot through the trees and bushes.

Relief chugged through Danger's veins. He keyed his mic. "He's got her again."

Riot plowed up an incline, the jungle floor one giant slide. Danger slipped several times. Nearly face-planted into a tree. The team behind him fought the same battle.

When the terrain flattened, Deke called a break and they moved off the trail.

Chowing down on an energy bar, Danger filled Riot's collapsible bowl with water—but the lug veered toward Stallion, sniffing his ruck like crazy. Riot parked his backside next to him.

Paisley laughed and clapped. "He did it! Amazing!" She squatted at Stallion's gear and dug into a side pocket. Drew out the pill.

Danger's brain caught up with the mini test and couldn't help the stupid grin that hit his face. "The nose knows."

"Maybe I made it too easy."

Cute. "Try again."

"I will."

He watered Riot, then fed him his joint meds with a treat. The only reason they were on to Lyric was thanks to this four-legged whiz. Without him, they'd have nothing.

He thumped the Dutchie's wet side. "Once we find her, you've earned yourself a fat steak. And a lot of KONG time, especially if you keep winning us brownie points with you-know-who."

Riot's big ears swiveled, and he licked his chops.

Smirking, Danger roughed up his neck. His gaze struck Paisley. She leaned against a tree, bandana plastered to her head like the rest of her clothes to her body. His gut contorted. Hated to see her like that. Couldn't fathom how uncomfortable she must be, crawling through mud, soaked to the bone, and muscles burning. Unlike the team, she wasn't used to this.

"Holy smokes, man. You've got it bad." Sitting next to Danger, Stallion grinned, his left eye swollen from Danger's thrashing in a nightmare.

Humiliation crowded him anew. The entire team had witnessed him lost in a fight that didn't exist except in his mind. He hadn't missed that he'd had no nightmares when he'd fallen asleep with Paisley in his arms.

His gray matter snapped back to their kiss. Man, he'd really tried to suppress that scene so he could focus on the mission. But holy Hades. The way she'd practically inhaled him, no hesitation whatsoever . . .

Stallion was right—Danger was under her spell.

A low rumble broke into his thoughts. Hackles raised, body tense, Riot stared down the undergrowth.

"Unfriendlies approaching from the east," Abel comm'd from his position thirty yards down the trail.

"Copy," Deke replied. "All elements, take cover and do not engage. Let them pass."

Punching to his feet, Danger ordered Riot to his side, then pivoted to Paisley. "C'mon."

"What's going on?" Her eyes darted over the thicket.

When he took a step, he spotted fronds moving. He jerked back, gaze careening toward their rucks—which were sliding backward out of sight under the stealthy move of Stallion, who gave them an acknowledging nod.

Danger seized Paisley's arm and pulled her to a massive tree with wall-like roots. "Hide and don't come out till ordered."

She blinked. Faltered. "But—"

"Now!"

She nodded. Climbed over a root and disappeared under a blanket of thick leaves.

Confident she was well concealed, Danger grabbed Riot's vest and pivoted.

Snap, crack.

The twigs breaking were close. Too close—the Guerreros must've left the trail and were coming right for them.

Not wasting a second, Danger flattened himself under a cluster of ferns and palm branches. Adrenaline surged as he pulled Riot to his plate carrier. Wrapped his legs around him. He clasped his snout with one hand and his SIG with the other. The Dutchie was perfectly still.

Voices and shuffling neared. Black boots thudded into Danger's range of vision. Two men spoke rapid-fire Spanish, but there were at least five different step patterns. The third Latino stopped inches from Danger's face.

Chatter morphed into whispering. Weapons cocked.

Danger shallowed his breathing. These men spent so much time in the jungle that they detected the slightest changes in the air and vegetation.

One of the unfriendlies snapped a command, and the squad started moving again. Guerrero number four . . . number five . . . but that one closest shifted back, his boot landing near them. He muttered something into a handheld radio.

Nothing to see here. Keep going.

The Guerrero took another step back.

Another one.

Another—

Right onto Riot's tail.

15

BOLÍVAR, VENEZUELA

CRACK-CRACK-CRACK.

Amid the yelp-bark of Riot, Paisley flinched in her hideout at the loud reports from Beau's gun. Watching over the top of the root serving as her cover, she saw the three Guerreros Beau had hit from his prone position under the plants—right across from her—all drop a split second apart.

Somewhere nearby, more shots and shouts punctured the stuffy air, the rest of the team engaged in their own battle.

Shoving up, Riot with him, Beau holstered his handgun and slipped the rifle to the front. They whipped around behind a tree just as a spray of bullets devoured the bark.

Paisley couldn't see where the Guerreros were, but they sounded close. Digging her nails into the root, she lifted a prayer. Searched for Beau. Was she supposed to move with him? Had he forgotten her? She edged to the side. Shifted out.

Suddenly, he emerged from behind the thick trunk, Riot his shadow. "Stay down!" He fired twice, two tiny sparks igniting even as the sonic boom met her ears.

Crack-crack.

He jerked back. Went down.

No! Paisley clamped a hand over her mouth to keep the scream in. Tasted mud along with mortal terror. *He's hit. He's hit!*

His foot twitched.

Oh, thank God!

Even as he rolled over, Riot clamped his choppers into his vest and dragged him, with powerful bursts, behind the closest tree. Beau sat up, leaning against it, breathing heavily.

Two Guerreros neared from behind, one going left, the other right.

Paisley's heart vaulted into her throat. She wanted to scream, warn Beau, but it was too late—both Guerreros stepped around the thick trunk, rifles raised.

Riot lunged. Thudded so hard into the Guerrero on the left that his legs were ripped out from under him.

Crack-crack-crack.

The other Guerrero went down in a heap from Beau's shots.

Riot wrestled his target, mud whipping so hard it nearly hit Paisley in her hideout. The guy emitted a blood-curdling scream. Beau swiveled and started in their direction. Aimed . . . but did nothing. Why wasn't he shooting? His expression went taut, his gaze dropping to the weapon. Two quick hand movements and he aimed again. This time, she saw his finger draw back the trigger. Still nothing.

He slung the rifle to his back and produced a handgun, intent howling in his every move, his expression cold as ice. A series of loud cracks echoed around them. A Guerrero came out of nowhere and slammed into Beau. They went sprawling.

Meaty thuds of fists hitting jaws thundered right before Paisley as the two men went at each other.

She whimpered. Squeezed her eyes shut. Her mind spun back to her captivity. To the man killed for trying to help her. It was . . . too much . . . too familiar . . .

No, no, no. I can't!

She pushed around. Didn't want to look at the fight. Couldn't stand the violence of it, the lethality necessary for her to stay alive.

Grunts and a brutal thud were followed by a pained growl. A shout.

It'd been raining that night too. Andres had gotten her just beyond the bunker, but the guards caught him. Her. Forced her to watch as they executed him.

She couldn't watch this time. Wouldn't. God, forgive her! She scrabbled from behind the root. Worked to stay calm, steady her racing heart. A wet slurping noise—and the only thought was a knife being plunged into a chest.

The thought sickened her. Forced her to scoot away. She didn't want to hear. Didn't want to see. Just a little farther, though she knew she was trying to escape the visceral memories of the past too. She wanted to be free. Branches scratched her arms and whipped into her face, but she kept running, deeper and deeper into the jungle.

The memory of Lyonel pummeling Andres assaulted her. Running even faster, she tried to unsee it, that moment he'd driven the dagger into his chest. Her legs gave way and she plunged into mud. She crawled to a tree on all fours, slumped against it, and hugged her knees to her chest. Lowered her head onto them. Her soaked clothes clung to her, chilling her to the bone. Reason struggled to push into her awareness. It was Beau. Defending her.

But the sounds were the same. The result was the same—one man dead.

It was different . . . Beau isn't evil . . .

He was protecting her. He perpetrated violence against evil. That was good. Twisted, but good, she guessed. *Go back.* She dragged herself up and turned. She'd scrambled away, lost in her fear . . . *So much for trusting God, Pais.* What if . . . what if Beau came looking for her and got killed because he didn't have the team to protect him? *Who will protect me?*

You idiot!

Crunch.

Paisley froze. What was that?

Heart thundering, she scanned the swaying fronds and underbrush. It all looked the same. Towering trees with massive branches. Thick-leafed plants and vines looking like they wanted to grab her. Mist hung low. She'd come that way, hadn't she? No, she didn't remember that thick trunk. Maybe . . .

Break the rules, people die. *Like me!*

An invisible hand closed around her throat. Why hadn't she paid more attention to where she was going? And why did it feel like someone was watching—

A thick arm shot around her waist and jerked her up. She screamed, only to have a slimy hand clamp her mouth. The smell of tobacco and musk filled her nose. She kicked. Thrashed, twisting side to side. Dug her nails into his arm and scratched.

The man cursed in Spanish, but instead of letting her go, his hold tightened, crushing her ribs. *Help!* Tears stung as she fought for a breath.

He yanked her backward, dragging her, despite every effort she gave to free herself.

Why had she run away? No one knew where she was. No one was coming to save her.

The man slipped his hand from her mouth and hooked his arm around her throat, choking off her air.

Gasping, Paisley clung to him for support, desperately trying to avoid being strangled. He must've realized how hard he was squeezing, because he lessened the pressure. And she seized the freedom. Screamed for all she was worth.

He drew her tight against himself, provoking a wave of nausea.

Her mind raced, unconsciousness sucking her in. All the self-defense lessons she'd taken after being freed from the Guerreros seemed to evade her. Hours and hours of training—gone.

Jesus, please help me.

Wait. Beau's lesson!

Bracing herself, she wrapped her right leg around her attacker's. He stumbled, halted, his grip slipping. Paisley shifted her hip to the side and slammed her hand back. Once. Twice—

Grunting, the man dropped her into the mud.

She scrambled to her feet, spun and stomped her boot into his knee.

Mind enlivened, she barely heard his howl. She whirled and ran. Ran like she used to when it was all just a game, jumping over roots and dogging vines. Only this wasn't a game. It was life and death.

Her heart pounded so loudly in her ears, her breaths heaving through her chest, she couldn't tell if it was her boots thudding against the jungle floor or her attacker's. She imagined his beefy paws reaching for her. That made her run even faster. *Don't stop. Keep—*

Her legs were whipped out from under her. She crashed into the ground. Hot pain exploded across her forehead and her shoulder. She moaned.

Up. She had to get up. But her legs . . . they were tangled in something.

A presence loomed behind her. Pressed in.

No, no, no.

She was yanked up by her braid, a cry of pain breaking out of her. Through the tears pricking her eyes she caught a flash of camouflaged uniform. The kind the Guerreros wore.

God, help me!

The fist came out of nowhere and sent her world spinning. Arms noosed around her. She heard the clatter of an engine. Smelled gasoline and exhaust. Whoever had captured her would bring her straight to Lyonel, and this time, the man wouldn't let her get away. She tried to free herself and felt a solid crack against her skull. Consciousness making its escape, she fumbled with the pill bottle. Opened it . . . felt one hit her palm and dropped it . . .

Beau, find it. Please. Mercy, why had she run away? Let fear drown her?

He would come for her. She knew that without a doubt.

But the Guerreros did, too, and they would be ready.

Please, Lord—please!—*protect the team.*

A barrage of gunfire echoed from behind the wall of trees, plants, and vines to Danger's two, announcing more Guerreros. Fifteen yards ahead, Stallion materialized from the undergrowth and pushed toward the raging battle.

Muttering an oath, Danger released the now dead Guerrero from his rear naked choke and quickly fixed the double feed in his M4 as he shoved to his feet. This place was crawling. He patted his left leg, bringing Riot to his side.

Muzzle bloodied, the four-legged hero's attention homed in on him. He'd saved Danger's sorry hide. Twice. Danger's chest still hurt where the two bullets had hit his plate carrier center mass.

He ran his hands over the brindled body. No injuries. Tail was okay too.

Suppressing the urge to check on Paisley, he started toward the fresh fight. Hated that he had to leave her alone beneath that pathetic cover of roots and leaves, but that's where she was safest.

Crunching twigs at his six made him halt. He glanced over his shoulder and scanned the foliage—movement at a spitting distance from Paisley's hideout. Hushed voices wafted to him.

Danger slipped behind a tree and keyed his mic. "More unfriendlies converging from the south."

Tapping his side, he made sure Riot was ready. The Dutchie's alert eyes absorbed his every move as he panted.

Let's rock 'n' roll.

Danger plucked a flash-bang from his war belt. Pulled the pin and tossed it to his right.

Bang! Hissssss.

M4 raised, he swept through the smokescreen to the other side with Riot's shoulder warm against his leg. He sighted the first unfriendly and neutralized him. Fired at the second guy. Pushed through the thick gas swallowing trees and bushes, eliminated a third cartel member, then took cover behind a fallen log. Listened for more threats.

Riot panted steadily, tongue a mile long. He'd need to hydrate soon.

The Dutchie's head snapped to Danger's five, ears swiveling straight up toward the incoming threat.

Danger whipped his M4 in that direction. Spotted the barrel of an FN SCAR aimed at him the same time the Guerrero seized and dropped to the ground.

A figure stepped through the receding fog, rifle raised. Deke, followed by Jude and Anna Mara.

Holy Hades. Ticker throwing a ruckus, Danger huffed out a breath. He'd nearly gotten Swiss-cheesed. He straightened, and the chief swung his weapon toward him. "Blue, blue," Danger called.

"You two alright?" Deke eased up to them as the team secured a perimeter and confirmed targets were neutralized.

"Thanks to you, still in one piece." Danger pulled out Riot's collapsible bowl from his ruck Stallion handed him and filled it with H_2O from the CamelBak. "You?"

"Cyprus took one in the shoulder—a through-and-through." Deke indicated to the man standing ten yards to the side, his jacket blood-caked. "Anna Mara patched him up." His mustache twitched. "God's definitely on our side."

Danger had to admit . . . at least everyone was alive. That was something. Did that have to do with God? Maybe. He grabbed Paisley's pack and stalked to her hideout. "Pais, come out. It's over."

No answer.

"Paisley." He leaned over the root and shoved a branch aside. "It's o—"

Empty. What—

He swiveled, glancing back. Did he have the wrong spot? He scanned the area, then back to the spot. Saw in the wet jungle litter the depression of where she'd been.

But she wasn't now.

Hauling in draughts, Riot climbed over the root. Frantically worked the spot where they'd left her.

Danger did a three-sixty, scouring every tree, bush, and crevice. Was she hiding somewhere else? He pushed past a frowning Deke and stepped over a dead Guerrero. Wanted to holler her name but knew better than to give away their position.

"What's going on?" the chief asked.

Clasping the rear grip of his M4 against the increasing sense of foreboding, Danger faced him. "She took cover behind this root during the firefight. Now she's gone." He dug into the ruck and drew out the poncho she'd worn in the village. Went to a knee. "Riot. Here, bud." When the Dutchie came to him, he held it out. "Seek. Seek-seek."

Knowing exactly what was expected of him, he sniffed the leaf-strewn ground.

"Let's move!" Deke called as the team fell into step behind them.

Powerful muscles flexing, Riot worked the scent cone in a serpentine pattern through the dense maze of trees and tangled undergrowth. From time to time, he lifted his head to sniff the humid air, then brought it back down to move on with unwavering determination.

Riot's ears swiveled and his tail flagged. He rounded a massive tree trunk.

Danger's heart malfunctioned, much like his M4 earlier. Paisley's bandana lay in the mud amid drag marks. The kind that looked a lot like there'd been a struggle.

Riot nosed the olive cloth. Whined.

"Good boy." Danger picked up the soggy fabric. Ran his thumb over it.

"Hers?" Deke asked.

Swallowing against the acid pooling at the back of his throat, Danger nodded. "Yeah."

"Then we're on the right trail. Let's go."

Letting Riot sniff the bandana, Danger told him to seek. The Dutchie swept the area around the tree, his head swiveling left and right, then forged ahead until they came upon tire tracks of a four-wheeler.

The iron cord around Danger's chest tightened. Why had he left her alone? She was in serious trouble. Gripping the bandana, he kept following Riot to a creek. Monitored as he worked the bank back and forth, constantly throwing glances Danger's way.

"Must be where her trail ends," Anna Mara said.

"Trail doesn't end—he just . . ." Danger flared his nostrils.

"Four-wheeler tracks," Deke called from the far side.

"Here too," Jude muttered.

"Creating confusion," Deke suggested. "To throw off the dog."

"Let me try something." Danger escorted Riot through the six-foot-wide creek and had him sniff the other side. *C'mon, find her trail . . . please don't let me have failed her too.*

But the Dutchie hiked back through the water to the waiting team, sniffing around the bank again.

Danger scraped a hand over his mouth. His bad gut feeling was right—Paisley had been kidnapped, and whoever had taken her had made sure Riot couldn't track effectively. The thought of the Guerreros, especially Osorio, laying hands on her—

He whirled and sent his fist into the closest tree, rage burning his insides. He'd promised to keep her safe, and now she was gone! He lowered to his haunches and held his head. First Tyron. Then Lyric. Now Paisley. The latter two at the Guerreros' mercy.

And only one could be blamed—himself. Should've never separated from Paisley.

Wrong call yet again. He deserved a medal for this outstanding accomplishment. Only thing he was good at— failing those he cared about.

A wet snout nudged the back of his neck, then seventy pounds pressed down on him. Hot breath huffed into his ear.

"Maddox."

Acknowledging the chief, Danger rose. Didn't like the grave expression he found on the boss's face. "Sir."

Deke took each team member in. "The dog can't track Reyna, and we've lost eyes on the girl, so that's a solid indicator they figured out she's our tour guide. Chance of an ambush just escalated dramatically. They're messing with us, letting us run around till we're spent and weak. We have one wounded, and we're short on ammo and food." His gaze hit Danger. "I won't sacrifice the team."

Danger swallowed hard. He understood Deke bore the responsibility of the team. But this couldn't be it. He wasn't going anywhere. Not without Lyric or Paisley. "What about leaving no man behind?"

Deke held up a hand. "Wasn't done yet. We'll hoof it another two klicks, see if Riot can pick up Reyna's odor."

Ticker picking up speed, Danger nodded. "He will. His snout's some serious stuff."

"Good. We hike down the creek, half of us on each side."

As Danger followed Riot along the bank, his attention—for whatever reason—was drawn to one of the pouches clipped to the back of his belt. He dug his fingers into the bag. Touched something wrapped in plastic. Kala. Had totally forgotten he'd brought her with him.

Keeping his eyes peeled on Riot and their surroundings, he brought the monkey out, unwrapped it, and let the smell of vanilla engulf him. Paisley's face flashed before his inner eye, and a sense of peace came over him. In the raging war called life, she was the anchor to his sanity.

His gaze caught on the dog tag. *The Lord is with you, mighty warrior.*

Something speared into his chest, into his gut. He hadn't exactly asked God for help. Maybe it was time. He wrapped the monkey back in the plastic and shoved it back into the pouch. *Alright, God. Let's cut a deal. If You let me get Lyric and Paisley out of here, I'll do whatever You want for the rest of my life.*

A bold call—maybe too bold—but he'd do *anything* to bring them back home, even deep-six his future as an operator and join a sewing circle, if that's what God called him to do.

Yes, for Paisley too. She was ranking pretty high on his Most Important People list. Dead even with Lyric.

Ahead, Riot lifted his head and sniffed the air to his nine. Brought his nose back down and continued hauling in odors only to lift his head again. Must've picked up an odor that didn't belong to Paisley. Drugs out here?

"He's picked up a scent," he said to Deke, who walked behind him.

The chief gave a nod. "See where it leads."

"Seek-seek."

Veering away from the creek, Riot led them back into the maze of the jungle. The ground was drier and strewn with jungle litter, no tire marks visible.

Riot punched on until he worked the same spot for a moment, then sat. Shot a look over his shoulder at Danger.

"Whatcha got, bud?" Chest thick with anticipation, Danger hunkered down and brushed the leaves aside.

A jolt went through him. The oxy pills! "Holy—"

"What is it?" Deke asked from behind.

Danger rose and, turning, held up the pill. "I gave her these to hide in rucks while we hiked. A distraction to show her how he tracked."

"You think she left a trail."

Danger grinned. "We're about to find out." No doubt she was sly enough to come up with an idea like this. "Riot, seek-seek."

Three hundred yards farther north they discovered another pill.

Adrenaline pumped through Danger's system. "Definitely a trail."

"Or it's the Guerreros luring us into an ambush," Deke warned. "Wouldn't surprise me if they destroyed Reyna's scent to then leave a false trail."

Danger adjusted his ball cap. "They don't know Riot's a narcotics detection dog." At least, he hoped not. It was hard to explain why a black ops team had a dog, but he needed the chief to trust him on this one. He fixated on Deke with newfound resolve. Solid, undestroyable resolve. "Whatever your call, I respect it. But if you guys exfil, our paths part here."

Hard eyes bored into him. "Won't let you go in there alone. That's a suicide mission."

Cocking his head, Danger smirked. "It's not like we're staring down the abyss for the first time."

Deke turned to the team standing guard nearby. Back to Danger. "You'd better start praying this is Reyna's doing and not the Guerreros'."

Danger would—had been. As they kept following the oxy trail, he prayed hard. Because if he was wrong, not only the team's blood would cake his hands but also Lyric's, Paisley's, and Riot's.

16

BOLÍVAR, VENEZUELA

A TANGY AFTERSHAVE PIERCED THE DARKNESS SURROUNDING Paisley. Lyonel! A shudder seized her. The Guerreros had brought her to him.

Great mercies, she had to get away from here. Away from *him*. But where was *here*? Why was it so dark, and what was the soft thing under her?

"Jesus loves me, this I know, for the Bible tells me so."

The sweet child's voice and something caressing her forehead stilled Paisley's racing thoughts. Was she dreaming? A singing child and Lyonel didn't make sense.

Wait. It did!

Her eyes popped open—and she found an angelic face framed by unruly dark curls hovering over her. "Lyric!" Ignoring the stabbing pain behind her temples, she lifted her head from the girl's legs and shifted around, gathering the little one into her arms. The bed they were on creaked, its comfortable mattress and plush pillows building a stark contrast to the bleak, concrete-walled room. It held no other furniture, and the long, rectangular window abutting the ceiling allowed little daylight in.

Paisley craned her neck to see what lay behind it, but it was too high. Where had the Guerreros brought them? Ice spread through her veins. Lyonel would make her pay for escaping all those years ago. And then he'd force her to again do all those things she'd thought would stay buried in her past.

And what sick plan did he have for Lyric?

Nope, she wouldn't allow that. No matter what, she'd protect her.

Holding the girl's shoulders, Paisley set her at arm's length and looked her over. "Are you okay? Did they hurt you?"

Apart from the rumpled clothes and her hair being a little more unkempt than usual, she seemed unscathed. She wasn't even dirty.

"I'm okay." Lyric's big brown eyes searched Paisley's face. "But you are wet and hurt."

Only now did Paisley realize she was shivering and, yes, soaking wet. They had stripped her of the vest and knife. Thankfully, after she'd dropped the pills. She prayed the moisture of the jungle didn't disintegrate them before Riot found them.

She winced, clearly recalling when the Guerrero had punched her. "It's okay," she reassured Lyric with a smile. "It's only a bruise." She took the blanket from the bed and wrapped herself in it, then touched her puffy cheekbone.

But Rachel's daughter didn't seem to need reassurance. She beamed. "I'm happy you're here, Auntie Paisley."

What? How was she so calm and collected? What had the Guerreros told her that she didn't even ask for her mother?

Paisley pulled her back into her arms and cupped her head. "Me too, sweetie." As Lyric snuggled up to her, Paisley silently thanked God that the girl was unharmed, then prayed the team would find the oxycodone trail. The Guerreros had made the mistake of securing her hands in front of her, so she'd managed to drop one after another from the back of the ATV, where they'd tied her.

The *click* of a door being unlocked jerked Paisley out of her prayers. She shoved Lyric behind her, eyes glued to the aluminum door. Her heart raced against her thoughts.

The door groaned open.

Her breath caught at the figure standing there—Lyonel.

He swaggered into the room, a smug smile displaying his pearly whites. "*Mi reina.*"

My queen. His pet name for her was a wordplay with her last name, Reyna, and brought back memories like she'd cracked open an old photo album. Lyonel had given it to her on their first "date." A date she wished had never happened.

"You are even more beautiful than thirteen years ago. A real woman now, eh?" Slipping his hands into the pockets of his black slacks, he ambled closer. The left sleeve of his button-down was bloodied and torn, and she glimpsed a bandage under it. Was that Riot's doing? "I'm so glad you came back."

He'd changed too. His features were sharper, his shoulders broader, and those dark eyes harder. But he still wore his hair slicked back. And the aftershave—crazy that he used the same after all these years. Then again, he'd always been nostalgic.

Shielding Lyric, Paisley rose. "I'm not here for you." She was grateful her voice sounded collected. Inside, she trembled. Too many times had she imagined this moment when she'd confront him, tell him she'd forgiven him. But now . . .

The past flooded in, threatened to rip her back into that black hole she'd gotten out of by God's grace alone. *Don't let me fall back in, Jesus.*

Lyonel pursed his lips. "I was hoping we could catch up on old times." His expression softened as he stepped up to her and used a finger to tip up her chin. "I missed you, mi reina."

An urge to slap his hand away seized her, but she knew he fed off violence. So she poured some steel into her glare instead. "A six-year-old? Really, Lyonel? This is low, even for you."

His hand fell away, his mouth tightening. "Do you really think I harmed her? I'm not a monster."

"Says the guy who is an *enforcer* of one of the most lethal cartels in South America."

"There was a time you would have been happy for me."

Nope, she was done playing his little mind games. "What do you want, Lyonel?" she snapped.

He sighed deeply, then his eyes lasered into her. "Your boyfriend."

Boyfriend. First instinct was to clarify that Beau wasn't her boyfriend, but maybe it was better Lyonel believe that. "Haven't you tortured him enough?" She threw a glance at Lyric, who watched wide-eyed from the mattress. Thank goodness she didn't understand Spanish. "You killed his entire team, and then you tortured him. Poured acid over him and cut out one of his kidneys without anesthesia. You're sick!"

Lyonel's mouth curved downward. "You call *me* sick? He killed the boss's brother with his bare hands!"

The lethality of Beau's actions in confronting the Guerreros in the jungle rose to the fore of her thoughts—it didn't surprise her that he'd done something like that. Warriors were a different breed of men. She knew that, as hard as it might be to accept.

"What do you do with this man, mi reina? He is a savage, a barbarian." Lyonel started pacing the length of the small room. "I'm a little torn, you know. No matter what we did, we couldn't break him. And we did a lot," he said with a haunting chuckle. "He is more beast than man, which has me disgusted. But on the other hand, I'm *muy* impressed. He lived through the unthinkable, then managed to escape. After killing the boss's *hermano*, he is starved and tortured. Yet he escapes. The guy is *loco*."

Hearing Beau's story all over again brought Paisley back to the ABA ranch, where he'd bared his scars—not just the ones on his skin. She closed her eyes as a battle of emotions unfolded. There was the deep longing to never again leave his side. And then there was the awareness of how she'd broken his rule—he'd told her to stay. It terrified her to think he might end up dead because—as she knew—he *would* come for her. And that was very likely to get him killed.

Break the rules, people die. How hard was that to get through her thick skull?

"Tell me," Lyonel said, smiling, "does he know about your past? That you were with more men than he personally knows?"

The words made her ache. Because they were true. "Yes, and loves me anyway. He loves me not because of what I have to offer but because of who I am." Her own answer drew her back.

Watching him take down one Guerrero after another, that brutal fight at the end, had triggered old fears, pitched her back to Andres's death. Haunted her. She'd let fear drive her away from the one man who could have been her protector. He'd risked his life to save hers. More than once.

"Uncle Danger will rescue us," Lyric said from behind her as if reading her thoughts.

Lyonel smirked. "Yes, he will," he answered in English.

The way he said that made Paisley's stomach roil. And he was right—Beau would come. It was only a matter of time until he showed up. Stepped right into a very well-prepared and lethal Guerrero stronghold.

Lyonel would slowly torture them to death.

No. She wouldn't let Beau—or any of his team—die here if she could help it. She and Lyric had to escape and find them before it was too late.

She glanced out the window. A dirt yard stretched beyond it, surrounded by a massive, at least eight-foot tall, concrete wall. Heavily armed guards marched through the downpour, patrolling the area.

Her heart sank. How were they supposed to get out of here? They'd never make it out of the room let alone the bunker, and even if they did, there was no way they'd get past the guards and walls.

Unless God worked a miracle, their fate was sealed.

Maybe God had given Danger's prayers a listen after all, because the oxy might save Paisley's and Lyric's lives. He'd known Paisley was a smart one, but man. Leaving this trail wasn't just smart, it was downright genius.

Riot sniffed out one pill after another, leading them up a leaf-strewn slope around logs, gnarled trees, and thick plants. Whoever had driven the four-wheeler had chosen a path that wasn't easily traceable. It reinforced Danger's belief that Deke had been right—the girl's trail was a distraction, which had cost them time. But it sucked for the Guerreros that Paisley had thwarted their plans while simultaneously providing Danger and the team the perfect opportunity to pounce.

At the top of the hill, Danger felt an old adversary—fear—coldcock him at what lay below. The compound, almost exactly like the one in Caracas. Must've had the same architect. Heart hammering, he eyed the stadium-sized area cut out of the lush valley below—the two-story concrete building, thick walls, and guard towers. His gaze skipped over the dozen or so visible guards. Curses and shouts from months ago assailed his mind. Seized his ability to process or assess the concrete jungle where they'd beaten the snot out of him.

"I remember this place," Jude said, taking it in. "Didn't realize we were so close. There's another building behind those trees."

Stallion huffed. "It's a stronghold. How do we get in?"

"There's a tunnel somewhere," Danger muttered. Recalled the hollow rustling of his shoulders scraping the dirt walls as he'd crawled out of the Caracas compound. If the surface was the same, was the underground too? Probably . . .

"Somewhere?"

"On the backside of the compound," Jude put in, eyeing Danger.

Deke peered through his binoculars. "Gate's not an option. Walls exclude any other infil." He stowed his nocs. "Let's find that tunnel."

Danger grunted his agreement, knowing the longer they waited, the higher the risk the Guerreros would discover their ambush had failed and attempt to relocate the girls.

As they backtracked down the hill, Danger found himself praying. Again. Funny how a couple days ago he wouldn't have wasted a single breath on prayer. Now, twice in one day. A record. But that odd feeling—a peace?—said this time would end differently. They'd live. Get out now, and alive.

Or was that the thirst of his vendetta?

Edging toward the trees, Danger and the others fanned out, maintaining line of sight on each other as they walked the area to search for the tunnel opening. The contradictory concoction of dread and anticipation jacked his adrenaline. It was here. They were close. Even as he alternated looking at Riot and the ground while verifying they still weren't seen, he reached for that feeling, that cool sensation that he could liken only to peace.

"Got it," Cyprus subvocalized in their comms.

The team converged on the spot and discovered a hatch. Abel crouched and cracked it open.

Deke did a quick look-see to verify it was safe. "Stallion and Cyprus, set up overwatch. Rest on me."

One after another, they descended the rungs, Danger hiking Riot into a fireman's carry. Couldn't shake the feeling that this time he was handing himself over to Osorio.

Then again, he'd do that if it meant Paisley and Lyric went free.

The surprisingly wide and solid concrete tunnel led them to a closed steel door. While the team backed out of the blast radius, Abel put his EOD specialty to work.

With a not-so-subtle boom that rained down dirt and concrete dust, the explosives popped open the door.

Grating claxons warned the element of surprise was lost.

They flowed into the adjoining room, finding it empty. Disturbingly empty.

Deke froze for a split second. The same one in which Danger saw the tendrils of wires running above the opposite door and the counting-down timer.

"Bomb! Go!"

The team filed back into the tunnel.

BOOM!

A wall of hot air slammed into Danger's back and punched him forward. He crashed into the wall, then hit the floor hard. His gray matter swam, a single thought dominating: despite their efforts to avoid one, they'd rushed straight into an ambush.

17

BOLÍVAR, VENEZUELA

THE CONCRETE FLOOR QUAKED UNDERNEATH PAISLEY'S FEET. DEBRIS rained from the ceiling, showering her, Lyonel, and Lyric, who was huddled on the bed covering her ears. Wailing sirens proved deafening.

Through the smeared window, Paisley saw the guards in a flurry, most of them sprinting across the yard toward the building they were in.

Yelling something into his radio, Lyonel stormed out of the room. Locked them in.

"What was that?" Lyric whined.

Your uncle, I hope . . . Paisley's heart lurched at the hope of that idea, but since she could be wrong, she didn't say it aloud. The Guerreros had a lot of enemies. Or if they had any labs in this building, something could've caused an explosion.

Didn't matter. What did was the distraction this provided. She whirled to Lyric and crouched at the bedside. "Come on. I'll get you out of here."

Big brown eyes met hers. "I'm scared."

"I know, me too. But Jesus is watching over us."

He stilled the storm to a whisper; the waves of the sea were hushed.

Yes, He was the One in control. Not Lyonel, not Querales, but God alone.

Tentatively, Lyric scooched off the mattress.

Paisley pulled at the bed, but it didn't budge. This thwarted her plan to get level with the oblong window so she could break it with her elbow. She'd have to use her fist. She grabbed the blanket and wrapped it around her hand, then faced their obstacle to freedom. Who would've thought Beau's demonstration on her Bronco would one day save her life?

If she managed to break it like he had. The glass crusted with dust and dirt looked fragile enough, but she was no powerful Navy SEAL.

For a moment, she hesitated. What if Beau and the team were on their way here? If she left . . . they'd miss each other. But again. That explosion could've been caused by any number of factors.

No, they had to leave. Now.

Recalling what she'd seen Beau do, Paisley drew her fist back—

A violent stinging erupted in her hand. With a yelp, she snapped it out and dropped the blanket. Pain unlike any she'd ever experienced speared her index finger. Moaning, she lifted it. Two tiny spots marked the outside. What . . .

She glanced at the blanket on the floor. A brown furry thing skittered away. Even as a shudder seized her, she stomped at it. Caught it and twisted her boot, just to make sure . . .

"What's wrong, Auntie Paisley?" Lyric squeaked above the sirens.

"I . . . I think . . ." No, she had to do this. Escape. Before it was too late. Her finger burned, the fire spreading into her hand as she shook out the blanket. Thwapping it, she verified no more spiders. This time she wrapped her left hand, then faced the window anew. Did her best not to crumple under the excruciating pain. *Just get it done.*

She reared back and drove her fist into the glass. It shattered, shards raining down on her. Gasping, she tucked her head, then glanced up. She'd done it—the window was broken. *Thank You, God!*

Her right hand still on fire, she cleared the frame of the remaining shards, then dropped the blanket back on the bed. The room—wall and broken window—spun. She gripped the ledge.

"What's wrong, Auntie Paisley?"

"N-nothing." Whoo, she did not feel right. The amount of pain wasn't normal. And her chest was tight, as if a heavy weight pressed down on it. Weren't these symptoms after—

Stop it! Even if it was a deadly spider, she had to keep going. Wouldn't let fear paralyze her. That's all it was. And the stuffiness of this room explained why she was sweating buckets.

A muscle in her left leg cramped, causing her to trip. She caught herself on the concrete wall. Straightened. She felt so . . . heavy . . .

She tripped again, and this time her body surrendered. Pitched into the ground. Her muscles spasmed. *Can't breathe. Can't . . .*

"Auntie Paisley! Auntie Paisley!" Lyric's cries spiraled through the air.

Paisley was slipping out of her own body. Floating heavenward . . .

Smoke and the acrid odor of explosives burned Danger's lungs. His ears rang, the tunnel's concrete walls acting as a funnel for the chaos. Coughing, he fought onto all fours, his lower back throwing a ruckus. Pressed on anyway. Knew that staying down made him vulnerable against threat. Shifting his M4 around on its sling, he blinked against the grit in his eyes. "Ri—" He coughed again. Where was Riot? They needed to get out of this tunnel. Only a matter of seconds till the Guerreros showed.

Scanning the floor, he instinctively drew on the lead. Saw nothing but whirling dust and fog in the light of his SureFire. Once more tugged the lead, realizing there was no resistance.

Yanking it back, his heart lurched. "Riot!"

A wet tongue slathered his chin.

"Okay, okay." Chuckling, Danger ran his hand over Riot's body. Found a sticky spot on his hind leg. Probing it with his fingertips, he was fairly confident it was only a small cut. Took two minutes to wrap gauze around it so nothing got in to agitate it.

Expecting to hear the chief giving orders—but he wasn't. Danger stilled. Glanced over to where he'd seen him. Only then did he realize—Deke wasn't up and moving.

"He okay?"

Anna Mara was assessing him, taking his vitals, checking a wound.

"Nothing can take down the boss," Abel said over his shoulder, monitoring one entrance of the tunnel, Cyprus the other.

"He's coming to." Anna Mara squeezed Deke's arm. "Bossman?"

He groaned. Sat up. Pressed a hand to his head. "I'm fine. Let's get out of here."

Danger snorted. Typical Deke. Could crash hard—and bounce right back. He extended a hand and pulled the chief up. Steadied him when he swayed.

"Um, Chief?" Anna Mara caught his shoulder and pressed a hand to his back. "You got shrapnel in your backside."

"Well, get it out and bandage me up."

Took a couple of minutes for field triage, then Anna Mara tapped his shoulder. "Best I can do here. Liquid stitches may not hold for long."

"Long enough," Deke grunted. "Charlie Mike. All elements

on me." He brought his M4 up, moving as if nothing had happened. Crazy knucklehead.

Bringing Riot to his side, Danger fell in behind Abel. The Dutchie plodded next to him, his panting echoing in the confined space. Tensions were high and the movements crisp, practiced. A black hole yawned where the door had been, smoke rising from the ragged edges. The team lined up on both sides along the wall.

Abel pulled the flashbang pin and tossed it into the hallway.

Clank. BANG!

Ahead of Danger and Riot, Deke dropped two hostiles, Abel another. They streamed into the hallway, smoke rising around them. Danger and Riot were on Deke and moved to the left, Anna Mara trailing, while Abel and Cyprus headed right.

Bullets spat concrete at them. Deke neutralized the firing Guerrero at the end of the hall, Riot and Danger covering the chief's six. Sweat poured down Danger's neck, the still-blaring sirens echoing in his head.

A room opened to the left. They cleared it. Found endless bricks of coke. Back in the hall they rejoined Abel and Cyprus, who returned from clearing the other end. Tension building, knowing each door could be the one, they moved in fluid lethality.

They climbed a flight of concrete stairs, emerging in another murky hall with several doors on both sides. Three unfriendlies streamed out of a room. Deke dispatched two, Danger the other.

The claxons stopped as they pushed on, a haunting silence settling. This place was bigger than it'd looked from the outside. A darned concrete maze.

"Actual, this is Stallion."

"Go for Actual." Deke's voice was still raspy.

"Chopper inbound," Stallion comm'd. "Sounds heavy."

"Copy." Deke sent Danger a tight look. "Getaway bird?"

"Probably, but that means Osorio's still here, and if he is, so are they." He went to a knee. Drew out the monkey and held it to

Riot. "Here, bud. Seek-seek." He released the lead, and the Dutchie started sniffing.

His movements weren't focused but more searching. Working the cone, he backtracked a couple of times. Started down one passage to their nine, then returned and went down one to their three.

Pace quickening, Riot's serpentine pattern narrowed.

"This looks good," Deke commented.

Danger worked to keep up with his four-legged partner.

Crack-crack.

"Contact front!" Danger shouted, returning fire and stalking ahead, unwilling to abandon his partner. Staying right protected him from the shooter, who'd have to move into the open to hit him.

From behind, Deke tossed a flashbang. It *clink-clink-clink*ed down the hall.

Danger turned away to protect his vision.

Bang!

He rushed ahead, counting on the disorienting effects to slow the enemy. He did a quick look-see, spotted the tango in the corner, and sent a short burst. The Guerrero slumped into the wall.

Riot had bypassed him, ever on the trail of the scent. He was hauling in heavy draughts at a threshold.

"Deke." Danger made quick work of reaching the Dutchie. Caught his collar and drew him back.

Abel and Deke checked the aluminum door—locked.

A noise came from the other side, and Danger's pulse ratcheted. Sounded like mewling.

No—crying! A child. "Lyric!"

The noise stopped. "Uncle Danger?"

It's her! He sucked a hard breath, palming the aluminum. "Get back from the door. We're coming in!"

He drew Riot back to give Abel space. The demolitions expert drove his booted heel into the lock of the door. It bucked but held. He repeated it. Lucky these weren't steel doors. Abel tried again, and the door flew open.

Riot charged into the room, and Danger feared the worst—a Guerrero welcoming his furry partner with a raised weapon. He rounded the corner and stopped short, nearly tripping over a body. Shifting aside, he glanced down. "Paisley!"

She was laid out, pale, unmoving.

Biting back an oath, he went to a knee. Even as he did, a blur of a child flew at him. Collided with his chest, small arms coiling around his neck. He hugged Lyric close, even as he eyed Paisley. "It's okay, princess. It's okay. I'm here now."

"I think Auntie Paisley is dead," she sobbed, her tiny frame shaking.

Her words sliced right into his chest, razor sharp and ruthless. No, she couldn't . . .

And then it hit him. Losing her would be like losing Lyric—it'd be the end of him.

God, don't take her. I'll never ask for anything again, but please let her live.

"Is she . . ." His words emerged hoarse, his insides twisting as he watched Deke examine her.

Riot sniffed her face, nudged her cheek.

"No," Deke said. "But she's barely breathing. Thready pulse. No visible injuries."

Danger set Lyric back on her feet. "What happened to Auntie Paisley?" Tried not to bark even though he was going haywire. There had to be *something*, or Paisley's breathing wouldn't be shallow.

Lyric said something, but she was crying so hard he couldn't understand a single word.

"Hey, it's okay." He dug out the monkey and handed it to her. "Hand on me, okay? Like at the park." And his tried-and-true method of keeping track of her worked here too as a small touch came to his thigh. He turned his attention back to Paisley. Again scanned her body— "Right hand." He lifted it and drew her fingers apart. There. Two small punctures on her index finger. "Something bit her."

"A spider," Lyric whimpered, pointing to a tan blob.

Danger dug into his AFAK and snagged the epinephrine pen he'd brought, anticipating trouble in the terrain and wanting to be prepared in case Riot got bitten.

The Dutchie licked Paisley's face as if urging him on.

Danger drove the pen into her outer thigh and started the ten-count. One thousand one, one thousand two . . .

"Is she going to be okay?" Lyric whined.

One thousand four . . .

"What've we got?" Anna Mara asked as she swung into the room.

"Where've you been?" Danger growled, pinning her with his gaze. Spotted the blood on her sleeve. "You got hit?"

"Anaphylaxis," Deke bit out, glowering at Danger. Keying his mic, he turned away. "Pita, we have the packages. Moving to exfil in five."

Paisley drew in a breath, her eyelids fluttering open. She jerked her hand up, and Danger blocked it.

"Paisley! Easy." He released the pen and tossed it into his ruck. Sent up a thank-you.

"What's the reaction from?" Anna Mara asked as she sat down her pack and donned latex gloves.

"Spider." Danger jerked his chin toward the smooshed guts. "No idea what kind."

Paisley mumbled something, trembling uncontrollably.

Squeezing her arm, Danger leaned closer. "What's that?"

"Brazilian . . . wandering . . ."

Anna Mara went to work. "Brazilian wandering spider." The combat medic ripped open her ruck and threw a small pack at Danger. "Keep her warm." She unearthed a kit from which she took a vial and a syringe. Drew up that liquid.

"Do you have antivenom?" Danger unpacked the foil rescue blanket and wrapped Paisley in it.

"Yep, and I'll give her morphine and thread an IV."

The tight fist in Danger's chest eased. If this wasn't God's doing . . .

"All elements," came Jude's calm intrusion. "Ready for pickup at the west wall. We scored two bulletproof Chevy Colorados. Raúl will meet us at a clearing two klicks east."

Anna Mara gave Paisley a morphine shot into her thigh, then slipped an IV into the inside of her elbow. "She's good to go."

Danger lifted Paisley upright.

"Wait-wait. I'm okay, I can stand."

Not liking that idea, he hesitated, well aware of how much support he was providing. "You sure?"

Eyes hooded, she nodded. Hooked an arm around his shoulder. "I'll need help, but yeah . . ."

Riot's lead in a loose but firm grip, Danger escorted her into the hall. They banked left, back in the direction from which they'd come. Ahead, Deke had his weapon trained on the passage, stalking forward with Abel carrying Lyric. Anna Mara stayed close, trying to reassure Danger's niece, who strained to make eye contact with him.

"It's okay," he said with a nod, helping Paisley continue forward. Angling around a tight corner, he found it too congested to get himself and Paisley through.

She steadied herself on the edge. "I can do it."

He hesitated. "You—"

Her glower as she moved tentatively into the passage silenced him. And made him smirk.

"Stop," she said with more than a little teasing warning, continuously using the wall for a little extra support—but she was a tough cookie. "Don't baby me."

"Wouldn't dream of it."

She eyed him and a smile crept into her beautiful features. But then she faltered, bracing herself as she looked at the juncture ahead. "That . . ."

Danger glanced there, and his gut tightened in the split

second Riot planted his backside, signaling a hit, and he spotted the team ahead, shuffling—Anna Mara tripping.

Tripping . . . tripped.

"Down!" Danger whipped to Paisley and threw himself at her, the collision sending them into the wall. He forced her to the ground even as a small detonation punched him in the back and popped his ears. Heat swarmed his nape but receded just as quickly. "You okay?"

She nodded.

His gaze jerked to the juncture, where he'd last seen— "Riot!" Hauling Paisley to her feet, he strained through the haze of the explosion. "Riot!" The brindled coat wasn't anywhere to be seen. And the opening that had been there ten seconds ago was now caved in, rock, concrete, and dust billowing. He shoved at the pile, trying to shift it, but the thing seemed to have been pounded into place by some invisible hammer. "Riot!" Though he traced the floor for sight of a tail or other hints, he saw nothing. Hoped that meant his partner had gotten to the other side.

A hollow sound came from behind the cave-in.

"I thin—"

"Shh-sh," he interrupted Paisley, angling his head toward the debris. "I heard something. Riot!"

"He's here—okay!" Deke's shout sounded as if it came from the other end of the passage. "No chance to move the debris," he comm'd.

Breathing a little easier, Danger keyed his mic. "I know. Lyric?"

"She's fine."

"There." Paisley pointed down another passage. "We should see where it leads."

Danger swept the SureFire of his M4 in that direction, a long narrow hall that banked to the right. Didn't have many options, did they? He keyed his mic. "We're going out the packing facility. Meet you there."

"Copy. Stay frosty."

"Let's go." Danger took Paisley's hand again and set it on his drag strap. "Stay tight."

And with that, they moved decisively but carefully, clearing corners, junctures, and turning right, then left. Up a flight of concrete steps. They came out in a musty corner surrounded by large wooden crates. Through a stack of three—that easily cleared thirty feet high—he saw rows of tables with materials, lamps, and stools. A large, open middle raced straight up to a lowered, oversized garage door.

"There." Paisley pointed to his nine, where a small door with a window broke up the enormous corrugated steel wall. Vehicles were lined up along with a small grouping of chairs and a makeshift counter and struggling fridge. Lounge area, he guessed. A haze—likely permanent—lingered in the air.

He caught her hand and they started for the door.

Grating and squeaking erupted through the large warehouse-like building.

"Run!" he shouted. But even as he lunged forward, bullets spat at his feet. He skidded to a stop, Paisley crashing into him. As he straightened and she did the same, he pivoted, weapon tucked into his shoulder as they faced the steadily rising door that allowed the flood of light from vehicle headlamps to blind them.

"Thank you for making it easy to get mi reina back."

18

BOLÍVAR, VENEZUELA

THEY HAD BEEN TRAUMATIZED AT HIS HANDS, AND NOW THEY would die at his hands. It seemed poetic.

More like demented.

Paisley looped a finger into Beau's tac vest when he stepped in front of her, his boots planted and shoulders squared. Using his body to shield her.

No, she wasn't dying here. Neither was he.

Lyonel stood flanked by a couple of his guards. Headlights from two vehicles glared at them, turning him into some dark apparition. Like his personality had assumed an ominous physical shape. "Lay down your weapons."

Beau cocked his head. "A little ironic that you call her your queen but treat her like a slave."

Crack!

"Augh!" Beau faltered in front of her, gripping his leg. "Son of a—"

What . . . Paisley felt him jerk to the side even as a crimson stain grew on the back of his left thigh. He was shot! She lunged from behind him. "Are you *insane*?" she spat at Lyonel. "You—"

223

Crack!

She ducked at the report that echoed through the packing house. Cringed, waiting for the explosion of pain . . . that never came.

"That was a warning, mi reina. The next will not be." Lyonel's footfalls bounced off the walls as he marched closer. "Weapons on the ground. Now."

That demeanor and tone . . . Paisley knew exactly what was coming—Lyonel was done playing games and out for blood.

Maybe Beau perceived it, too, because he shoved her back behind him, then unclipped his rifle. Set it down, followed by his handgun. The way he positioned them seemed . . . intentional. "There," he ground out.

Lyonel brandished his weapon as one of the other Guerreros scooped Beau's up. "Hands in the air and down on your knees."

Beau complied, raising his bloodied hands and sinking to the concrete.

"I thought you prided yourself on being reasonable," Paisley said. Trying to get into Lyonel's brain was futile, but she wanted to buy precious minutes to figure out what to do.

"Time for reason is over. You made that so by coming back here . . ." His brows knotted. "Where is the child?"

With the team, thank God, wherever they were. "Far from you."

"You disappoint me, mi reina. This is another reason why I must punish you. You have aroused my boss's anger by hurting his operation. My job is to make you regret it, and I will."

Beau sniffed. "Hope you're not too picky. There ain't much space left on my skin."

Challenge glinted in Lyonel's dark eyes. The smile splitting his face as he pressed the muzzle of his gun to Beau's head made him look like a lunatic. "I am happy with shooting you right now."

"C'mon, Osorio. We both know you won't."

With a sneer, Lyonel tucked the gun into his shoulder holster.

"You are right, of course." He waggled his fingers at one of his guards, who handed him a jagged knife. "You deserve a slow death, and she"—he stabbed the tip at Paisley—"will watch."

Blood rushed in her ears, her gaze stumbling around the warehouse. The morphine made it hard to think straight, made her feel drowsy. She had to do something. Find a weapon. Maybe gasoline to throw at him.

Right, start a fire with yourself trapped in here.

Okay, so no gas. This was the packing house. Bricks of coke sealed, a couple cut open—he'd been testing it?—paper, along with tables and stools. Nothing useful.

Hands behind his head, Beau waggled his fingers. What . . . He jabbed a finger toward the packing table. A signal? *Pointing—* he was pointing at something.

Careful not to be obvious, Paisley glanced to her right. Coke. Cord. Paper . . . What was he trying to tell her?

"Mi reina," Lyonel said, extending a hand. "Come. Now. And I will let him live." His eyes rested on her, almost pleading. When she didn't respond, they darkened. "You know the rules. Follow them, and no one will die."

Paisley swallowed. Yes, she knew the rules. And yes, believed Lyonel would let Beau live if she went with him. He wouldn't, however, let him walk unscathed, but Beau was strong. He'd survive, and then he could go back home with the team and Lyric. Finally be free from the Guerreros' clutches.

So, following the rules . . .

Her gaze dropped to Beau, still kneeling with hands behind his head. Slowly bleeding out, yet so calm. An anchor in the storm of adrenaline and fear raging within her.

And she had an even stronger anchor. *"He stilled the storm to a whisper; the waves of the sea were hushed."*

God was greater than her fears, and following rules wasn't what determined the outcome. *He* did. He was in charge, and nothing that happened was out of His control.

Yes. The only rules she followed from now on were His.

225

"No." Lifting her chin, Paisley met Lyonel's gaze, feeling that peace-infused steel slide into her spine and heart. "I won't come with you. I choose the real man."

Beau chuckled. "Ouch." Again, he pointed to Paisley's right. *What . . .*

Even as she looked, she saw in her peripheral vision that Lyonel threw a signal she was far too familiar with. Instinct flared in a split-second understanding of what Beau had meant—the coke! She grabbed it and pitched it up at the rafters. The low-hung beam hit the brick like a bat. White powder plumed over the area. She ducked, covering her mouth and eyes.

Crack-crack. Crack-crack-crack!

She heard rustling and grunting. Scrambling of feet.

Beau's hand hooked her arm. "C'mon!" He pulled her around. "Run!" He pushed her toward the side door, where light fractured the dark in anemic lines. They burst into the open, coughing, glad for the downpour to wash away the narcotics from their faces.

Beau hauled her through the spacious fenced courtyard toward a parked pickup.

"Stop!" Lyonel's shout vaulted into the air.

Paisley's heart lodged in her ribs even as Beau shoved her ahead of him, again using his own body to shield her.

"Go. Don't stop!" he barked as he whipped back in the direction of Lyonel.

Crack-crack-crack.

Bullets zinged off the truck's grille in front of them.

Paisley flinched. Ducked. Scrambled for cover behind the vehicle.

Heavy footfalls thudded closer.

Why wasn't Beau shooting? She glanced back and— "Beau!"

On the ground, rain pouring over him, he wasn't moving.

"No!"

A hand grabbed her by the hair. Wrenched her around. "Mi reina."

She kicked. Dropped hard to try and free herself, only to have hair ripped from the roots—Lyonel still had a hold. She kicked again, growling. "Let go! No!"

"Look what you did, mi reina," he snarled into her ear, forcing her head in Beau's direction.

Unwilling to look, to see the man she loved dead, she closed her eyes.

A demonic snarl and clapping of teeth erupted. Wet fur blazed along her face, brushing her temple. She felt more than saw the primal attack. Heard the thudding impact of the moment Riot collided with Lyonel. Heard the violent snarl as he thrashed. Heard blood sluicing.

Knowing what was happening, she looked away. Couldn't watch.

Instead, she focused on Beau. "Please." She dropped to her knees. "Beau, please—"

He groaned, straining his next breath. A roar, then he was upright, though pain gouged his rugged features. His weapon swung toward Lyonel. Then slowly lowered. "Riot. Out." He patted his leg, then growled as he clamped his hand over the bullet wound there.

After extricating his teeth from his target, Riot shot to Beau's side. Rain mixed with blood dropped from his muzzle.

With a ghost of a smirk, Beau rubbed the Dutch shepherd's ears. "That's my lethal teddy bear."

Paisley grasped his arm. "I thought you were dead."

"Armor caught it," he said, pained, swiping the rain from his face. "Again. Must've blacked out for a sec." Wincing, he plucked his ball cap out of the mud and donned it. Looked at her, his blue gaze intense. Taking her in.

Warmth curled through her as her thundering, racing heart slowed and adrenaline crashed over her. Mind spiriting through the last few moments, straight back to the most important part— "You came . . ."

"You lived. God does answer prayers, I guess."

With an exultant breath, she pressed her lips to his.

Steps thudded in, and Beau shouldered her aside and snapped up the gun.

"Friendly, friendly!" came Stallion's call. "Gotta move. Chopper inbound. Likely hot."

Anna Mara rushed in and knelt as distant firefights warned of Deke and the others neutralizing the last of the threats. She quickly wound gauze around Beau's leg, then nodded.

Stallion hooked his arm under Beau's and hauled him upright. Together, with Paisley holding Riot's lead, they hustled out of the courtyard to where the rest of the team waited in two pickups.

Jude held open the passenger door of the back one. "Someone order an Uber? This baby is bulletproof."

"Yeah, for food, not a ride," Beau grunted as he climbed in.

The chuckles of the team were suddenly drowned out by a jet-like screech. An army-green helicopter looking like a huge, terrifying insect shot from behind the treetops.

"Get in!" Deke yelled from the driver's seat.

Right before massive bullets peppered the path behind them.

Lead hailed down, piercing the steel fence panels of the courtyard as the Mil Mi-28 "Havoc" thundered overhead. Lyric screamed.

Danger whirled in his seat, relief flooding his system when he saw her, Paisley, and Riot crammed into the back along with Jude, all in one piece. The door that'd just been open was ripped off.

"Stallion, what's your status?" Deke comm'd and gunned it after the other Chevy Colorado.

"Unharmed," Stallion reported. "Maybe I should teach them a thing or two about aiming."

There was no more denying that God was on their side,

because no matter the protection level of the Colorados, if those 30mm armor-piercing rounds had hit them, their bodies would be riddled with gigantic leaks.

"Copy." Deke squinted out the rain-streaked windshield as he followed the others down the dirt road snaking into the jungle. "Look alive."

They reached the tree line, the canopy now shielding them from the attack bird. Somewhat.

Danger stretched out his leg, the bullet wound—a clean through-and-through—burning, the dents in the plate carrier where Osorio's two rounds had hit pressing into his back. Not the first time he'd eaten lead, but never had his armor caught so many shots. Nothing short of a miracle.

Something in the side mirror snagged his attention.

A massive fireball erupted from the compound.

BOOOOM!

The ground rattled and the concussion bucked the truck. They slid sideways, nearly crashing into a tree. Deke jerked the wheel, tires bucking wildly over roots and shrubs, maneuvering the Colorado back onto the road behind the others.

The Havoc zipped overhead, visible through holes in the canopy. It banked.

"Hold on!" Deke yanked the wheel to the right, bullets spitting up dirt where they'd just been. Shredding the trees to their left like paper.

"There's a rocket launcher in the back of our truck," Stallion comm'd. "I'll see if I can hit them."

Deke said nothing for a moment, then, "Copy. Get shot and you got a problem with me."

As the Colorado ahead of them slowed, Stallion hopped out and lunged into the bed. Grinned like an idiot as he kneeled and shouldered the launcher.

"It's coming back around!" Abel's shout came over comms.

A blaze from Stallion's launcher lit the gloominess, and the rocket shot into the air.

BooOOoom!

The canopy far overhead exploded, a fireball blinding them. Wood rained. Screaming from the backseat.

"What was that?" Paisley yelled. She was hunched over Lyric, shielding her, Riot sitting between her feet.

"Stallion hit the other rocket," Danger said, looking for a sign of his buddy.

The sniper emerged in the truck bed, launcher ready.

Just as the canopy gave way to a large clearing, the Havoc came around for a third run. Stallion maintained his position and launched another rocket. It ripped through the rain, leaving a smoke trail in its wake. Hit the bird head on. A bang tore through the air. Fire and sparks flew. The bird tilted, but Stallion wasn't done. He'd already loaded another rocket. Sent it. Hit the tail.

The Havoc whipped into a spiral and vanished from sight. There was no sound of an explosion.

"Everybody okay?" Deke asked as they rumbled along the tree line over the field, and received a chorus of affirmatives.

"There's another one!" Paisley's hand trembled as she pointed at a black helo descending into the clearing.

"That's Raúl," Jude said.

Danger could literally hear Paisley deflate.

They stopped the trucks thirty yards from where Raúl touched down and jumped out. A plume of smoke rose from the position where the Guerreros had gone down. Rotor wash whipped at them as they hoofed it through the tall grass, eyes out for more threats.

And then they lifted off, once again escaping the Guerreros' diabolical claws.

19

ONE WEEK LATER

PEDERNALES FALLS STATE PARK, TEXAS

PAISLEY'S STOMACH TIGHTENED WITH EACH STEP DOWN THE BROAD forest path as she clung to Jordi's urn with one hand, to Beau with the other. Lyric hung on his back like a little monkey. Rachel had Paisley's other side, Riot plodding ahead of them, stopping every once in a while to explore an interesting odor—the natural work of a K-9. The beautiful morning, the singing of birds, and gentle rushing of the Pedernales Falls built a stark contrast to the turmoil inside her. It was finally time to let Jordi go.

"This is it," Rachel said as they reached the rocky river shore. They had chosen a spot where the water was flowing gently enough that they could get in.

Barking his excitement, Riot sloshed into the river only to be recalled by Beau.

"Give us a minute, bud." He rustled her dog's ears, then pointed at Lyric sitting on a rock. "Guard."

Tail wagging, Riot plodded to her, nosed her, then planted his rear by her side. The two were so sweet together, and Paisley was certain that Riot had helped with Lyric's mental recovery from the abduction. He had helped them all, including her.

It'd been a week since they'd returned from Venezuela. She'd left Riot with Khat Khouri for some tending and evaluation after the mission, then collapsed into her bed and slept eighteen hours straight. Even now she still relished the warmth of her bed, the clean and dry clothes, the delicious food, and her lattes. Every now and then, Lyonel popped into her mind. But he was gone. And she was glad he couldn't hurt anyone else. Ever again.

Clutching the urn to her chest, she stripped off her Chucks and socks, then stood at the water's edge and stared into the blue.

"Wanna do it alone?"

She looked up at Beau beside her. "I'd like you both to come." So with Rachel and Beau, she waded out to the middle of the river.

"Do you want me to say something?" Rachel asked.

All Paisley could muster was a nod. Her entire chest burned.

Rachel interlocked her fingers and lifted her chin heavenward. "Dear Father, we thank You for Jordi and the light You made him to be down here on Earth. We know he is in a better place now and gets to embrace Your full love and mercy. Please comfort Paisley with Your healing presence in this challenging time. In Jesus's name, amen."

Silent tears streaked down Paisley's face, and when Beau wrapped his arm around her shoulder, a sob broke free. She took a steadying breath, opened the urn, and released the ashes, just as she released her cousin to the Lord. The ashes danced on the surface as they were carried downstream by the current. *Goodbye, Jordi.*

"Sure hope nobody's swimming down there."

Rachel gasped, then punched Beau in the stomach. "You're so insensitive!"

He doubled over with a grunt the same time a laugh bubbled out of Paisley.

And she couldn't stop. She laughed until the happy tears turned into sad tears and she began sobbing again. Rachel wrapped her into her arms, then Beau took over.

She didn't know how long they'd been standing in the middle of the river, him rocking her gently.

"Look at that," he said, his chest rumbling.

She peeled away and followed his chin-jerk toward the rock. Gasped. Riot had curled up on her Chucks. "Impossible!"

"Not really. Probably smell better than mine."

Paisley laughed. "Probably."

"Hey." He cupped her face.

She found herself caught in Beau's blue gaze. Intense. Roaming over her.

"I love you."

Her heart stuttered. Plunged. Soared. "I love you too."

And then Beau claimed her lips, the world dropping away. He was trust. Home. Family.

An inconceivable joy flooded her, and she poured out her thanks to Jesus. She might still not understand why Jordi had committed suicide, but she saw all the good the Lord had brought out of it. That she lived down the road from Rachel and Lyric. That she had a crazy and wonderful dog like Riot. That Beau, fierce and courageous, protected and loved her. And that her relationship with God was stronger than ever.

She slightly pulled back from Beau. "We tied up my loose ends. Now it's time for yours."

HARMONIA, TEXAS

If knocked down, I will get back up, every time.

The last time Danger had been at his father's grave was ages ago, but the letters were carved into his soul just as they were into the tombstone. He'd never thought he'd appreciate that Mom had insisted on having his grave here instead of at Coronado, where they'd been living when he died. That choice made it easier for him to do this.

He slid a glance over his shoulder. The small cemetery with headstones in all shapes and sizes was empty except for Paisley and Riot, who were in the middle of a rope tug-of-war. Danger couldn't help the grin. Sure was one lucky son of a gun.

Clutching Paisley's dog tag in his cargo pocket, he turned back to his father's grave. Pulled a deep breath and squatted, the healing gunshot wound stretching. Time to make peace with the past. Which he should've done years ago. He cleared his throat. Here went nothing. "If knocked down," he said quietly, "I will get back up." He nodded. "Every time."

When he fist-bumped the slick, cool headstone, he felt a part of the weight he'd been carrying around for years suddenly drop. Running a hand down his neck, he lifted his gaze to the crisp blue sky. Here he was, back on his feet—thanks to God.

The past few days, Danger had found himself cracking open Dad's old Bible over and over. He'd discovered a verse in Proverbs that'd been seared into his brain: *Do not say, "I'll pay you back for this wrong!" Wait for the Lord, and he will avenge you.*

Osorio's death hadn't brought the satisfaction he'd expected. Maybe because he knew Querales would simply replace him with another lunatic. But Danger now understood that it wasn't revenge that brought peace, but knowing that, one day, the Lord would deliver justice.

It was time to let the past go, including forcing his way back into the spec-ops world. If God had a mission for him, he wouldn't say no. Until then, he'd enjoy life with the woman he loved and her annoying four-legged sidekick.

Throwing one last glance at Dad's grave, Danger rose and strolled over to them. It still felt surreal to have them both in his life, as if he were living one of those corny fairy tales Lyric always wanted him to read to her.

"Are you ready?"

Not really, but he had no choice. "Let's get it over with."

Half an hour later, he parked his Tacoma in front of Hank's mansion and killed the engine. Strangled the steering wheel.

A warm hand rested on his lower arm. Squeezed. "You can do this." Paisley smiled, the shiner on her left cheek now yellow.

He appreciated that encouraging smile. Wondered where he'd be if it weren't for her. "Okay."

They got out of his Tacoma, let Riot out, and made their way to the backyard over the manicured lawn.

"Uncle Danger!" Lyric hopped up from the chair she'd been sitting on by the pool and came racing toward them.

"Princess." Danger caught her mid-lunge. When he tossed her over his shoulder, she squealed, and man, he loved that sound.

"I missed you," Lyric whispered as he started carrying her to where his family had gathered around a bar-height table.

"You know what? I missed you too," Danger whispered back. Didn't matter that they'd just seen each other this morning.

Lyric giggled, and Danger couldn't stop thanking God that, after everything she'd gone through, she was back to her old self. She squirmed in his arms. "Auntie Paisley."

He passed her over to Paisley, whose face glowed as she wrapped Lyric into a tight hug.

"I brought Kala with me," Lyric said, holding up the monkey.

Riot's eyes snapped to it, and he licked his chops.

"No, Riot." Paisley's command was firm, and the Dutchie folded his ears, tail wagging.

The two were really starting to mesh.

"Lyric takes Kala everywhere we go," Rachel said as she strolled up to them, Mick flanking her. His buddy apparently hadn't left her side since Lyric went missing. Had to talk to him about that later.

First, he had to take care of business. He excused himself, quickly kissed Mom on the cheek, then walked up to his stepfather, who was conversing with Collin at the pool bar. Danger gave his brother a look, and Collin retreated.

"What's so important that you have to disrupt my peace?" Hank grabbed a bourbon bottle and poured a glass. "Want one?"

Low blow. The guy was well aware of his addiction.

Past addiction, though he knew they said "once an addict, always an addict." Still, he had no desire to go on a bender. Even going to a bar with the tribe hadn't fazed him.

The only reason he'd accept the tumbler was to crack it over Hank's skull. Chances were, a month ago he would've done exactly that. But the past few nights he'd spent on his knees were paying off—he was slowly regaining self-control.

Yeah, God *was* with him, had his six, even when it didn't feel like it.

Danger sniffed. "I'm good."

Hank took a sip, then held his drink against the setting sun as if inspecting the clarity of the amber liquid. "Shame. This is a single-barrel, seventeen-year-old . . ."

His voice drifted into the background as Danger slid his focus to his family talking and laughing, Paisley and Riot with them. The two fit in like they'd always been a part of the Maddox clan. A sliver of warmth spread through his chest. He could see what God had done there. That bond he'd once shared with Dad, then with the Teams, God had returned to him. Now his new tribe was Paisley and Riot. And ABA.

"I forgive you, Hank. For all of it." The words hadn't come easily, but Danger looked his stepfather square in the eye. "Now I'd appreciate it if we could move on, for Mom's sake. She's the one suffering the consequences." He pulled his hand out of his pocket and extended it to Hank.

His stepfather squinted at it. Then he threw his head back and guffawed.

When he didn't make a move to accept the olive branch,

Danger nodded. "In case you change your mind, you know where to find me." With that, he returned to his family.

Paisley, ever attuned to him, skated him a wary look. "How did it go?" she asked quietly once he'd reached them.

He drew her away from the others for some privacy. "I did my part."

"I'm proud of you," she said, smiling.

Danger wrapped an arm around her and leaned in. Kissed her, and she kissed him back with the same fire that burned inside him. He pulled her closer, savoring her taste and the feeling of her body molded against his. Man, he didn't know how much longer he could leave it at those kisses. Had to get married soon, because—

Deafening barking had Paisley breaking away from him with a gasp.

Scratch getting married. Having a mutt who constantly needed attention worked better.

"Ignore him." Danger claimed Paisley's mouth again. Dove back into that place of heat and—

Claws dug into his outer thigh and arm. Warm breath in his face, then a full-on lick over the side of his face. And it wasn't from Paisley. Whose beautiful laughter lifted into the humid evening air.

Danger did his best to hold his glower and turned to Riot. "You'll never learn what a wingman is, will you?"

The Dutchie gave off a bark, his tail rotating so hard he was about to go airborne any moment.

"Don't give me that innocent Bambi look."

Paisley giggled as she bent and buried her fingers into that beautiful brindle coat Danger was about to pull over the mutt's ears. "Don't worry, boy," she said. "You're still my number one."

Yeah, that's what Danger feared. He already saw them married, in bed one night with Riot wedged between them. But frankly? He was cool with that. The Dutchie was one of the greatest blessings God had given him.

"Riot, wait!"

The Dutchie ignored Paisley and darted over the lawn up to the barbecue area, where Hank was grilling steaks. Before the old man could even react, Riot had snatched the two biggest pieces and bolted off under a hail of curses.

Danger grinned to himself.

See? Greatest blessing.

EPILOGUE

TEXAS HILL COUNTRY

The A Breed Apart kennels were some of the finest in the country. The concrete runs had shielded "homes" that allowed the dogs inside air-conditioned areas but also afforded them a length of fenced-in space for romping around. The long bay down the middle of the facility allowed the staff to check in and retrieve dogs without bothering others.

"Better by a mile than what you'd find at the local humane society," Crew Gatlin said as he opened the chain-linked gate, pitched a KONG into the inner section, and unclipped the lead from Riot—who glanced at Paisley and Danger, then snapped back to his favorite toy. "Get it!"

Riot vaulted into the kennel, and Crew secured the gate.

"He'll . . . be okay?" Paisley asked.

Crew hooked his hands into his armpits. "It's nice to be sentimental—he's special to you. But he's a working dog, and they're happiest working. And he doesn't have to stay here all

239

the time. Give us time to do some counter-conditioning for his negative behavior, then he could spend the weekends with you." He shrugged. "Some dogs need the structure. Others are okay without it."

"Thank you." Paisley smiled, then scrunched her nose as she looked at Riot trotting up and down the outer kennel.

Crew cocked his head. "Look at that. Already flirting with Trinity. Don't tell Ghost." He nodded, then walked them out. "You have my number. And I'll send you texts. Let you know how he's doing."

"Again, thank you." Outside, she turned to Danger, hazel eyes glistening.

Danger tugged her close. "You did the right thing."

Her arms came around his waist, and she pillowed her head on his chest. "I know. It's just so . . . hard."

"It's not a goodbye." Crew paused and considered her. "It's a 'thanks for letting me keep working so I don't get bored and eat the interior of someone else's vehicle.'"

A jolt went through Paisley, and Danger thought she was crying until he heard her quiet chuckle.

Crew sloughed his hands together. "Time for barbecue."

They made their way down to a place on the ranch called The Watering Hole. There the staff and handlers of A Breed Apart were gathered for an evening of relaxation—good food, swimming, and conversation. After a hot late-summer day, this was the perfect team-building event.

Carved into limestone, the swimming hole offered the perfect opportunity for cliff diving. The sun hung low in the pristine sky, casting its last rays onto the blue water and scatter of greenery surrounding it. There was a guy Danger didn't recognize. A new handler? Whoever he was, definitely the no-nonsense type—tall and ball cap pulled deep over his eyes.

While the ladies spread blankets on the flat rocks at the water's edge, the guys hauled the coolers and food down. Sweat poured down Danger's chest and back. Couldn't wait to dive into that inviting blue. But first had to take care of something else.

He found Paisley getting the paper plates arranged and grabbed her hand. "Ready?" When she nodded, he emitted a whistle, causing everyone to stop what they were doing. "Ladies and gents, we have an announcement to make."

"About time you guys tied the knot," Crew hollered.

"Where's the ring?" Timbrel asked. "Needs to make her hand heavy to hold up."

Paisley jerked her head up to Danger, a question mark etched into her face.

Huffing, Danger shot Crew a look. "That's not—we're not." He roughed a hand down his nape. Couldn't miss how Paisley started. Apparently that's what she'd hoped too.

Made him feel like a jerk . . . Well, it might've if he didn't already have an ace up his sleeve.

He cleared his throat. Jerked his chin at Paisley. "Go on."

Paisley took their friends in. "I'm not sure why he said it that way, but I've got a full-time job in Austin working with trauma victims. In light of that, I've decided to transfer ownership of Riot over to A Breed Apart. It's best for him—he wants and needs to work. Hard for me. I want him with me. But he's what's important."

The team whooped and clapped.

"So, no wedding plans?" Foxtrot—Vienna Foxcroft—asked.

A rare smirk built on Ghost's face. "Am I the only one who thinks he deserves a dunking for that?"

Before Danger could react, the guys wrestled him to the ground, grabbed him by the hands and feet and hauled him up the nearest cliff. Swung him back and forth. "One . . . two . . . three!"

Gravity took over and Danger sailed six feet into the air, then sixteen down. Tried to rotate to avoid a painful landing and narrowly sliced his hands into the water first. It still smacked. A hollow thud punched the oxygen from his lungs.

When he surfaced, the guys at the top of the cliff were laughing their heads off.

Danger smirked. It was a privilege to call these boneheads his new tribe. And Ghost was right—he probably deserved this for stringing Paisley along.

That was about to change.

He swam over and climbed out of the water. Peeled off the soggy T-shirt and sneakers. Figured people were staring, but what could he do? They were there. Couldn't change it.

Shouts came from Foxtrot and Crew, wrestling each other near the lake's edge.

"Give me my leg back," Crew ground out, his gaze flickering over the watching crowd, then back to his fiancée.

Danger knew where the guy was coming from. "Gatlin."

Huffing, Crew turned. "*What?*"

"Good thing you got an inflated ego, or I'd be worried you'd drown."

"You're just jealous of *all this*." Crew puffed his chest and motioned up and down himself. "And for the record—I don't take advice from a guy who can't own his mistakes."

Even as a grin ripped across Danger's face, God reminded him of that one pressing matter. He growled inwardly. Would rather join that sewing circle than crawl to his boss.

Sucked to be him, since he'd promised the Lord to play His game from now on.

Fine. He angled over to Ghost. Time to take ownership. "Got a sec?"

When his boss nodded, he moved out of earshot. "What's up?"

Down at the water, Foxtrot held Crew's titanium leg out of his reach, blocking him with her rear. "You want it? Come get it."

Savage.

Running a hand behind his neck, Danger squeezed his aching muscles. "I'm ready to, uh . . . talk." There. He said it.

Ghost tucked his hands into his armpits and considered Danger. "You asking me for help, Maddox?"

Way to make a guy beg. He squinted at the team, then to the ground under his feet. "Guess I hit rock bottom."

Somehow, Crew had gotten his leg back and set it down. Instead of straightening, he wrapped his log-like arms around Foxtrot's waist and vaulted them both into the water. The tribe laughed.

"Took you long enough." Ghost grinned, then sobered. "Whatever you need—we're here for you, man."

Danger cleared his throat. "Appreciate it." He scanned the water and found Paisley lounging in an inflatable chair, chatting with Rio and Darci. She looked good in that white one-piece. Too good. He wrenched his gaze from her. "We still good on the weekend?"

Ghost nodded. "Absolutely."

That was all Danger needed. "Thanks, man." He broke into a sprint and dove off the fifteen-foot cliff into the water. Stayed close to the bottom until he could make out Paisley's floatie above him. When he brushed one of her feet, she pulled both legs up. He pictured her frantically looking into the water.

Placing his hands under the seat, he pushed. The thing flipped, and Paisley joined him in the water. Thrashed. He grabbed her and pulled her to the surface.

"You!" she sputtered, her eyes wide, then she laughed.

Smirking, Danger found purchase on a rock and drew her against him. Felt her slick skin on his. "Do you wanna get married?"

"What?" Paisley went limp in his arms. "Are you saying . . ."

Danger cocked a brow. Challenged her.

"Of course I do," she whispered. "Yes!" Her arms looped his neck.

"Then let's get married this weekend," Danger murmured into her ear, his mouth suddenly as dry as the Afghan desert. "Hit the municipal courthouse. Hightail it to the Ozarks, where a buddy of mine has a cabin. Just you, me, and Riot. We'll be back in time so you can start your new job on Monday."

Paisley leaned back. Blinked at him out of those huge hazel eyes. "You mean *elope*? The day after tomorrow?" The last words emerged in a squeak.

"That's exactly what I mean." He lowered his lips to that dip in her neck he couldn't stay away from. "Been praying about this for a while." He kissed her wet skin. "Answer's always the same. Whenever you're ready."

She threw her head back, laughing. "You're just impatient, admit it."

"Busted." With a growl, he buried his nose in her neck. Earned a squeaked laugh. After planting another kiss, he straightened and looked her square in the eye. "I'm serious about what I heard from God." Had spent night after night on his knees, asking the Lord for permission.

Paisley's face radiated like the sun melting into the horizon behind her. "I've been hearing the same thing."

"That a yes?"

She nodded. Pressed her lips together, her eyelids fluttering. Kept nodding. "Rachel will kill us."

"Only after we're back." About to lose it, Danger leaned down and captured her perfect lips. Poured everything he had into that one kiss while thanking the Lord for his future wife, a crazy dog, and his new tribe—who commented on their act with catcalls and whooping. He raised a fist heavenward, broke off, and shouted, "She said yes!"

Thank you for reading *Riot*! Gear up for the next A Breed Apart: Legacy thriller, *Fury* by Ronie Kendig and Steffani Webb, releasing this Summer. Turn the page for a sneak peek!

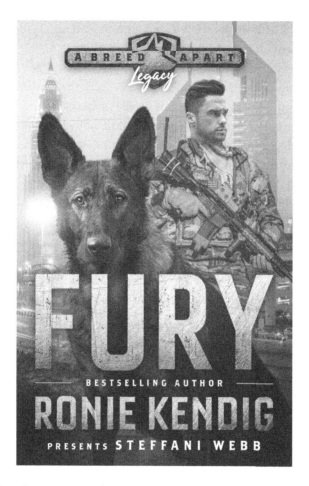

Amidst the glittering heat of Abu Dhabi, Hollyn Reinhardt's world shatters in one tragic night. Once a child prodigy, now a leading AI scientist, she's left reeling from her parents' sudden death—and the haunting suspicion that it was no accident. Vulnerable yet defiant, Hollyn must protect her life's work from unseen enemies.

Enter Davis Ledger: former Green Beret, owner of a keen-nosed military working dog named Fury, and the slightly older man whose rugged charm once captured Hollyn's young heart. Medically discharged and disillusioned, he's ready for peace in the US, but walks back into the line of fire when he discovers his friends have been murdered and that their daughter Hollyn—now all grown up—needs his help.

Following an attempt on her life, Hollyn realizes the USB containing her code has been stolen. Code that, in the wrong hands, could kill thousands. But Davis's sable German shepherd, who has been specially trained to sniff out electronics, is the perfect dog to ensure this doesn't end in disaster. They have no choice but to join up with a black ops group to protect Hollyn and hunt down the tech.

As they're pursued by killers, Hollyn struggles to douse her reigniting crush, while Davis finds it harder and harder to deny his feelings and stay mission-focused. With the clock ticking down to an unthinkable catastrophe, Hollyn and Davis face the ultimate test. Can they thwart the threat and reclaim the code, or will their second chance at love end in heartbreak—or worse . . . disaster?

A masterful blend of breathless suspense and heart-stopping romance, this tale of danger, devotion, and rekindled love will have you at the edge of your seat.

FURY | A BREED APART: LEGACY, BOOK 4
PROLOGUE

UNDISCLOSED LOCATION, AFGHANISTAN

Drool ran down the back of his hand.

"Knock it off, you goon," Davis Ledger muttered to his military working dog. He swiped at the liquid. Shifted his prone position on the rocky ground so he wasn't in the slobber LZ. "Down," he commanded the sable German shepherd.

Panting, Fury conceded, lowering his muscular frame. Like the wretch he was, he licked Davis's cheek, hot breath puffing against Davis's skin.

When the wet snout hit his ear, Davis jerked his head away. It reminded him of the wet willies his childhood best friend used to give him. He'd hated it then. Hated it now.

Fury yawned, clearly happy with himself, as suppressed chuckles from the rest of the nearby team filtered over. Davis shot a glare at his partner through the dusk slowly seeping into darkness. Resumed his patient watch of the mud-brown area below.

The compound was tucked between the craggy hills that were surrounded by parched, cracked dirt. Dust, dust, and more dust. That's all this part of the region was. A cluster of guards relaxed by the faded blue gate, smoking, AKs slung over their shoulders. Davis could have sworn the same company made the security gates for every Third World country he'd been to. They all looked the same. But it also meant they were familiar and easy to breach when you'd done it a few dozen times.

"Trouble in paradise, honey?" His friend Luke Ross razzed him. They'd been buddies ever since clawing their way through Basic. The guy was solid as they came but never missed a chance to joke around. Even from a few feet away, Luke's bright white smile was visible. It'd earned him the name Pearly.

"That's all he's got," team leader, Shaw, chimed in.

"Yeah, but what a way to go." Luke again. The inflection in his tone drew another round of quiet chuckles. "When's the last time you took a girl out? Second grade?"

Davis shook his head. Not everyone found the love of their life on the first day of school like Luke and his wife Jana. Davis admired their relationship. It resembled only one other that he'd seen. They were more devoted to each other than any of the relationship examples his mom had shown him growing up. Gave him hope that someday he might find the same thing.

Thought he'd found it once. He'd been wrong.

Least, that's what he told himself.

Wind started picking up, and Davis heard Luke's MWD, Reza, shift in her down position. She and Fury were two of the best electronic detection dogs in the military. They could find a mini USB in a sandstorm. Which was why they were both on the mission to acquire a USB drive with missile codes that intel claimed some fool had decided to sell to a warlord with ties to Al-Qaeda. Namely, the warlord camped out in the compound below.

Fury held up a giant paw. Swung it in the air in Reza's direction. She ignored him completely.

"Hey," Davis whispered loudly to his partner. "Pull yourself together. No flirting on missions."

Luke smirked at Reza. "Tell him he can flirt all he wants." He ran a hand down the Malinois's neck. "It'll just prove how much more dedicated you are to the job when you find the USB first because lover boy can't see straight."

"Yeah, we'll see who finds it."

"Loser buys?" Luke held out a fist.

"You're on." Davis leaned over and tapped his gloved hand to his friend's.

"VT6. Seller approaching the compound," came the gravelly voice of their team sniper, Rafkin, who was perched uphill, farther behind the team. Ten yards to their left, Zaid and Niles were set up and waiting for the signal to move in.

Fatigue poking his neck from the prone position he'd been in, Davis narrowed his eyes at the faint dust trail marking the progress of a small approaching convoy. The quasi-uniformed guards at the gate straightened their caps and unlatched the main gate. Swung it wide as three meticulous HiLuxes pulled into the courtyard.

"Buyer's coming out to meet him." Rafkin's calm voice could've been announcing sports scores. "Identity confirmed. It's Hardy."

After shifting his scope to the middle truck in the convoy, Davis watched a man in a suit step out of the vehicle, leather briefcase in hand.

"Confirmed seller onsite. Laurel." Rafkin again.

"Cleared to engage," came the order from VT6.

Shaw's voice nearly stepped on Command's transmission. "Lock and load."

With a flick of his right thumb, Davis rotated the selector switch on his M4 from SAFE to SEMI.

Just outside the front door of the main compound building, Laurel and Hardy—the code names for the warlord and seller—greeted each other. The lead truck in the convoy crept ahead a few feet before stopping again.

Rafkin growled over the comms. "No joy," he hissed.

Laurel and Hardy disappeared inside with five personal

security as gate guards returned to their posts—and two lit cigarettes. Clearly not expecting trouble.

Happy to disappoint, gents.

Davis glanced sideways at Fury.

The lug met him eye to eye, eager for the signal to work.

Time dragged by as they waited for Shaw to make the call. The hills around them turned purple-gray and finally disappeared into the night.

Still, they waited. It was above Davis's pay grade to know the ins and outs of why. All he and Fury were there for was to ensure mission success.

Compound lights winked out.

"Go, go, go." Shaw's voice broke the extended quiet.

Sliding backward to avoid silhouetting himself above the horizon, Davis pushed off the dirt and trekked stealthily toward the compound. Fury padded at his side, his NVGs breaking up the moonlit outline of his head. Davis paused at the expanse between the hills and building. Crouched, M4 tucked to his shoulder, he hid behind a cluster of scrub bushes ten yards from the gate to his right. Grasped Fury's harness. He didn't need to look around to know the rest of his team had moved into position as well.

Crack!

The sound from Rafkin's sniper rifle rippled through the night a few seconds after the bullet's impact threw one of the guards back. Davis took out the second gate guard even as the guy's startled companions brought up their weapons, looking around.

Crack! Crack!

Stalking forward, Shaw and Niles took out the remaining guards.

"Gate clear!" Luke shouted.

"Moving." Davis crouch-ran for the gate. "Fury, let's go." The green cast from his NVGs gave him a haphazard line of sight as he hustled forward. Slipped past the iron entry, attention trained on his highly skilled MWD. Over fifty-thousand dollars had gone into training this four-legged warrior, and Davis had learned to trust the dog.

Fury slightly ahead and sniffing, Davis also depended on the team to do their jobs, which allowed the MWD handlers to focus on the dogs. Luke and Reza swept the left side of the area.

Gaze locked down the barrel of his weapon, Davis continued his visual sweep along the left wall. The courtyard was empty from what he could see. Tail up, Fury continued to seek. Didn't alert to the presence of any explosives. Guess they wouldn't be blown to kingdom come just yet.

Skirting around the north edge, they came up to the front door. Luke gave him a thumbs-up.

"Courtyard clear," Davis affirmed.

Like water through a sieve, the team filtered past the iron entrance.

The first level of the building still sat dark and quiet in the ominous night. "Fury, *fuss*." Suspicious, nerves buzzing, he waited, weapon trained on the metal door the warlord and buyer had disappeared behind hours earlier.

No response fire greeted them. He hustled back a few steps with Fury to take cover as Niles picked the lock. Luke and Reza stood ready opposite him. They'd search for the USB containing missile codes after he and Fury cleared the rooms for any explosives. Reza wasn't cross-trained for that.

Fury jerked like he was trying to go behind Davis. "Easy," he hissed in a whisper, firmly gripping the handle on the dog's tac vest. Fury always got amped up before a search. His one downfall. "Stay."

The MWD whined but complied.

"On your six." His squad leader's low words over the comms warned him before the man melted from the shadows, M4 at the ready.

Niles shoved the unlocked door open, and Shaw breached first, quickly dispatching two tangos with brutal efficiency. The house was silent as Davis slipped inside, pulse thrumming, eyes out.

"Fury, seek-seek!" Muscles tense, finger against the trigger well, Davis stalked forward with his MWD into the combined dining and lounge area.

No alerts, nothing out of the ordinary. Various other rooms, all clear. No bedrooms on the lower level.

Clicking his tongue, Davis drew Fury toward the stairs. M4 firmed, he carefully ascended the rickety steps. Sweat trickled down his back under his personal protective equipment as he continued, breathing a sigh of relief when Fury reached the top, glanced around without alerting. Shadows hung on every inch of the walls, the air heavy with the stagnant smell of body odor and old smoke. But he saw no one through his NVGs.

Luke and Reza reached the landing. "Go, go."

He moved forward.

The door to the first bedroom hung slightly ajar. Davis reached for it. Shoved it open with the muzzle of his M4. Glanced around the room. Faint moonlight fell through the window onto a man lying in bed. His frame was similar to the seller Rafkin had ID'd earlier. Fury trotted over to the bed and sniffed.

Tense for a reaction, Davis eased closer for a better look, M4 trained on the guy. Something felt off.

Adrenaline spiked. He closed the gap. Saw blank eyes staring up. Mouth agape. Davis shoved the muzzle of his weapon against the guy's sternum a couple times. No response. Davis keyed his mic. "Laurel's dead," he said tersely. His gaze stalled on an open plastic container—empty—on the nightstand. "Looks like they didn't trust the guy." He indicated to the table. "Fury, seek."

The sable GSD glided from his side, searching the room quickly. Efficiently.

Luke and Reza entered and went to work. The Malinois sniffed swiftly back and forth, snout tracking.

Davis felt his adrenaline ratchet another notch as he watched. Waited. The MWD made her way across the room. Thrust her sensitive nose into every corner and crevice.

Nothing.

Fury growled softly, shoving past them back into the hallway.

Taking the cue, Davis followed, weapon up, expecting trouble. Saw that sable tail vanish into a second room. Checked it. Still nothing except a bleary-eyed man, who stumbled and brandished a weapon.

Davis neutralized the threat as Reza and Fury headed to the last bedroom, single-minded in their efforts. Under the empty bed. In the wardrobe. Around the nightstand. Frustration coiled and he keyed his mic at—again—coming up short. "Target and buyer rabbited." Made sure his tone didn't betray the irritation they all felt. "Likely together. Don't let him leave the compound."

The team copied.

"Movement at the front," Rafkin's voice warned from his nest on the hill.

Davis bit back a curse.

Fury was still sniffing around. Intensity in the GSD's body language ramped up. He was lead team. Should be the one heading outside first, but if he had something…

Davis turned to Luke. "I'll finish here. Go."

Luke nodded. Double-patted his leg, recalling Reza, and they raced down the stairs.

Fury turned to Davis. Wagged his tail. False alarm. "Let's go."

They retraced their steps to the lower level. Hustled to the front.

"Nonlethal measures!" Shaw growled into the comms. "We need him to talk."

Crack! Crack!

Gunfire outside snatched Davis's attention as his boot hit the bottom step. He booked it to the front door. Paused to clear it before hurrying into the courtyard. Saw Luke engaging Hardy, who seemed to be impervious to the bullets flying at him. Davis drew down on the warlord. Hit his leg and the guy pitched forward. Tumbled. Came up running toward the parked convoy.

Luke slipped the lead off of Reza. "Get him!"

Through the green oculars, Davis watched the Mal charge off with Luke close behind. Hardy lifted a fist near the truck he was closing in on.

What was he holding?

Whoosh!

Even as the fireball erupted, Davis felt himself punched backward amid the bright flash that lit the night. His NVGs were shoved out of place. Black spots dotted his vision.

Boom!

Vibration from the blast shook around him before he collided with a plaster wall. Hot pain tore through his shoulder despite his PPE. He bounced against the ground. Rolled. Came to a stop face up. He opened his mouth. Gasped for air.

His lungs refused the request.

He tried again. Oxygen rushed in, thick with gasoline and smoke from the fully engulfed HiLux. Coughing, gagging, ears ringing, head bombarded by warbled voices he couldn't place, Davis scrambled but got nowhere. Blinked through the haze. Where was Fury? He couldn't move. Was pinned to the ground. By what? His shoulder screamed at him, and he felt like a truck was lodged in his ribs.

Gingerly, Davis looked down the length of his body. Spotted jagged metal sticking out of his side. It'd managed to lodge itself between the cracks of his PPE. That was gonna leave a mark.

He groaned. Choked on another wave of pain dragging him toward unconsciousness.

Gotta stay awake. Get Fury.

Wait. Fury. Where was he?

Davis looked around, not caring about the pain it caused.

Ears still ringing, he saw flames from the truck coiling and twisting upward. They snapped at the night sky. Then he saw.

Fury. Lying a few yards away.

"Fur—" He coughed—which sent shards of pain through his chest. "Fury!" His diaphragm seized, and fear clutched his chest. Squeezed tight as he strained through the dust and smoke hanging in the air.

The big lug wasn't moving. Davis twisted to look over his shoulder. Call for help. Nausea rose in his throat.

Luke. Or what was left of him.

Davis cursed.

In the light from the fire, he saw his friend's body lying in a heap, cut nearly in half by a chunk of the pickup, eyes open and unseeing. Reza, a few feet beyond her handler. She was—

Davis retched.

No, no.

A guttural half yell spilled from him. He tried to scoot closer. Tried to get to his friend, but the metal in his side held him fast. Pain had him seeing black spots. The contents of his stomach nearly made another appearance.

"Luke!" The yell vibrated in his chest. His head.

"Ledger. Keep still." Shaw appeared. Dropped at his side, combat lifesaver kit open. "Pearly's gone." He shook his head and went to work on Davis. He activated the quick-releases on Davis's vest, then carefully ran his fingers around the edges before checking for a clear airway and moving on to extremities. Expression hard, Shaw finally began packing field dressings around the metal object projecting from Davis's side.

Pain ripped through him.

"Reza..." Davis could feel himself teetering on the edge of blacking out.

Shaw shook his head somberly. "Medevac is three mikes out."

What had he done? Had Hardy been outside the whole time?

Was that what Fury'd been trying to tell him before they entered the home?

Luke. He'd gotten his friend killed. Should have been him out the door first.

"Whoa! Fury, out!"

Davis blinked. Looked for the source of the shout. Fury was up—*alive!*—and trotting around the truck. Looking. Searching. For Davis? For his furry friend? He wouldn't be working any more missions with her. The landshark snapped at Niles, who jumped back, gripping his rifle.

"Quit, man!" Niles screeched.

"Fury, here!" Davis gruffed, the pain excruciating at the effort of calling his dog off.

The GSD's large head whipped in his direction and he charged. Shaw leaned back slightly as Fury came in hot. The lug's wet tongue was all over Davis's face the second he got close. He dug his fingers in his dog's hairy coat.

"Hey, buddy." He chuckled, distracted for a split second from the agony. "You okay, then? Just wanted to give me a heart attack?" He did his best not to look at Luke's body. Tried not to think about Jana and the notification she'd be getting.

The sable German shepherd lay down beside him and set his head on Davis's good shoulder.

The *thwump-thwump-thwump* of chopper blades whirling in the sky preceded the CH-47 Chinook that soon hovered over the compound. Dust swirled around as it lowered.

As combat medics raced over with a stretcher, Davis felt his head swimming. His side and shoulder were on fire. His hearing was hollow. Vision graying…

"Boss…" His words were lost in the thunderous sound of the helo.

Shaw turned just as Davis felt his body go slack.

We hope you loved the action, adventure, and romance in this riveting story. Discover more exciting romantic suspense from Sunrise Publishing!

A soldier, a Malinois, and a stuntwoman walk onto a TV set . . .

Former Special Forces operator Sergeant Crew Gatlin takes everything in stride, even the career-ending incident that separated him from the Army, half a leg, and his beloved working dog, Havoc K027. Putting his life back together and lying low, he takes a job with A Breed Apart and is unexpectedly reunited with Havoc. It's too good to be true—and the proof is in their first assignment: to work as a K-9 team for a television drama in Los Angeles. Miffed at being relegated to TV fodder, he's willing to pay the price when he sees the stuntwoman.

Being a stunt double allows Vienna Foxcroft to fulfill her acting dream—with a side of MMA—and stay out of the limelight. The same one that plagued her childhood and put her through a nightmare scenario. Now, her tight-knit stunt team are the only ones she trusts. Then in walks Mr. Mountain-of-Muscle and his tough-as-nails dog, and Vienna has a bad feeling her life is about to turn upside down.

Ticked as they head overseas for a location shoot in Turkey, Crew guts it up—after all, he has Havoc again. Okay, and yeah—Vienna is going, too. When an attack sends the cast fleeing into the streets of Turkey, Vienna must face the demons of her past or be devoured by them. And Crew and Havoc are tested like never before.

Experience the high-octane thrill ride that is the first book in the A Breed Apart: Legacy series.

Buckle up for an edge-of-your-seat trek through the dangerous jungles of the Philippines in this enemies to more, forced proximity, alpha hero, sunshine versus grumpy romantic thriller!

When Rio Silva is told her aunt and uncle are missing in a Philippine rainforest, she knows there is only one way to find them: the retired military working dog her dad entrusted to her. Chaos, however, has a mind of her own. A lot like Rio. Worse, they'll have to trust arrogant, demanding former Army Ranger Cathal McGowan if she hopes to get them back.

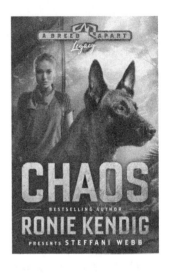

The last thing Cathal McGowan wants as he heads into the darkness of the rainforest is to be shackled with a young, pretty teacher who has no tactical experience. But she has heart—he'll give her that. And he has the expertise necessary to rescue her family.

Putting everything on the line, Rio and Cathal struggle to navigate the terrain, as well as their emerging feelings for each other. But the closer they get to mission success, the more things aren't adding up, including who might be behind the disappearances. It's not long before they realize the rainforest holds greater perils than deadly vipers . . . and the biggest danger of all might be to their hearts.

Dive into another thrilling A Breed Apart: Legacy adventure!

GET READY . . . THINGS ARE ABOUT TO GET HOT!

With heart-pounding excitement, gripping suspense, and sizzling (but clean!) romance, the CHASING FIRE: MONTANA series, brought to you by the incredible authors of Sunrise Publishing, including the dynamic duo of bestselling authors Susan May Warren and Lisa Phillips, is your epic summer binge read.

Immerse yourself in a world of short, captivating novels that are designed to be devoured in one sitting. Each book is a standalone masterpiece, (no story cliffhangers!) although you'll be craving the next one in the series!

Follow the Montana Hotshots and Smokejumpers as they chase a wildfire through northwest Montana. The pages ignite with clean romance and high-stakes danger—these heroes (and heroines!) will capture your heart. The biggest question is...who will be your summer book boyfriend?

FIND THEM ALL AT SUNRISE PUBLISHING!

CONNECT WITH SUNRISE

Thank you again for reading *RIOT*. We hope you enjoyed the story. If you did, would you be willing to do us a favor and leave a review? It doesn't have to be long—just a few words to help other readers know what they're getting. (But no spoilers! We don't want to wreck the fun!) Thank you again for reading!

We'd love to hear from you—not only about this story, but about any characters or stories you'd like to read in the future. Contact us at www.sunrisepublishing.com/contact.

We also have a monthly update that contains sneak peeks, reviews, upcoming releases, and fun stuff for our reader friends. Sign up at www.sunrisepublishing.com or scan our QR code.

ACKNOWLEDGMENTS

First of all, thank you. Yes, you holding this book. An author is nothing without his readers. I pray RIOT was more than just entertainment for you—an encouragement for your walk with God.

Susie and Lindsay—thank you for giving me this incredible opportunity and for letting me extend the deadlines a hundred times. Rel, Sarah and Essie—you guys put so much work in no one sees. The Lord does. Bethany, your funny comments made editing a blast.

My writing buddies Steff, Voni and Katie. It's been so much fun. Season 6 rocks!

Ben—you and your stupid prophetic dreams. This is all your fault. Love you, bro.

Steven, mentioning you is kinda a waste of space, but I have a promise to redeem. Thanks for keeping my banter sharp :D.

A huge mahalo to Teju, Miranda, Taz and Ewi, and everyone who cheered me on and prayed for me.

Robert—thank you for letting me glimpse the mind of a former combat medic and lieutenant colonel. You inspired me to write Deke.

The guys at STA. Thanks for answering my questions regarding all things ballistics. Still hoping that one day I'll be strong enough again to stop by your shooting range.

RONIE! Sheesh, your patience with me . . . lol. What you taught me went beyond writing—it deeply impacted my life. When I thought I have to throw in the towel, you showed up like a superhero. THANK YOU for all the blood, sweat and tears you put into RIOT, from the plot to the writing to the cover . . . I couldn't have pulled it off without you.

Micc. You've encouraged me, listened to my rants, made me laugh, and prayed for me more often than I can count. Even as an author, I can't put into words what your support, what you, mean to me. You're my warrior angel. Ha di liäb.

Last and most important—Jesus. I wish the world could've seen the miracles You worked while I penned this story. The energy and grit You gave me to keep going when pain and fatigue hit surpasses my understanding. I pray You use this work to draw one or the other soul closer to You. Now I'm ready for the next adventure.

ABOUT THE AUTHORS

Ronie Kendig is a bestselling, award-winning author of over thirty-five books. She grew up an Army brat, and now she and her Army-veteran husband have returned to their beloved Texas after a ten-year stint in the Northeast. They survive on Sonic runs, barbecue, and peach cobbler that they share—sometimes—with Benning the Stealth Golden and AAndromeda the MWD Washout. Ronie's degree in psychology has helped her pen novels of intense, raw characters.

To learn more about Ronie, visit www.roniekendig.com and follow her on social media.

Growing up in the beautiful east of Switzerland, **JJ Samie Myles** spent her childhood chasing adventures and crafting stories with her vivid imagination. Curious what the big wide world has to offer, she became a travel agent and later a missionary, collecting enough writing-inspiration for a lifetime.  Now she shares her passion for thrills and God's grace through her suspense and faith-filled stories.

Made in the USA
Monee, IL
02 January 2025